the Drifter

LORI COPELAND

MEN *of the* SADDLE

the Drifter

DOUBLEDAY LARGE PRINT HOME LIBRARY EDITION

Tyndale House Publishers, Inc.
WHEATON, ILLINOIS

TYNDALE is a registered trademark of Tyndale House Publishers, Inc.

Tyndale's quill logo is a trademark of Tyndale House Publishers, Inc.

Edited by Kathryn S. Olson

Scripture quotations are taken from the *Holy Bible,* King James Version.

The Scripture in the epigraph is taken from the *Holy Bible,* New Century Version, copyright © 1987, 1988, 1991 by Word Publishing, Dallas, Texas 75039. Used by permission.

Published in association with the literary agency of Alive Communications, Inc., 7680 Goddard Street, Suite 200, Colorado Springs, CO 80920.

ISBN 0-7394-5489-7

Printed in the United States of America

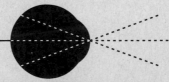

*To Jim and Helen (Little Bear) Adams
and Mac and Vivian McGinnis.*

*Thanks for the memories:
strawberry shortcake,
great Christian fellowship,
laughing so much it hurts,
and food, food, food.*

WE LIVE BY WHAT WE BELIEVE,
NOT BY WHAT WE SEE.

2 CORINTHIANS 5:7
New Century Version

the Drifter

PROLOGUE

Missouri, September 1867

The day started out like any other.

The pungent aroma of earth mingled pleasantly with the tangy smell of sweat rolling in rivulets down the back of the tall, powerfully built man gently urging the team of oxen to pull the heavy plow. Overhead, the bright sun hammered down on man and animals as they steadfastly went about furrowing the ground for fall planting.

Nature's elements rarely bothered Beau Claxton. Truth be told, nothing much bothered him because he was an inordinately happy man. The good Lord provided a roof over his head, food on his table, close family ties—and he had the prettiest, sweetest woman in all of Missouri for his wife.

As far as Beau was concerned, he had everything a man could ever want.

Oh, he had to admit that times were hard. The country was trying to put itself back together since the War Between the States, and many people still went to bed hungry every night, but he knew the Claxtons had fared better than most. God had been good to him, and life couldn't be better.

Beau's mother, Lilly, still lived on the old homestead a couple of miles down the road. His father, Samuel Claxton, had moved his wife and their two sons from Georgia to Missouri when Beau and his older brother, Cole, had been tykes. Cass, his youngest brother, had been born shortly before Samuel died. Cole and his wife, Wynne, now lived two miles on the other side of Beau's land. Fifteen months ago they'd produced a baby boy named Jeremy, who was growing like a weed and cute as a bug's ear.

Beau had to grin when he thought about how downright silly Cole was about his wife. They both acted like love-struck youngsters whenever they were together. He would've bet his spring crop that no woman could have worked Cole Claxton into such a lather, but two years ago the feisty little woman from Savannah had waltzed in and stolen Cole's heart and the man hadn't been the same since.

But Beau understood how Cole felt. He gave a sharp whistle for Sally to pull right, and his grin broadened. Hadn't Betsy Collins done the same thing to him? He recalled how they'd no sooner decided to marry than war had broken out. He'd left to join the fight, and when he returned, Betsy was waiting for him. Though they'd married two years ago, she could still make his insides go soft when she smiled up at him with those big eyes the color of a January sky.

Just the thought of holding her in his arms made his heart skip a beat. He thanked the good Lord every day for giving her to him. Any day now, they'd be having their own child—a son, he hoped, though a little girl wouldn't upset him any. It had taken forever for Betsy to get in the family way, but the doc had said she was healthy as a new pup and should be able to have all the babies they wanted. Beau wanted a large family.

"Easy, girls, easy." Beau turned the oxen and leaned over to wipe his dusty face on the sleeve of his sweat-dampened shirt. The days were still hot, even though they were nearing the end of September. He'd be glad to welcome the cooler days and crisp October nights. There was still a lot of work to be done before winter. He had to butcher the old sow, lay in a good supply of firewood, and stock the root cellar. . . .

The sound of Betsy's voice caused him to glance up and slow the team's pace. He grinned at her and waved. Must be close to noon, and she was bringing his dinner. His mouth watered at the thought of the fatback and corn bread she'd have in his dinner pail. She'd been making fried-apple pies when he'd left the house. No doubt she'd packed a couple of those too.

He heard her call again, and he whistled for Kate and Sally to stop. Strange, he thought, Betsy wasn't running toward him like she usually did. He enjoyed watching her move, smooth and graceful as the prairie grasses rippling in the wind. After their meal, they'd often lie under the old cottonwood tree talking and kissing. Like as not, it'd be well past his allotted rest hour when he'd finally go back to work.

Betsy called his name a third time, and Beau's smile began to fade. He dropped the reins and shaded his eyes against the hot sun to see her more clearly.

Her slender frame, swollen with child, was silhouetted against a broad expanse of blue sky. For a moment he hesitated, expecting Betsy to start toward him again. But she lifted her hand feebly in the air and then dropped to her knees.

Cold fear shot through him. Something was wrong. The baby. *Yes, that's it,* he reasoned. He started running. The baby was coming, and Betsy was scared. How many times had he told her not to be afraid; he'd be there with her when their child was born? He'd be there to share her pain, to hold her hand, to tell her how proud he was that she was the mother of his child. Together they'd share an incredible joy when their son or daughter came into the world.

He was running fast now, sucking long, deep breaths as he watched Betsy slump to the ground. His feet covered the hard-packed dirt with lightning speed. "I'm coming, Bets!" he called to her. *God, don't let her be afraid.*

She lifted her head once as if she was trying to answer him, but with growing horror, Beau saw her fall back limply to the ground.

"God . . . oh, God . . . please." Beau's lungs felt as though they'd explode. He ran harder. Something deep inside told him that this was more than labor pains, but he refused to listen. On he went, over rough tufts of ground, his boots gouging the dry, crusty earth, his eyes never once leaving the silent form crumpled close to the woodpile.

It couldn't be anything serious. . . . She was teasing him. . . . No, Betsy never tried to scare him. . . . It had to be the baby. . . . Maybe she was going to have a harder time than most. . . . The pains were sharp, and she'd dropped to the ground to wait for him. . . . That must be it. . . .

Gut-wrenching fear gripped his windpipe. Beau pushed himself faster. Betsy wasn't moving. She lay on the ground in deathlike stillness.

When he finally reached her, he fell to his knees and gathered her in his arms. His heart pounded, his breath coming in painful gasps as he cradled her head and called her name.

At the sound of his voice, her eyes slowly opened and she smiled at him. She reached up with trembling fingers to touch his cheek, and he saw his tears drop gently on her hand.

"What is it, sweetheart? The baby . . . is it the baby?" he prompted.

"My baby . . . ," she whispered softly, so softly that he could scarcely make out her words. "Dear God, Beau . . . our baby . . ."

"Bets, what's wrong? Tell me, sweetheart. Should I get Ma or Wynne?"

She lifted her hand to cover his lips. "Snake . . . over by the woodpile . . . rattler . . . don't worry . . . dead now . . ."

Rattler! The word hit him with the force of a bullet, and suddenly he felt his heart drop to his stomach.

He whirled, his distraught gaze searching the woodpile by the house until he saw the horrifying evidence. A timber rattlesnake, almost seven feet in length, was stretched out on the ground. Its head, severed by a hoe, lay in the dust some distance away. The small pile of wood Betsy had been gathering was scattered about the area, mute tes-

timony of what had happened. Betsy had
encountered the snake unexpectedly while
gathering wood for the stove.

Frantically, Beau began searching for the
fang marks. If she'd been bitten by a rattler,
there wasn't much time.

"Where's the bite?" Beau's voice trembled, but he fought to remain calm. He
didn't want to scare her more. She moaned
softly, and he remembered that she should
be still. The more she moved, the quicker
the poison would spread through her body.
"Don't move, sweetheart, I'll find it. . . . I'll
find it!" His eyes and hands searched her
body. It didn't take long to locate the two
small puncture marks on her right arm. He
bit back a curse when he saw the angry
swelling. The rattler's fangs had hit the vein
dead-on.

Beau swallowed the tight knot in his
throat. He knew without being told that the
poison would go straight to her heart; there
was nothing, *nothing* he could do to save
her.

Swiftly, he pulled his knife from his pocket
and cut two small slits across the vein. He
brought her arm to his mouth and sucked

the venom, then spat it on the ground while he stemmed the tears brimming in his eyes.

When he'd done all he knew to do, he talked to her in soft, reassuring tones. "I love you, Bets. More than I can ever say. We've had a good life together and we're going to have a lot more good days, you and me and our baby."

She didn't answer and he held her closer. "Don't be afraid, darlin'. I won't let anything hurt you."

Her eyelids fluttered open, and he brushed a lock of hair back from her forehead. "I'm sorry I was so neglectful. I'll keep that wood box filled every day from now on, I promise."

He should have done that anyway, he agonized, though Betsy had insisted on carrying the wood herself.

"Don't leave me, Bets," he pleaded when he heard her moans growing weaker. "I have to go for help," he murmured. "I have to get the doc out here—"

"No . . . no . . . stay with me, Beau." Her hands anxiously clasped him, and he rested his head on the swollen mound of her stomach. They both started to sob.

Beau lifted his face to the sky. Tears

streamed down his face. "Dear God . . . Oh, please, God, don't let her die. I know I've not been all I could be, but don't make Betsy pay for my sins. Lord, I love her so much. If You'll spare her, I promise I'll do better. I'll live my life for You every day."

Betsy's lashes fluttered, and he could see a change—but not the one he wanted to see. Anger filled him, anger at his Maker. "You're supposed to be a God who cares, a God who watches over us!" Just last Sunday the pastor had spoken of a benevolent God who wanted to do good things for His people. Surely such a God wouldn't take Beau's wife and child from him in such a cruel, senseless act.

"What kind of God are You?" he raged. "How can I trust You when You let this happen to Betsy? She trusted You!" He could see her slipping away from him, and his heart turned to stone.

Paralyzed with fear, Beau clutched Betsy and crooned to her, rocking her gently back and forth, back and forth, until the sun dipped low on the western horizon. The golden rays spread across the parched earth, enveloping the young couple in an ethereal light. Still Beau wouldn't let go.

He didn't know the exact moment she left him. His arms had grown numb from holding her, yet he would not release her. If he put her down, she'd be gone from him forever. He couldn't accept that.

His brother Cole found them.

Cole's tall frame swung out of the saddle as he dismounted and walked to where Beau sat cradling Betsy in his arms.

"Beau? What's wrong?"

Beau cried openly—deep, heartrending sobs that shook his entire frame. He clasped his young wife tightly to him, murmuring her name over and over. He saw Cole's concern, but he couldn't find the words to answer. He moved his head, indicating the snake.

Cole's eyes focused on the lifeless body of the rattler on the ground beside the woodpile.

The horror of his expression told that he realized the full extent of what had happened. "Oh, Beau. I'm sorry."

Cole gently reached to lift Betsy from his brother's arms.

"No . . . no . . . don't take her, Cole." Beau spoke for the first time, his voice steady.

"I have to take her."

Beau tightened his grip around his wife's body. He shook his head.

"Give her to me," Cole commanded softly.

Since the day Sam Claxton had died of a heart attack, Cole had been father and brother to Beau and Cass. He'd been there for them through the good and bad times, and they still looked upon him as head of the household. Beau couldn't go against years of strict obedience. He reluctantly relinquished his hold.

"Don't hurt her," he whispered hoarsely.

"I'll take good care of her."

Carefully lifting her in his arms, Cole stood and carried Betsy into the house. Beau stumbled after him. He'd built that house for Betsy, and they had lived and loved here, planned for their family. He'd thought they would grow old together here. Now the house they'd loved was an empty shell. Betsy was gone.

The Claxtons were a prominent family in River Run. Just about everyone turned out for Betsy's funeral. *Such a lovely young thing,* the townspeople whispered among themselves. *Why had tragedy struck such a fine couple when they'd only begun to live? What would poor Beau do now? She was so young . . . and the innocent baby she was carrying . . . why, it would have been born soon . . . horrible . . . just terrible . . . simply unthinkable . . .*

Beau hadn't shed a tear since the afternoon Cole had found him holding Betsy. Standing straight and tall between his two brothers, he kept his face an empty mask as the preacher droned on.

At the graveside, he watched as his mother, Lilly Claxton, wrapped her arms around Betsy's mother and suffered with her. He knew as far as Lilly was concerned, Betsy had been more than a daughter-in-law; she had been one of her own.

Beau showed no emotion until the first spade of dirt fell atop the simple pine coffin. When the sound reached his ears, he flinched as if he'd been burned, but he kept his eyes dry and his face stoic. Betsy, his Betsy, was in that pine box, lost to him forever, and he had nothing left to live for. After the burial he turned and walked away without a backward glance.

Wynne Claxton, flanked on either side by Cole and Cass, approached Beau. Wynne handed baby Jeremy to his father and enfolded her brother-in-law in her arms, hugging him tightly. "We share your pain, Beau, and we love you very much," she whispered.

"I don't know how I can go on . . ." Beau's brave facade shattered, and his voice filled with raw emotion. Even God had forsaken him.

"But you will. You will, Beau."

For a fraction of an instant Beau tightened his arm around Wynne; then he dropped it back to his side and walked on.

Cole matched stride with his brother's as Beau marched to his horse.

"Why don't you come over and spend a few days with Wynne and me?" he invited. "You don't have to go back home until you're ready."

"Thanks, but I'll be leaving for a while." Beau paused and turned to face his brothers.

"Leaving? Where you going?" Cass demanded.

Beau's gaze rested upon the small mound of newly turned dirt. "I don't know. Away somewhere."

"Aw, Beau, I can understand you feeling that way, but don't you think this is a bad time to be running off?" Cass protested. "Tell him, Cole. He shouldn't be wandering around by himself . . . not right now."

Cole shook his head. "I think he should do what he feels he has to, Cass."

Beau looked into Cole's clear blue gaze and saw a silent understanding. He nodded. "Thanks. Bets . . . well, she'd have appreciated all you've done. . . ."

Cole clasped Beau's shoulder. "Let us know when you're ready to come home."

"I will. I want you to take Kate and Sally and the rest of my stock."

"I'll see to them for you."

Beau reached out and touched Jeremy's nose, drawing a happy gurgle from the baby. "Take good care of this little fella." Bright tears stood in Beau's eyes. He thought about his own baby and what might have been.

"You take care of yourself," Cole said.

Beau nodded. "Tell Ma not to worry." Slowly, he mounted his horse and pulled his hat low on his forehead.

"She'll worry anyway—you know Ma," said Cass. Beau realized his younger brother still wasn't sold on the idea of his leaving. "A man needs his family at a time like this. Let us know where you are, you hear?"

Beau's eyes returned to Betsy's grave and lingered there. "I hear."

Trouble was, he didn't care.

CHAPTER 1

Kansas, November 1868

"Shoo! Shooeee! Get out of here you—you. Shoo! Shooee! Get out of here! You—you miserable . . . ungrateful . . . ham hock!"

Charity Burk was determined to show no pity as she swatted the old sow across her fat rump and herded her back out the front door. It was a sad day when a woman couldn't step outside to hang the wash without being invaded by pigs!

She slammed the heavy wooden door and leaned against it to catch her breath. She had to do something about getting the fence back up.

Her husband, Ferrand, had died in the

war four years ago, and since his death
Charity had been on her own. Not that
she wanted to be—far from it. She wasn't
equipped to homestead in this desolate
land, nor had she ever entertained the least
desire to do so, but shortly after they'd married, her husband had decided to take advantage of the federal government's Homestead Act, signed into law in May of '62.

She could still remember how excited he
had been the day he'd come home, swung
her into his arms, and announced they were
moving to Kansas. "A hundred and sixty
acres, Charity. Think of it! They'll give us a
hundred and sixty acres of whatever land
we stake out."

Kansas? For a girl who'd spent all of her
life in Virginia, Kansas sounded like the end
of the earth. Charity had paced the parlor of
her ancestral home, wondering aloud why
Ferrand would want to run off to some foreign land when they had a perfectly good
home right here with her parents.

Her husband had been patient, reminding
her that Kansas wasn't a foreign land. But to
a woman accustomed to nannies and servants who attended to her every whim without a moment's hesitation, the idea had

seemed foreign enough. Certainly Kansas was not a place she wanted to live.

Ferrand Burk came from an old, aristocratic line in Virginia. His father could have well afforded to buy any amount of land his son desired. Why, even her own pa had offered to purchase Ferrand a plantation on their wedding day. They didn't need to travel hundreds of miles to acquire a mere hundred and sixty acres.

But Ferrand wanted land of his own, not something her father or his had provided. The Homestead Act was the answer, as far as he was concerned. All a person had to do was begin improvements on the land within six months of the time he filed for application and then stay there for five years, and the land became his, free and clear.

Charity filled a bucket with the wash water and carried it outside, emptying it away from the path. The cold November sky threatened rain or snow. Folks in town were predicting an early winter. The wooly worms were completely black this year, which meant bad weather and lots of it. She'd cut open a persimmon seed back in October and found a spoon. A sure sign of a lot of snow, according to Laughing Waters and

Little Fawn, two Kaw Indians who had chosen her for a friend.

The Kaws were a friendly tribe and had often dropped by the homestead before they broke camp and moved away, leaving Laughing Waters and Little Fawn behind. The two women came and went whenever they chose. They'd never been known to knock, and sometimes they drove her to distraction, but they had taught her about herbs and native plants, and she had learned to accept their unexpected visits.

Charity leaned against the tumbledown fence and thought about the way Ferrand had held her close and kissed her, promising an adventure. Well, he had surely delivered on that. She'd had about all the adventure she could stand.

Sometimes she hadn't understood her husband.

She had loved him, and her papa always said a man was the undisputed head of his household, but still . . . given her choice, she would have stayed in Virginia. Charity carried the bucket back to the wash kettle, remembering how Ferrand had also promised her life wouldn't change much. There would be plenty of people looking for jobs in Kansas, and she could hire all the help she'd need to do the work. Turned out there had been virtually no one looking for a job. Everyone had enough to do trying to survive life on the frontier.

She straightened and rubbed her aching back. She'd had to learn to cook and clean, do all the things someone else had done for her. At first she had missed Mama and Papa and Jenny and Sue, her sisters. Ferrand had promised her family could come visit when they'd got settled on their homestead, but that hadn't worked out either. To tell the truth, she was sort of relieved Papa had never seen how she lived. Kansas was different from Virginia in more ways than one.

She'd worried about the war too, afraid her husband might have to leave any day. Her husband had laughed and said they'd worry about that when the time came. Well, the time had come a lot sooner than Charity had planned.

They hadn't lived on their new settlement for more than a few months when Ferrand decided it was his duty to join the fight for the Confederacy. She'd been left to face the bewildered looks of her neighbors when they found out he'd decided his loyalties still belonged to the South.

She emptied the last of the rinse water and propped the washtub against the side of the house to drain. Kansas was hundreds of miles away, and her family hadn't been able to make the long trip to visit. After they'd learned of Ferrand's death, they had written, urging her to come home. When she had informed them she was staying on to claim the land, Mama had begged her to reconsider.

Charity brushed her hair out of her eyes and stared out over the unrelenting landscape. She was a stubborn woman, too stubborn for her own good, she suspected. She was determined to stay in Kansas, though at times she hated every waking hour in this wild, uncivilized land, where the winds were fierce and the winters long and unbearably cold. The heat could be suffocating and the droughts endless. There were tornadoes and grasshoppers and Indians. And wolves. She hated the wolves, too. They prowled around her log cabin at night, snapping at her dogs, Gabriel and Job, while she huddled in a corner grasping

Ferrand's old rifle and praying they wouldn't break through the door.

Still, she couldn't bring herself to relinquish her right to the homestead. In a strange, inexplicable way, she felt a certain pride to think she owned the land—or would, if she could hold on one more year.

Then maybe she'd go home. The thought was mighty tempting. There hadn't been any servants or nannies out here to take care of her. In truth, she'd barely been able to manage.

She felt herself smiling, something she rarely did anymore, when she thought of how poor Ferrand had struggled to mold her into a pioneer woman. He'd been good to her. He'd seen her through her crying spells and days of loneliness. Sometimes weeks would pass before they'd see another human being, and at times she thought she couldn't bear the solitude.

But she'd survived. When the news of her husband's death had reached her, she'd had a good long cry, but by then she'd begun to adjust to the harsh realities of the world. Oh, she'd been furious at him for getting himself killed in that foolish war and leaving her all alone to care for a miserable chunk of worthless land. But the feeling had passed, and she'd started remembering what a really good man her husband had been, and then Kansas didn't seem all that bad. It was home now, her home, so she guessed she'd best make do and quit feeling sorry for herself.

A hawk hovered against the overcast sky before dropping like the weight on a plumb line, straight down. The hawk would devour some helpless rodent. Life was hard out here and not likely to get easier. She sighed and turned back to look at her home. Not fancy compared to what she'd left in Virginia, but what she and Ferrand had shared had been special. Despite all her domestic failings, she knew she had to do this one last thing for him. He had worked too hard in the brief time they'd been granted together for her to be fainthearted now. She'd see this thing through. Though she had to admit, she couldn't understand how she was going to do it.

From a purely practical standpoint, she needed a man. She'd have to make improvements on the land to keep her claim, but she simply didn't have the knowledge, the strength, or the necessary skill.

Thanks to Grandmother Pendergrass's personal tutelage, Charity knew how to piece a pretty quilt and bake a tasty blackberry pie, but she didn't know how to build a barn or plow a field. Oh, she'd tried. Her hands, once lily-white and soft as rose petals, were now calloused and beet red.

When it had come to setting posts and planting wheat, she'd done an embarrassing job. Ashamed for anyone to see the way her fence posts leaned westward when they were supposed to stand straight, she had ripped them out and cried herself to sleep that night.

A man was her only answer.

But a man was a rare commodity around these parts. It was unlikely that anyone would walk up and knock on her door and say, "Well, hello! I hear you're looking for a husband, Mrs. Burk. Take me." She laughed out loud at the notion.

Though the town of Cherry Grove wasn't far from her land, she rarely socialized. Once a month she made the trek into town to purchase staples and yard goods from Miller's Mercantile, but suitable marriage prospects weren't plentiful. Oh, there were the usual cattle drovers who came through town, bringing their longhorns up from Texas to ship them out by railroads. Of course, the travel-worn herders were always looking for female companionship, but Charity despised their slovenly ways and drunken antics. They carried on like the devil himself. Their cattle brought them a good price back East, but she wanted nothing to do with such men. They were rovers and drifters, and she needed a man who'd stick around for a spell.

She sighed in despair and turned her face heavenward, as she increasingly did these days. "Well, it's up to you, Lord. I'm at the end of my row."

Beau Claxton slowed his horse beside the stream and paused to let the animal drink his fill. Unkempt and dirty with a heavy beard covering the lower half of his face, he felt older than his twenty-eight years. He slumped in the saddle, body aching with fatigue. A light drizzle had been falling for the last half hour and his beard was caked in ice.

He'd been on the trail long enough for the sun to cook his skin and the wind and weather to lash him into a blank acceptance of a life that no longer held purpose.

He knew he looked bad but he couldn't seem to care.

He didn't eat the way he should. He was at least forty pounds lighter than he had been a year ago. During that time, he'd rambled down one winding road after another, going wherever the next one took him. He'd tried to get through one day and then the next and then the next. Sometimes he'd noticed when he crossed a state line, but if anyone had asked him where he was, he wouldn't have known or cared. Life was one long day after the other.

Betsy had been gone a year now, or close to it. Beau didn't know what month it was, but summer and fall had come and gone so he'd guess it was November now.

The memory of his wife brought a smile. Their baby would've been over a year old by now. Boy or girl? Suddenly, he realized he'd never let himself ask that question. Well, he guessed it didn't matter. Nothing mattered anymore.

He slid from his horse and knelt on the

bank to break the ice, then reached into the stream, cupping his hands for a drink of freezing-cold water. When he finished, he splashed a handful of icy wetness down his neck to wash away the stench.

He had straightened and prepared to mount when his horse shied nervously. "Whoa, girl, easy." Beau gripped the reins and pulled himself into the saddle as the mare whinnied and side-stepped. "Easy . . . easy . . ." He glanced toward the surrounding woods, wary now.

"What's the matter, girl?" His eyes scanned the area and his stomach tightened. Standing not twenty feet away, partially hidden in the undergrowth, was one of the biggest timber wolves he'd ever seen.

The horse trumpeted and pranced in alarm. The wolf's lips curled back above its fangs. It growled a low, ominous warning. Its eyes had a bright, feverish sparkle to them; its back paw dangled limply.

Beau could see fresh blood dripping from the wound onto the frozen ground. Probably been caught in a trap. Slowly, he backed his horse out of the stream, taking pains not to make any sudden moves. The animal would be in no mood for socializing, and neither was Beau. He could shoot it, but his draw would have to be lightning quick, and he didn't want to chance it.

Before he could choose his next move, the decision was out of his hands.

With a lunge the wolf sprang from its hiding place. The horse reared, pawing the air.

Beau reached for his gun at the same time the wolf charged. The air was alive with the screams of the crazed horse and snarls of the wild animal locked in a life-or-death struggle. Beau managed to pull his gun from his holster, but the wolf fell, regained its footing, and sprang again, clamping its teeth on his leg. Beau tumbled out of the saddle and landed in the water, trying to shield himself from the animal's sharp teeth.

He fought to get away. The wolf repeatedly slashed at his unprotected body.

Charity stopped kneading bread and cocked her ear toward the open window. The dogs were setting up a howl on the front step, and in the distance she could hear what sounded like animals in some sort of fight.

She wiped flour from her hands. *Pesky coyotes,* she thought irritably, reaching for the rifle. They'd probably attacked a stray dog or calf. The noise increased as she stepped out of the cabin and started toward the stream.

She'd be forever grateful to Ferrand for choosing this particular piece of land. In this part of Kansas, a shortage of rain, coupled with high winds and low humidity, sometimes left a pioneer at a serious disadvantage. But the Burk home was built near an underground spring that provided a stream of cool, clear water year-round.

A shrill squeal rent the air, and her footsteps quickened. Good heavens! Something had attacked a horse! Her feet faltered as she entered the clearing, her eyes taking in the appalling sight. A large timber wolf was ripping a man apart as his horse danced about him in terror.

Charity hefted the rifle to her shoulder and took careful aim. A loud crack sliced the air, and the wolf toppled off the man. The gunfire spooked the horse. The animal bolted into the thicket, and Charity waded into the stream, flinching when she edged past the fallen wolf. The gaping bullet hole in the center of its chest assured her that her aim had been true. Her husband had taught her how to be a deadly, accurate shot. She'd learned her lesson well.

She knelt beside the wounded man and cautiously rolled him on his side in the shallow water, cringing when he moaned in agony. He was so bloody she could barely make out the severity of his wounds, but she knew he was near death.

"Shhhh . . . lie still. I'm going to help you," she soothed, though she was afraid he could neither see nor hear her. His eyes were swollen shut from the lacerations on his face. As she watched, he slumped into unconsciousness.

She hesitated, not sure whether to hitch Myrtle and Nell to drag him out of the water. He was a tall man, but pitifully thin. Though she was small and slight, she was a lot stronger than when she'd first come to Kansas. She decided she wouldn't need the oxen to move him.

It took several tries to get him out of the water. He wasn't as light as he looked. She tugged and heaved inch by inch, pausing periodically to murmur soothing words of encouragement when he groaned. Though she handled him carefully, his injuries were so great she was sure he suffered unspeakable pain.

Once she had hauled him onto the bank, she hurriedly tore off a small portion of her petticoat and set to work cleaning his wounds. He fought when her hands touched torn flesh.

"Please, you must let me help you!" she urged.

She was accustomed to patching wounds on her stock, but she grew faint looking at this man's injuries. But she shook off her queasiness and looked after his needs.

As her hands worked, she studied him, recoiling not only at his injuries but at his general condition. He was so unkempt, so dirty, so . . . slovenly. She wasn't used to that. Ferrand had always kept himself clean and neat. No doubt this man was a drifter, or perhaps one of those drovers. He certainly hadn't had a bath in months—maybe even years—and he was in need of a shave and haircut.

She peeled away the torn shirt and

washed the blood from his broad chest. She could count his ribs. Obviously, he hadn't had a square meal in months. With more meat on his bones he'd be a very large man . . . powerful . . . strong . . .

Strong enough to build a barn and set fence and work behind a team of oxen all day. . . . Her hands momentarily stilled.

A man. Here was a *man*—barely alive perhaps, but a man all the same. He could be the answer to her problems. Her hands flew feverishly about their work. She had to save him! Not that she wouldn't have tried her best anyway, but now, no matter what it took, she'd see to it that this man survived!

As far as men went, he wasn't much . . . disgusting, actually, but she reminded herself she wasn't in a position to be picky. She'd nurse him back to health, and once she got him on his feet, she'd trick him into marrying her. No, she amended, she wouldn't trick him . . . she'd ask him first, and if that didn't work, *then* she'd trick him.

But what if he has a wife? an inner voice asked.

Don't bother me with technicalities, she thought. *I'll cross that bridge when I get to it.*

Her hands worked faster, a new sense of confidence filling her now. He *would* live. She knew he would. The good Lord wouldn't send such a gift and then snatch it back. Would He?

The man moaned, and Charity lifted his head and placed it possessively in her lap.

He was a gift from God.

She was certain of that now. Who else would so unselfishly drop this complete stranger at her door?

Charity gazed down at her unexpected gift and smiled, lifting her face heavenward.

She would be able to claim her land.

In her most reverent tone, she humbly asked for the Lord's help in making this man strong and healthy again, at least strong enough to drive a good, sturdy fence post.

She closed her petition with heartfelt sincerity. "He's a little . . . well, rough looking, Father, but I'm not complaining." She bit her lower lip and studied the ragged, dirty, bloody man lying in her lap. With a little soap and water, he'd be tolerable. She shrugged, and a grin spread across her face. "I suppose if this is the best You have to offer, Lord, then I am surely beholden to You."

CHAPTER 2

Charity dragged the stranger up the ravine and then the quarter of a mile to the house. By the time she managed to pull him onto her bed, she was gasping for air.

She sighed and surveyed his pitiful state. The nearest doctor was over an hour's ride away. The stranger would die before she could make it to Cherry Grove and back.

No, if his life was to be spared, she'd have to use whatever skills she possessed, and she had to admit they were deplorably few.

It would take a lot of nursing, and the mercy of God, to see him through this, she realized.

Though he remained in a state of unconsciousness, the man's face was swollen and contorted with pain. The angry six-inch gash across his chest oozed blood. She knew he would bleed to death if she didn't stem the wound.

She rolled up her sleeves and moved to the hearth. After filling a wash pan with scalding water from the teakettle, she tore an old petticoat into soft bandages. She'd stitched up livestock, she reminded herself. Her hands automatically went about her task. When Nell had gotten tangled in Ansel Latimer's fence last year, she'd been the one who'd cleaned the torn flesh and stitched it back together. She took scissors and a needle from her sewing basket. Of course, Nell's wound had been nothing like this poor man's, but the ox had healed beautifully.

And she'd assisted with a few births, but helping a woman deliver a baby was easier than sewing a man back together. She selected a spool of black thread and absently closed the lid on the basket. Doctoring wasn't her favorite thing, but then she had no choice if she wanted the man to survive. God would ultimately decide his fate, but she'd do all she could . . . and not for purely selfish reasons. She had an obligation to her fellow man.

It took a half hour to cut away his clothes. She choked back nausea as she bathed his wounds in cool water. Drawing deep breaths of fresh air to quell the urge to empty her stomach, Charity turned back to the injured man.

She wasn't sure she could go on. Most likely the man would die in spite of her efforts. No one could survive such injuries, she reasoned. But she thought of her own miserable plight and resolved anew to save his life.

The laceration across the middle of his back was the deepest. She carefully rolled him onto his stomach, cringing as she poured a small amount of carbolic acid into the wound. The man stiffened, screaming in anguish. He tried to twist away, but Charity held firm, throwing her slight weight against his large frame, pinning him down until he drifted back into unconsciousness.

She found herself biting her lower lip till she could taste her own blood. Her hands worked feverishly to stitch the open gash. When she finished with his back, she rolled him over and continued to stitch the other lacerations. At any moment he could wake up and overpower her, and then what would she do?

The darning needle, which she'd held in the fire, slid in and out, in and out . . . until she thought she'd faint. The room was stifling. She dipped a cloth into the bucket of clean water and pressed it to her flushed features. Once the lightheadedness passed, she continued.

The afternoon shadows lengthened, and Charity's back felt as if it would break, but she worked on. She heard Bossy standing near the front door, bawling to be milked.

"Not now, Bossy," she called out softly, praying the old cow would wander off.

It was nearing dark when she finished. Tears welled in her eyes when she listened to the sounds of his suffering. She dropped weakly into the rocker and stared unseeingly at the cooling stove, numb with fatigue. She'd felt every agonizing prick the needle had made in his bruised flesh as surely as if she'd been the one injured.

Her body, as well as his, was sticky with sweat and blood, and she knew she must bathe the both of them before she could rest.

The man mumbled and thrashed about on the bed. Charity feared he'd reopen his wounds. If he did, she wasn't sure she'd have the strength to sew them again.

There was nothing to ease the stranger's agony except the bottle of brandy Ferrand had kept for medicinal purposes. If this wasn't a medicinal purpose, she didn't recognize one. She hurriedly pulled the bottle from the cupboard and carried it to the bed. He moaned when she scooped his head up from the pillow and cradled it in the crook of her arm. She tipped the bottle to his lips, letting the strong brown liquid trickle down his throat.

When he choked, she set the bottle aside and patted his shoulder, trying to soothe him. He screamed in torment when the wound across his chest threatened to escape the bounds of the slender thread.

When he regained his breath, she tipped the bottle again, and the nerve-racking choking started all over again. It took several minutes to get enough of the liquid down him to dull his senses.

He'd fought her with a strength that was surprising for a man so gravely injured. Twice he'd nearly knocked the bottle out of her hand, but she was as determined as he. The spirits took full effect, and he lay so still that she leaned forward to be sure he was still breathing.

Assured that he was she released a long sigh. *He's going to make it. He has to.* If she could clean and stitch his wounds without fainting, then he could live! She eyed the unconscious male lying in the middle of her bed.

He was a pitiful sight. His chin was covered with stubble; his ribs poked through his sides like those of some half-starved animal. But it didn't matter, she told herself, trying to bolster her sagging morale. He *was* a man, and good Lord willing, she was going to see that he lived. He obviously needed someone to take care of him, and she needed a man. Surely a satisfactory arrangement could be worked out, once he regained his health.

He was still breathing, and she took small comfort in that. By morning he'd be awake, and she'd find out who he was and where he'd come from. Mustering up enough strength to walk to the fuel box, she tossed a few buffalo chips on the fire, then stumbled back to the rocker and dropped into an exhausted sleep.

Wind howling down the chimney penetrated Charity's dulled senses. Her eyes opened to slits, then closed again. For three nights, she'd hovered over the stranger, alternately bathing him in cool water and changing the bandages.

His wounds didn't look good. The long, angry lesions were beginning to fester, and her heart pounded with fear when she looked at them.

The man was hot and feverish—delirious at times, calling out for "Betsy." If she had known Betsy, she'd have gladly fetched her. She'd try anything to ease his torment, but nothing helped.

Only once had he shown a sign of consciousness. Last night, when she'd been sponging his burning forehead, his eyes had opened to stare at her with a blank plea in the deep, tormented pools of indigo.

Charity had smiled and spoken to him in soft, reassuring tones, running the damp cloth gently across his reddened skin. "There, now, you're going to be fine." Her heart had skipped a beat when his eyes had grown incredibly tender and he'd returned her smile.

It had been so long since a man had looked at her that way. Then she realized that it wasn't Charity Burk he'd been seeing but his Betsy. His feverish mind continued to play tricks on him.

The stranger had grasped her hand and brought it to cradle lovingly against the rough stubble coating his jaw. His eyes had slid shut, and she'd heard him whisper faintly, "Bets, I knew you'd come back, darling." Charity watched with an aching heart when tears rolled from the corners of his eyes to dampen the pillow.

Slowly his eyes had opened again, and she'd caught her breath when he pulled her head down to meet his. She had been transfixed when their lips touched and lingered. Because he was so ill, the kiss had lacked substance, but nothing could have disguised the love he'd transferred to her. His kiss had taken her breath, and she'd felt herself growing weak.

When their lips parted, Charity had seen

a look in the stranger's eyes that she'd seen before in Ferrand's. It had been such a look of love, so strong that Charity felt warmed by the adoration shimmering in the tormented depths. Then he smiled at her again and said softly, "Bets, I love you."

Charity had never encountered such striking eyes: clear, vibrant blue . . . the color of morning glories that grew on the trellis beside the porch when the first rays of summer daylight nudged them gently awake. Somehow she knew those eyes, now bright with fever, could sparkle with merriment during better times. Despite his pitiful condition, the stranger was still the handsomest man she had seen in a long while.

And he loved a woman named Betsy.

The wind was rising. Charity noticed a chill in the air, and she rose to throw more chips on the fire. She stoked the glowing embers and thought of the stranger. A frown played across her features. Maybe he wouldn't be able to help her. Then what would she do? She'd lose the homestead, that's what.

She thought of Ferrand and how hard they'd worked together to build the cabin. It hadn't been easy traveling to the Great American Desert, as Kansas was sometimes called.

They had taken a steamboat part of the way. My, what a glorious time that had been, churning up the wide Missouri on a big old paddle wheeler. By then, Ferrand had convinced her that an exciting new life awaited them; all they had to do was reach out and take it.

Charity walked back to the rocker and sat. It was still early; the sun wasn't up yet, so she could dawdle for a spell before she milked Bossy. Rocking back and forth, she let her thoughts remain in the past.

How she had loved Ferrand Burk.

When they'd arrived in Kansas, they'd immediately found a piece of land, staked their plot on good level ground, and stripped the spot of grass. They'd worked from daylight to dusk, clearing the land of rocks and debris.

From sunup to sundown, they'd cut logs to build the one-room house. A tough job for a pampered Southern woman raised a lady. No sitting on a cushion sewing a fine seam here. She'd worked like a man, like one of the slaves on her father's plantation.

You never know what you can do until you have to do it, she thought.

After the logs had been hewn, she'd helped load the heavy timber into the spring wagon. Working together, they had built their house and more important, they had created a home. Tears sprang to her eyes when she remembered how happy they'd been. She dabbed at the wetness with a corner of her apron and tried to push memories aside.

What good did memories do her anyway? Ferrand was gone, and crying wouldn't bring him back. She wouldn't cry again. She was just feeling tired; that was all. Sitting up with the stranger for three nights straight had taken its toll.

She returned to the bed and touched the stranger's forehead. Still hot. She didn't know how much longer the fever could rage before it either broke or killed him. It would do one or the other soon.

She settled back in the chair and sighed. Ferrand seemed to hug the fringes of her mind this morning. Perhaps because he'd always loved this time of day. Charity let herself dwell on her husband's quiet strength, and somehow that eased her mind.

She leaned her head against the smooth wood of her chair and thought about how he'd made the rocker and given it to her on their first Christmas together. She tried to remember his eyes . . . blue, like the stranger's . . . no, they were hazel, weren't they?

The slow creak of the rocker ceased. Blue . . . no, hazel. She frowned. Blue or hazel? Which one was it? Strange, she couldn't recall. Setting the chair in motion she thought about how tall and handsome Ferrand Burk had been. She could remember clearly what an attractive man he was. Oh, he might not have had a broad-shouldered frame like the stranger, but Ferrand had had a firmness about him that she'd found most attractive.

And he'd held his own when it had come to working the land. He might've been raised in a home where servants had done all the backbreaking chores, but he hadn't been afraid of hard work. Neither was she.

Her eyes wandered lovingly around the room. The cabin was all she had left of Ferrand, and if she lost it, she feared she'd lose what remained of his memory. Oh, she knew this house they'd built wasn't fancy like her ancestral mansion in Virginia. But it was home.

Charity's gaze surveyed the meager furnishings. Not much—a buffalo-hide carpet on the floor, a wooden bed with a straw-filled mattress, some goods boxes fashioned into tables, and a few barrels Ferrand had hewn into chairs. She'd managed to save enough egg money to buy material to make pretty gingham curtains. The two richly patterned patchwork quilts that had once belonged to her grandmother brightened the room.

All things considered, Charity loved this home. That's why she had to keep the stranger alive. He might be pitiful, but if she could enlist his strength once she nursed him back to health, he could save her homestead.

She didn't know how she'd make him stay once he recovered—provided he did recover. This Betsy would be an obstacle, but perhaps the stranger could be persuaded to help out while he was mending. It would take a good long while for him to regain his full strength.

Suddenly she slapped the arm of the chair and her frustration erupted. Oh, it cut her to the *core* to have to depend on someone else! Her life should have been so different. She hated the miserable, senseless act of war that had snatched Ferrand away from her!

Wind whistling down the chimney added to her fury. While she was mad at everything, she thought angrily, she might as well include the Kansas grasshoppers, tornadoes, and blizzards, along with the incessant wind that had withered what little crops she'd planted.

Wearily she rose from the chair and blew out the tallow candle on the kitchen table. The sun was up now—a new day. Maybe this one would shine more favorably on her and the stranger.

She poured water into the kitchen basin and washed her face and hands, then pulled the pins from her hair. The soft black cloud fell like a shawl around her shoulders. She picked up a brush and pulled it through the tangled locks, pausing to stare at her reflection in the mirror. Frontier life had been hard, and she feared her beauty—what there was left of it—was fading.

Her hand absently fingered the faint crow's feet around her eyes. Come next month, she'd be twenty-three years old. Twenty-three years old! An old widow.

Most women her age were busy raising families and tending husbands, but she had neither. Instead she had a dead husband, an unclaimed piece of land, a few chickens, a few old sows, two dogs, a cow, two oxen, and a gravely ill stranger about to meet his Maker.

The sound of a buckboard rumbling into the yard caught her attention. Charity hurriedly repinned her hair, wondering who could be calling at this hour. She took a final glance in the mirror, then quickly smoothed the wrinkles on her dress and answered the knock.

She was surprised to find her neighbor, Ansel Latimer, standing on her doorstep, his face pale, his mouth set in a grim line.

"Good morning, Ansel." Charity peered on tiptoe around his large frame. "Is Letty—?"

"Letty sent me to fetch you," Ansel interrupted curtly. "She's—she's feeling right poorly this morning, and I don't know what to do for her."

"Is it the baby?"

"I don't know. It ain't time for the young'un to be born, but Letty—she's been hurting all night."

Ansel and Letty Latimer had been Charity's closest neighbors until a few months ago when the Swensons and several other families staked their claims. The Latimers lived a good five miles away, but Letty and Charity visited back and forth once a month, excitedly planning for Letty's new baby, due in late November.

The women were about the same age, and they had developed a close friendship while the Latimers and Burks homesteaded their properties. Ansel and Letty were the closest thing to family Charity had, now that Ferrand was gone.

Charity was reaching for her shawl when she remembered. "Of course I'll come, Ansel, but will you step in for a moment?"

Ansel removed his hat and walked into the warmth of the cabin. "We'd best hurry, Charity. I hate to leave Letty alone any longer than need be."

"Of course. I'll only take a moment." Charity motioned for him to follow her to the bed. "I want you to see something."

He strode across the room, a tall man,

still handsome at forty-three, with brown eyes and dark hair streaked with gray. He was twenty years older than Charity, and she valued his intelligence and common sense. Many times since Ferrand's death she'd gone to him with her problems. If anyone would know what to do about the stranger, Ansel would.

Slowly his puzzled gaze focused on the bed. A frown crossed his rugged features. "Who is he?"

"I don't know. Three days ago I found him in the stream. A wolf attacked him. I shot the animal and managed to drag the stranger to the house."

Ansel bent over and lifted one of the bandages. Charity watched his frown deepen. "Infection's set in."

"I know. I've tried to keep the wounds clean, but they look worse every day."

Ansel lifted the other bandages and shook his head as he viewed the angry lesions. "He needs a doctor, but even then, I don't believe he'll make it."

"I know. Oh, Ansel, what should I do?" Charity heard the quiver in her voice. "He's going to die!"

Ansel patted her shoulder reassuringly.

"Looks to me like you've done about all you can. I've never seen a better job of stitching. But the man's wounds are too serious. It'd be more merciful to let him go to his reward in peace."

Her eyes filled with tears. She stared down at the stranger's flushed features. His face was pathetically swollen and hot with fever. She felt such a closeness to the man, yet she couldn't explain why. She'd fought so hard to save his life that it seemed unthinkable to let him go.

Still, she knew Ansel had spoken the truth. Wouldn't it be kinder to let him pass away? In three days she'd managed to get only a few drops of water and a couple spoonfuls of broth down his parched throat.

The man was so weak Charity could barely hear him call for Betsy. She wondered how much longer she could bear to watch his suffering.

Ansel gently touched her arm. "Let him go, Charity. You've done all you can. He's in the Lord's hands now."

She nodded, tears of resignation trickling down her cheeks. Ansel was right. She had to let the stranger go. There was no mercy in letting him suffer this way.

"Come with me. We'll tend to Letty; then I'll bring you back this evening and help you bury him," Ansel said.

She nodded again and reached to tuck the sheet tenderly over the man's chest, realizing Ansel expected him to be dead by sunset. "I know it's best, but it . . . it seems awful just letting him pass away alone." Her voice caught. Tears ran in swift rivulets.

"Nothing more you can do." Ansel put his arm around her shoulders and led her away from the sight.

She knew he was right. Ansel was always right, but it seemed wrong, leaving a man to die alone. Charity wanted to be with him when it happened. . . .

"Letty needs you," Ansel reminded gently.

"Oh . . . yes, Letty . . . of course." Charity had almost forgotten her friend. Letty should be her first concern, but her eyes raced back to the still figure lying on her bed. Ansel helped her with her shawl.

"Bundle up real good. Chilly out this morning."

"Put plenty of chips on the fire. I—I don't want him to be cold."

Ansel did as she asked, then opened the

door and quietly commanded, "Charity, Letty needs our help, girl."

"Yes . . . yes, of course." She glanced one final time at the bed before she turned and walked through the door.

"May the mercy of the Lord be with you," she whispered, wishing desperately that his Betsy could be here to see him safely home.

CHAPTER 3

The old buckboard rumbled along the rutted trail, bouncing Charity back and forth on the wooden seat, but she barely noticed. Her thoughts were on the stranger. She wondered how long it would be before he . . . He could be dead at this instant, she realized, and the thought made her shiver. Another time a ride across the prairie would have been a source of pleasure, but not today.

The roadbed ran along Fire Creek. She, Ferrand, Letty, and Ansel had enjoyed picnics here on lazy Sunday afternoons. Willow trees lined the bank along with grapevines and hazel bush. In warm weather, Charity and Letty had spent hours gathering the wildflowers that grew in colorful profusion along the roadbed while the men discussed their crops.

A killdeer sang his tuneless note. A meadowlark called. The old buckboard lumbered across the shallow stream and rattled up the steep incline toward the Latimer homestead.

Charity noticed Ansel had said little during the ride, commenting only occasionally on the weather. His face remained pensive; worry lines were grooved deep at the corners of his eyes.

She knew how much he loved Letty, and she sympathized with his concern for his young wife. He and Letty looked forward to their first child like youngsters waiting for Christmas. Charity sighed deeply, wishing Ferrand had left her with a child. It would have been a part of him to love and to hold when the nights were long and the wind wailed around the cabin. A child to carry on Ferrand's name. Her heart ached with the loss. Best not to think about such things. What was done couldn't be undone.

She couldn't imagine what was ailing Letty this morning. She'd seemed fine at church on Sunday. After the service the two women had lingered outside, discussing the new dress they'd make for Letty after her baby came. They'd use the fine blue-and-yellow sprigged calico they had dawdled over the last time Charity had ridden to Cherry Grove with the Latimers for supplies.

Charity suspected Letty's weakness for dried-apple pie was the source of her discomfort, but she didn't think Ansel had any notion to hear her opinion.

The buckboard clattered along the prairie, and soon Charity could see the chimney pipe of the Latimer dugout poking out of the ground. Whenever she visited Letty, she always came away thankful that Ferrand had built a cabin instead of a dugout.

Letty was forever complaining that her home was dark and damp year-round, and she said it was practically impossible to keep things clean, what with dirt from the roof and walls sifting down on everything. Whenever it rained, water poured in through the roof and under the door. Letty had to wade in mud until the floor could dry out.

Bull snakes got into the roof made of willows and grass. Letty said sometimes one would lose its hold at night and fall down on the bed. Ansel would jump up, take a hoe, and drag the snake outside.

Charity shuddered at the thought. There were no snakes in her cabin. In summer it was cool as a cavern; in winter, a snug, warm refuge from the howling Kansas blizzards.

"Looks like Letty's allowed the fire to burn down," Ansel remarked. He drove the buckboard alongside the dugout and drew the horses to a halt. Only a faint wisp of smoke curled from the stovepipe.

He set the brake, jumped down, and lifted Charity from the wooden seat.

"I bet she'll have dinner waiting," Charity predicted, trying to ease the worry lines on his face.

When they stepped inside the dugout, her optimism faded. It took a moment for her eyes to adjust to the small room. A ray of sunshine filtered through the one window and Charity squinted to locate Letty, who lay on the bed, her hands crossed over her swollen stomach, her lips silently moving.

Charity hurried across the room and knelt beside the straw-filled mattress, reaching out to smooth back the damp tendrils of carrot-red hair. "Letty, it's me. I'm here."

For a moment she thought Letty hadn't heard. Then Letty's lips moved, and Charity leaned close to understand her words. "Ansel . . . make him go outside. . . ."

Charity's heart started to hammer. Something was terribly wrong. This was far more serious than a case of eating too many dried apples. She touched her friend's delicate hand and discovered it was unusually cold. "Ansel's here, Letty, and so am I. Can you tell us what's the matter?"

"Ansel . . ." Letty's voice was stronger. "Make Ansel . . . go *outside,*" she repeated.

"Letty . . . why?"

Letty's tears fell across cheeks sprinkled generously with girlish freckles. "Just make him go, Charity. . . . Make him leave. . . ."

Charity turned in bewilderment to face Ansel, who was standing quietly in the shadows. "She wants you to leave."

"I heard." Without questioning his wife's unusual request, he turned and walked out.

Charity turned to Letty and began smoothing the rumpled bedding. "Now, let's get you comfortable." She paused, frowning when she felt a warm, sticky substance on the sheets. Shock moved through her. She stared at the blood on her hand.

Gently, she shifted Letty's body. The girl was pitifully thin except where she was swollen with child. Charity pressed her hands to the bottom sheet and discovered it was saturated with Letty's blood. Her gaze flew back to her friend's pale features, and the young woman on the bed whispered softly, "It's the baby. It's coming . . . and there's something wrong."

Letty cried out, then bit her lower lip, muffling an agonized scream. She reached to grasp Charity's hand, holding on tightly until the spasm passed.

As soon as she could turn loose of Letty's hand, Charity snatched up a clean sheet and used it as padding to stem the flow of blood, but already she could see the crimson fluid soaking through the wadded-up cloth. How could anyone bleed like that and live?

Charity grabbed a rag from the basin on the floor beside the bed and gently sponged Letty's flushed face. She spoke in low, soothing tones. "There now, everything will be fine. The baby might be a few weeks early, but I'm sure it'll be strong and healthy. Perhaps Ansel should go for the doctor?"

Letty reached up and halted the movement of the wet cloth, her dark eyes fearful. "There isn't time, Charity. Something's wrong."

Charity tried to speak with assurance even though she was afraid. "It's going to be all right. I'll help you and God is with us." Now was the time to pray if there ever had been one. She wanted to help her friend so badly, but she didn't know what to do.

A violent seizure racked Letty's slender frame. Sweat stood out across the girl's brow. She buried her face in Charity's shoulder to muffle her scream. "Don't . . . want . . . Ansel . . . to . . . hear," she panted.

"Don't worry about Ansel," Charity soothed. When the pain abated, she ran the wet cloth across Letty's pale features. "How long have you been in labor?"

Letty shook her head and stiffened with the onset of another contraction. This time the seizure was so violent, so savage, that Letty screamed and clung to Charity's hand so tightly that Charity bit her lip to keep from crying out. The baby was very close to being born. She needed to tell Ansel to stoke the fire, to bring the kettle to a boil.

Letty's amber eyes grew wide with fear, her body shook with convulsions. She called Charity's name. The horrible shaking subsided. Still trembling, Letty began the Lord's Prayer with whispered fervor, " 'Our Father, which art in heaven . . . Hallowed be Thy name. . . .' " She screamed and clutched the sides of the bed, then continued, " '. . . Thy kingdom come. . . . Thy will be . . . done . . .' "

Charity couldn't think straight. She knew it shouldn't be happening this way. She'd assisted at other births, and they hadn't gone like this.

" 'Give us this day . . . our daily . . . ,' " Letty whispered. Another contraction seized her. "Ansel!" she pleaded in a high-pitched wail.

The dugout door flew open and Ansel rushed into the room, his eyes wild with fear. "Letty . . . Oh, dear God!" His words sounded like a prayer.

"Leave!" Charity tried to shield him from the pitiful sight. Letty thrashed wildly on the bed, screaming Ansel's name over and over.

"Charity—do something for her!" Ansel watched his wife in stunned horror. Letty's body was consumed with spasms as the child pushed from the confines of its mother's womb.

" 'And lead us . . . not . . . into . . . temp- tation . . . ,' " Letty murmured, stopping to pant, her eyes squeezed tight in torment. "Ohhhh . . . Ansel, help me!"

Throwing her full weight against his frame, Charity tried to shove Ansel toward the doorway, hoping to spare him further agony. "Go outside," she pleaded, raising her voice above the sound of Letty's terri- fied pleas. "I'll tend to her. She'll be fine. . . . She'll be fine. . . ."

But Ansel wouldn't leave. He leaned against the heavy wooden door, mumbling to himself. "God, help her, she's dying, Letty's dying."

He sagged against the doorframe and then slid down in a crumpled heap on the dirt floor, pressing his hands over his ears to block out her screams, tears of helpless frustration rolling down his cheeks.

Charity reached to support the baby coming out bottom first.

Letty's screams ran together. She clawed the sheets, her eyes bright with terror. "I'm goin' to die, Charity. Take care of . . . my . . . baby. . . . Take care of my baby. . . ."

"No!" Charity protested, her voice rising in hysteria. She couldn't permit Letty to die!

"You have to hold on, Letty—you have to fight!" The baby was nearly out now. Charity grasped the small mound of flesh and pulled, blinking back tears.

"Tell Ansel . . . I . . . love . . . him . . . take care . . . of . . . baby!"

Before Letty could finish she convulsed violently one final time. The baby slid free of her body into Charity's waiting hands.

Charity stared at the scrap of humanity. "It's a girl, Letty! You have a daughter! Look! She's beautiful!" Charity held the squalling, red-faced bundle up for Letty to see, her words slowly fading in her throat.

She blinked back tears when she realized Letty would never know she had a fine, beautiful daughter. She lay peacefully in the folds of the soiled linen, her screams silent now. Deathly silent.

Ansel glanced up when Charity held out the bundle in her arms, tears running down her face.

"Ansel?" she spoke softly, knowing how much he must be hurting.

He gazed back at her, eyes blank.

"You have a lovely baby daughter." She carefully pulled back the folds of the blanket and held the baby so that her father could inspect her.

He stared awkwardly at the tiny wrinkled face. "A little girl?"

"Yes. She looks real healthy."

His eyes slowly lifted to search Charity's. "Letty?"

Charity shook her head. For a moment the anguish in Ansel's eyes was more than she could bear.

Tears streamed. He looked at Charity. "She's . . . gone?"

She nodded, her own tears blinding her.

His gaze dropped to the baby. "A little girl. We was hoping for a boy," he said. All trace of emotion was gone from his voice.

"Would you like to hold your new daughter?"

"Oh . . . no . . . not now . . ." He turned and stumbled from the room. "Think I'll take a walk right now," he murmured.

"Ansel, don't go. . . ." Charity's heart was breaking. She wanted to go to him and lend him comfort, but she couldn't. He needed time to grieve.

"I'll be all right. You'll—you'll see to my wife's needs, won't you?"

"Of course." Charity would bathe Letty

and dress her in her Sunday best for viewing.

"Good, good." Ansel stopped and drew a deep breath, then looked up into the sky. "It's a fine day, isn't it? Couldn't ask for any finer. Letty would have found it real enjoyable."

"Ansel." Charity watched numbly as he ambled off alone. She glanced down at the tiny bundle in her arms and recognized Letty's pug nose and thatch of bright red hair. Letty would live on in this child, she thought with sad jubilation. Letty would live on, but what would happen to poor Ansel?

She lifted her face to the sky—and as if Letty could hear her, Charity finished Letty's last thought in a heartfelt whisper.

"'For Thine is the kingdom, and the power, and the glory . . . for ever. . . . Amen.'"

Beau drifted in and out of consciousness, neither awake nor completely under. He had no idea where he was, nor did he care. The pain was unbearable. Voices drifted around him. Were they speaking Kaw, or was he dreaming?

"White Sister asleep."

The words meant nothing to him. From a long way off another voice answered, "This no White Sister."

Something touched his chest, and he wanted to scream with the sudden jolt of pain.

"Gold Hair lives, but sick."

A clucking sound. "Ohhhh, big sick. Heap big sick."

Beau clutched the tattered edge of sleep around him and drifted off on a sea of dark water. He knew he was dying and he welcomed the release, but something drew him back to the light.

Rough hands stroked his fevered forehead. "This good man. *Good.*"

Good?

He didn't know about that. He wasn't *wicked,* but he wasn't a saint. He'd done his share of bad things, but those days were behind him. Truth be told, he'd been a better man after marrying Betsy. Now Bets was gone, and there wasn't any reason to live.

"No, Little Fawn, man White Sister's," the stern voice admonished someone. Didn't make sense, though. He didn't know anyone named White Sister.

"You wrong, Laughing Waters. White Sister gone. She leave Gold Hair to meet Wa-kun-dah alone. I take care. Make Gold Hair *strong* again."

A ripple of interest skipped through Beau's mind. Laughing Waters? Little Fawn? Where was he? Gold Hair? If this was a dream it was a strange one. No pictures, just voices talking babble.

"He fine strong buck." The voice came again. "When he well, Little Fawn call him Swift Buck with Tall Antlers. He be fine father to many papooses."

"I think he fine man too. I make him well, call him Brave Horse with Many Wounds."

Beau struggled to open his eyes, but it was too much for him. He must be dying. Maybe he was hearing angels, but he'd never heard of angels speaking Kaw. . . . But who was he to question almighty God? The voices had stopped and he drifted off again.

Hours—maybe days passed. He stirred uncomfortably on the bed. Hot! It was hot.

He wanted to force his eyes open, but the effort was too much. Every inch of his body ached, and his mouth was so dry he could spit cotton.

Where was he? He willed his legs to move, but he found them so heavy they refused to budge. A trickle of sweat ran down the sides of his head; when he tried to wipe it away, he realized his hands wouldn't move.

Paralyzed. He was *paralyzed*! The wolf's image with its great slobbering jaws rushed back, and he realized with a sinking sensation what had happened.

He was dead. The wolf had killed him.

The thought was strangely disappointing. He had to admit that he hadn't wanted to live since Betsy died, but he hadn't necessarily wanted to die either.

That must be what had happened. The wolf got him.

So this was what dead felt like? Somehow he had expected something different, like harp music and angels singing. He'd never counted on hurting and feeling heavy and hot. So hot!

He drew a shaky breath and found the air stifling, like a furnace. A new, even more disturbing thought surfaced. If he was dead . . . and it was this hot . . .

He groaned and willed his eyes to open. If he was where he thought he was, he might as well face it. Slowly, his lids fluttered open, and his eyes roamed the darkness. He was lying in some sort of bed . . . in a room. Did they have private rooms here? He'd never heard of that, but then he'd never known anyone who'd actually come back and said anything about the facilities. His heart hammered, and sweat rolled in rivulets off his forehead and dripped into his eyes.

The rosy glow of red-hot flames danced wickedly across the wall in front of him, and he groaned and clamped his eyes tightly shut. "Oh, God, help me," he prayed, limp now with fear. He really was here. Hell.

Well, it wasn't fair, he thought, resenting the fact that he hadn't had a chance to explain the bad things he'd done in life—not that there'd been all that many.

You'd think God would have cut him a little slack. He'd lived a good life after marrying and settling down. Been a good husband. Loved the Lord with all his heart . . . until Bets died. That ought to count for something, but his luck must be running true to form. This last year had been one thing after another. And now this. What would Ma say?

He did have a few things on his conscience, like that hundred-dollar debt he owed the general store, which he meant to pay once he got back to Missouri. But it would have been nice to be allowed to tell his side of the story, even if God did have his transgressions written down in some big book.

No, it wasn't fair. Ma had taught him to obey the Ten Commandments, and with a few minor exceptions, he'd done it.

Cole had been worse.

His younger brother, Cass, even worse than Cole.

He wondered if he could talk to someone and get this mess straightened out. He hadn't seen anyone when he'd opened his eyes. Maybe he was in some kind of holding pen.

He carefully opened one eye and moved it slowly around the room, surprised to discover hell looked much like the inside of a log cabin. He'd never stopped to think what hell would look like, since he'd never had any intention of going there.

But it sure was *hot* down here. Preacher Adams had got that right.

He tried to wipe the sweat off his forehead only to discover he was wrapped tight as a tick in some sort of blanket. He shifted, trying to free his hands. Suddenly he glanced up and his heart jumped into his throat.

Standing over him was the biggest squaw he'd ever seen. On closer examination he saw she was young and she was smiling a wide, toothless grin.

"Gold Hair wake. Good."

Gold Hair? Where had he heard that name before?

He wondered if he was expected to say something back, though he preferred not to. He might be in hell, but he didn't have to socialize this soon. From all he'd heard, the people who came here weren't the kind he'd choose to associate with.

A second woman suddenly loomed above him, her massive bulk blocking the flickering flames on the walls. She began to unwrap the tight blanket.

Beau groaned and jerked away. "No! Don't!" he pleaded. Pain shot through his side. "Listen, there's been a mistake."

"No talk, Gold Hair," the second woman grunted. "Save strength."

His eyes widened when the first woman reached out and touched a lock of his hair, smiling as she fingered the silken locks. "Pretty, like rocks in water."

"Listen, who's in charge?" Beau asked. What was going on here? A stench filled his nostrils. The second woman hurriedly stripped off the blanket.

"No hurt, Gold Hair. We make well," the first woman promised.

He tried to fight them off, but he didn't have the strength of a stray kitten, and who was this Gold Hair they kept nattering about? There'd been a mistake. He was in the wrong place; why couldn't they see that? Someone had gotten the records mixed up and "Gold Hair" was up there with the streets of gold, where he was supposed to be, and he was down here being roasted like a spit pig.

The women ignored his protests. They dipped their large hands into a pail beside the bed and slapped moist, vile-smelling mud all over his body.

He gagged and winced when a series of sharp, excruciating pains shot through him like stray bullets. He realized that this must be part of his eternal punishment, though he'd never imagined it would be administered by a pair of loud-talking squaws.

Preacher Adams had never mentioned a word of this. What Bible verses said that he had to put up with this sort of treatment? Some of those minor prophets, he'd bet. That was his last rational thought before he mercifully slipped back into sweet oblivion.

CHAPTER 4

LETITIA MARGARET LATIMER
BELOVED WIFE
MAY SHE BRING AS MUCH JOY IN HEAVEN
AS SHE BROUGHT HERE ON EARTH

Charity's heart nearly broke as she watched Ansel lovingly carve the inscription onto a wooden cross for Letty's grave.

She had dressed Letty in her wedding gown, made of the finest ivory silk. When she'd unpacked the dress, she'd found a pair of satin shoes tucked beneath the folds. She had slipped the shoes on the young girl's feet, thinking of her well-to-do family back East, who'd married their daughter to Ansel Latimer in grand style, only to have her die in a dugout on a Kansas prairie. They'd have to be notified of her death, but that was Ansel's job.

She brushed Letty's hair until it was the color of a fiery sunset and fastened a cameo brooch at her neckline. Ansel had given the cameo to Letty on their first Christmas together. It had been her most cherished possession.

Charity gazed down at her friend, and her eyes filled with tears. Letty looked so small, so young . . . so helpless.

She draped the kitchen table with Letty's grandmother's lace tablecloth, then called Ansel in from the lean-to, where he'd been building the small pine box.

When he stepped hesitantly into the room, she slipped past him to leave, allowing him time alone with his wife. Her thoughts returned to Ferrand. She hadn't been there when he died—no chance to say good-bye. Maybe that had been for the best. She'd been spared the memory of seeing him suffer. Ansel would never forget the horror of Letty's death.

She remembered the stranger lying on her bed back home. By now he was dead.

Maybe in heaven with Letty. Maybe not. She didn't know his faith or if he had any.

Was there a special place up there for newcomers, one where they could get acquainted? Were Letty and the stranger looking down right this minute, watching them today? If they were, would the man she had tried so hard to save forgive her for leaving him to die alone? Could she have done anything to help Letty? Not the way the lifeblood had poured out of her.

Charity leaned against the rough bark of a sycamore tree and cried for Letty, for Ansel, for the stranger, for Ferrand, and for herself. Most of all she cried for that poor motherless baby girl who would never know the wonderful woman who had given her birth.

When she went back into the dugout, she and Ansel hoisted the simple pine box onto the middle of the kitchen table, then gently placed Letty in it. Charity lit a single candle that would burn until they buried Letty in the morning.

She stood for a few moments looking down at her friend, fondly recalling how they'd sat around that same table, laughing and giggling like two schoolgirls. For hours on end they'd made plans for the new baby, stitching tiny gowns and lace bonnets and knitting booties. So many dreams had come to an end with Letty's death; so many hopes would be buried with her.

The funeral was small. Only a handful of neighbors stood in a circle around the open grave, singing "Amazing grace, how sweet the sound, that saved a wretch like me. . . ."

Letty had known that grace. She was at rest now, gone home.

Pastor Olson held his worn Bible, looking over the small group of neighbors with compassionate eyes. "We are gathered here to say good-bye to Letty. This young wife and mother loved God. She lived in obedience to His commandments. And our lives are richer for having known her.

"She was a good friend, a good wife, and she would have made a good mother—but unforeseen circumstances took her from us. God did not cause Letty to die, and we must not place the blame at His doorstep. But we can be sure He received her with open arms, and He had a place prepared for her.

"Although she left this life, leaving behind a husband and daughter, she did not go alone. A loving heavenly Father sent His angels to carry Lazarus home, and those same angels cradled our friend in their arms and carried her to that place where there are no more tears, no more sorrow, no pain.

"We grieve today for Letty. We will miss her, but she is in a far better place, and someday we will be reunited with her. Until then we will remember her with love, and we thank God for the privilege of having had her with us for a precious while. Letty is not gone—she lives in our hearts and minds, and she will live on in her precious baby daughter. We will not forget her. Let us pray."

The baby cried, and Charity gently patted the tiny back until she quieted. Neighbors paused to shake hands and murmur words of condolence, leaving one by one until only Charity and Ansel were left.

She waited, letting him take the lead, but he only stood staring at the raw earth heaped over the casket. The baby whimpered, and he cast one blank look in their direction and turned away. Charity walked alone back to the dugout, carrying Letty's daughter. Ansel didn't come in to eat until long after she had fed the baby and rocked her to sleep.

Friday dawned dark and dreary. A cold, gray mist fell from a leaden sky and encompassed the buckboard as Ansel and Charity rode without speaking.

Occasionally she crooned to the tiny infant carefully wrapped against the weather and cradled closely in her arms. Ansel drove the team of horses with methodical movements, seemingly unaware of either her or the child.

Had it been only two days since she'd traveled this same road? To Charity it seemed an eternity had passed since Wednesday, the day Ansel had come to fetch her for Letty.

Dear, sweet Letty. It was still hard to comprehend that the fresh mound of dirt behind the Latimer dugout was all that remained of her friend.

Death had come so swiftly she hardly had time to get it all straight in her mind. Letty was in heaven, leaving her precious baby motherless, and poor Ansel, all his hopes and dreams dashed. No wife and a new-born babe to look after. Her heart went out to him.

The baby started fussing and Charity looked up. "She's hungry again." Without the benefit of her mother's milk the infant seemed insatiable.

It bothered Charity that the baby hadn't been named yet. When she'd mentioned the subject at breakfast, Ansel looked at her vacantly. Instead of answering, he'd responded vaguely about his crop for next spring.

Letty had wanted to name the baby Mary Kathleen, if she should have a girl, but Charity wanted Ansel's blessing on the name. He glanced down at the infant, and she wondered if he was aware it was his child. At times, she didn't think he knew. He'd barely acknowledged that the child had been born, leaving the baby's sole care to her.

She was sure Ansel was acting strangely because his grief was so profound. He didn't cry or express his sorrow overtly. Charity knew if he'd just hold his new daughter, somehow a small part of Letty would return to him.

The babe looked so much like her mother.

Letty's laughing, amber-colored eyes stared back at her. Letty would live on in this tiny morsel of humanity. She had to make Ansel realize that.

"We'll be at your place soon," he said quietly, his tone unchanged by the sucking noises the baby made on her fist. "The child can eat then."

Charity lifted the infant to her shoulder and gently bounced her up and down. The soothing motion stilled her fretfulness for the moment. She worried how Ansel would care for the baby alone, once he returned home. Perhaps, she sighed, it would be good for father and daughter to be on their own. She'd promised to help find a woman to care for the baby, but she knew that could take time. Most everyone in these parts had their own young'uns to see after. In some ways, though, she felt that might be for the best. Ansel could become acquainted with his daughter, and Mary Kathleen could help fill the void in his life.

The baby whimpered as the buckboard topped a rise and Charity's cabin came into view. Her thoughts turned to another, even more perplexing problem: the stranger in her house. He would have to be buried immediately. She'd been gone much longer than she'd expected, and his remains would have to be disposed of quickly.

She glanced at Ansel and prayed he'd spare her the unpleasant task. Her heart still ached from having left the man to die alone.

The buckboard rumbled into the yard, and Ansel brought the horses to a halt. Charity noticed a heavy plume of smoke roaring from the chimney.

Ansel jumped down from the wagon and lifted Charity and the baby to the ground.

"Someone has built a fire," she remarked, puzzled. She stared at the rising smoke. Was it possible the stranger was alive? A thrill of expectation shot through her though she quickly suppressed the unlikely hope. There had to be another explanation for the smoke.

She glanced around the yard, looking for a clue. The stack of buffalo chips next to the house was the exact height it had been when she'd left two days ago. The oxen grazed stoically. Old Bossy, her bag heavy with two days' milk, bawled from the small pen beside the lean-to. A few hens roamed outside, scratching in the dirt.

Gabriel and Job lay in front of the door,

lazily wagging their tails, apparently waiting for Charity to come and scratch behind their ears.

Everything looked exactly like she'd left it, except for the strong smell of smoke in the air. She turned to ask Ansel how he'd explain the strange occurrence, but he was already climbing back onto the seat of the buckboard.

"Ansel, why don't you rest for a spell before you leave?" She knew he'd need the wagon to carry the stranger's remains to the gravesite.

"Thank you, but I'd best be getting along." He picked up the reins and released the brake.

Charity's jaw dropped. "Ansel," she protested lamely, "you can't be leaving!"

"You take care now, you hear?" He whistled and slapped the reins across the horses' broad rumps. The buckboard rolled noisily out of the yard amid the jangle of harness and creaking leather.

Charity watched the wagon roll off in the direction it had just come. She glanced from the bundle in her arms to the disappearing buckboard. *Great balls of fire!* He *was* leaving.

"Wait!" she shouted, running after the wagon. "You forgot your baby!" But in moments she was out of breath. Her footsteps faltered.

She released an exasperated sigh and stared down at the infant in her arms. If this wasn't a fine kettle of fish! How dare Ansel ride off and leave the child in her care!

The baby started to cry, thrashing her fists angrily in the air, demanding her dinner. Charity trudged toward the house, wondering what had gotten into Ansel. Surely he'd have the good sense to remember he'd forgotten his daughter and come back. Meanwhile she was left to care for the infant, and face the unpleasant task of burying the stranger, by herself.

If her thoughts weren't disconcerting enough, the baby was screaming at the top of her lungs when she finally reached the cabin. She pushed the door open and sucked in her breath when a blast of suffocating air nearly knocked her to her knees.

"What in . . . ?" Charity pushed the door wider and stepped into the room, trying to adjust her eyes to the dim light. When her vision cleared she couldn't believe her eyes. Two squaws sat before the fireplace in rocking chairs they had pulled up to the hearth. They had built a roaring fire, and the flames were licking wildly up the chimney.

Charity wrinkled her nose, her attention momentarily diverted when she noticed the several large pans of herbs and roots bubbling on the stove, filling the room with a vile odor.

The stranger lay on the bed, swathed tightly from head to toe in a bedsheet. He reminded Charity of a picture of an Egyptian mummy she had once seen in a book.

The room was so stifling hot she couldn't breathe, and the smell rolling from the stove made her stomach lurch. She stood speechless at the door, clutching the baby against her bosom.

Little Fawn caught sight of Charity and gave her a wide grin. "White Sister return?" Her smile wilted. She scrambled to her feet, dragging Laughing Waters with her. "We take care of Gold Hair."

"Little Fawn? Laughing Waters?" Charity stared at the two disheveled women with growing bewilderment. The heat in the room had flushed their faces with perspiration. Buckskin dresses clung to their massive forms. Sweat rolled from beneath their dark hairlines and dripped off their chins.

"What is going on here?" Charity glanced to the bed where the stranger lay. Her heart leapt when she heard him moan weakly, trying to break free of the bindings.

Little Fawn crossed her arms over her ample bosom, and a combative glint came into her eyes. "We make Gold Hair better."

Charity couldn't believe he was still alive. It was nothing short of a miracle, but the man *had* survived. "He's better. . . . He really is? Oh, thank you, God!"

Laughing Waters grunted. *"Little Fawn and Laughing Waters* make Gold Hair better," she said curtly.

Charity hurried to the bed. Yes, he *was* alive. His eyes were open and staring. His nose was visible through an opening in the sheet.

"Why is he wrapped so tightly?" she asked in a whisper. Was he aware? fully conscious? She didn't know.

"Make medicine work," Little Fawn explained. She scurried to the bed and edged Charity out of the way with a large hip. Her fingers picked up a stray lock of his hair, and the man's eyes widened fearfully. She smiled and stroked the golden strand. "Pretty, like rocks in water. I keep."

The man groaned and clamped his eyes shut.

"I think he's trying to say something." Charity reached to unwrap the bandage wound so tightly under his chin that it prevented him from speaking. Little Fawn's hand shot out and stopped her. The squaw sent her a stern look. "*We* help Gold Hair!"

Charity glanced up, surprised to hear the possessive note in her voice. For months, Laughing Waters and Little Fawn had made a habit of visiting the cabin, making themselves at home. Whenever they came, they examined every nook and cranny, satisfying their natural curiosity.

She never scolded them, even when they peeked in the cooking utensils or pried open the storage bins. If she wasn't busy, she would let them watch her work the spinning wheel. Sometimes she would snip a piece of yarn or a colorful ribbon and give it to them. They always left delighted with their new treasures.

Apparently they'd happened by to visit two days ago and discovered the wounded man, and now they had laid claim to him.

"Thank you very much for tending . . . Gold Hair . . . while I was away," she said carefully. She would have to convince them that the man was hers, not theirs.

"Gold Hair heap good man," Little Fawn proclaimed. She grinned.

"Oh, yes . . . yes, I can see that. He's very . . . nice. He's . . . mine."

Little Fawn's face dropped.

Laughing Waters's eyes narrowed. "Why you leave Gold Hair? Heap big sick."

"I know he is." Charity wasn't sure how much they understood, but she sensed they were waiting for an explanation. Remembering the baby, she smiled and unwrapped the blanket, proudly revealing a grumpy Mary Kathleen. "See? I've been away helping my friend have her baby. That's why I had to leave Gold Hair."

The women lowered their heads in unison and stared at the child. "Papoose." Little Fawn tickled under the baby's chin.

Charity noticed Laughing Waters wasn't impressed. "Gold Hair heap big sick. We fix; we keep," she announced.

Since the Indians had never seemed threatening, Charity wasn't alarmed. Apparently the two women had been able to do for the stranger what she hadn't, and she was grateful. But not grateful enough to let them have him.

"You see, my friend, Letty, was very ill. She was about to have her baby, and she needed my help," Charity explained. "Since Gold Hair was asleep, I thought it would be all right to leave." That wasn't exactly true, but Charity knew the women would have no way of knowing otherwise. Broken English was their only means of communication. Actually they understood very little short of their native tongue.

Laughing Waters was clearly skeptical. "Where mother of papoose?"

"She . . . died," Charity admitted.

Laughing Waters still wasn't convinced. "Where papoose's father?"

"He's . . . not here right now . . . but he'll be back soon. Because my friend died, I was gone longer than I intended. I'm thankful to see you and Little Fawn have taken such good care of Gold Hair."

Little Fawn and Laughing Waters exchanged noncommittal looks. "If you'll show me what to do, I'll take over now." Charity prayed they'd buy her story. "He was attacked by a wolf, and I haven't been quite sure how to care for him. I see you have him on the mend."

Laughing Waters grunted. It seemed unlikely the two would relinquish their rights to the white man. They went off into a corner and gestured animatedly, whispering to each other.

Charity held her breath. She glanced at the bed and found the man eyeing all three of them warily. His eyes were as blue as she remembered, and she tried to reassure him with a discreet nod.

Laughing Waters returned and grudgingly handed Charity a large cup of vile-smelling liquid. "Make Gold Hair drink."

Charity nodded and released a pent-up sigh of relief. She set the cup on the bedside table. "Thank you; I will."

"We be back Big Father's Day," Little Fawn stated firmly.

The baby began to fuss, and Charity absently rocked her back and forth in her arms. She thought she'd faint from the heat. "Sunday? Yes, Sunday will be fine." They were not going to give him up easily.

"Keep fire burning. Heap big sweat. Make Gold Hair better."

"Yes . . . yes, of course," Charity promised, wondering why she hadn't thought to try and sweat the poison out of him herself.

"Put medicine on hurts."

Charity stared at the bucket of herbs and roots sitting next to the bed. "I will."

Little Fawn walked back to the bed and touched a strand of golden hair. She gave the man a flirtatious wink and displayed the wide gap of missing front teeth. He shut his eyes.

"We go now," Laughing Waters announced.

"I'll take good care of Gold Hair," Charity promised.

Laughing Waters started past her and paused to look at the baby again. "Gold Hair make stronger papoose," she grunted.

Charity watched Little Fawn and Laughing Waters open the door.

"We be back Big Father's Day," Laughing Waters repeated.

"We'll be here."

The door slammed, and Charity sank weakly onto a chair. The baby began to scream. *What a disagreeable day,* she thought numbly.

Most disagreeable.

Beau lay wrapped in his cocoon, relieved the two squaws had left. He didn't know what the women had in mind for him, but he had a hunch it wasn't anything he'd enjoy. The woman who'd gotten rid of them tried to soothe the infant.

She kept casting worried glances toward the bed as she rushed around the room, trying to calm the baby's wails, which were getting more frantic by the minute.

Even the warm milk squeezed through a clean cloth didn't help. The baby screamed at the top of her lungs, her tiny face turning red as a raspberry. The woman paced the floor, jiggling her up and down in her arms.

The more she jiggled, the louder the baby cried. Obviously she hadn't had much experience with babies.

Still trussed up like a Christmas goose, Beau lay on the bed watching the growing ruckus. When the infant erupted into a full-blown tantrum, holding her breath until her tiny features turned a strange, bluish white, the woman panicked and broke into tears. Both woman and child were sobbing noisily when Beau cleared his throat, hoping to get her attention.

He'd felt relief when he'd finally realized he wasn't in hell—at least he wasn't in the fiery pit described in the Good Book. But exactly *where* was he?

Wherever it was, it was strange. Two Indian squaws fussing over him, slapping foul-smelling something on his wounds. Now he was faced with a baby howling like a banshee and a woman who obviously didn't know the first thing about mother-hood.

He cleared his throat and squirmed about, but the woman and baby were too busy crying to notice. Glancing around, he focused on a tin cup filled with tea sitting on the stand beside the bed. He inched his way across the straw-filled mattress and nudged the cup with his shoulder, knocking it off the table.

The contents splattered on the bed, leaving a dark stain on the white linens, but the cup had the desired effect of hitting the floor with a resounding clatter.

Both woman and baby ceased their wailing at the same instant. She looked his way, and he tried to motion with his eyes for her to remove the tight bandage confining his chin.

The baby resumed screaming while the woman continued to stare at him.

"Were you speaking to me?"

"Ohmmhgtynm."

"You want me to untie the bandage?"

"Ohmmmhgtynm!"

"Yes, of course."

She used one hand to try to loosen the knot in the bandage, attempting to converse over the baby's screams. "I'm sorry, I know we're disturbing you, and I'm *trying* to get her to hush, but she won't!"

The knot came undone, and Beau felt like he'd been released from a bear trap. He worked his jaws back and forth, wincing at the painful stiffness yet grateful for the overdue freedom.

"I don't know what's gotten into her," the woman apologized. "Nothing I do seems to help."

"Get the scissors and cut me out of this sheet," Beau whispered hoarsely.

"Oh, I don't think I should. Little Fawn and Laughing Waters said—"

"I know what they said!"

Startled by the snap in his voice, the infant screamed louder.

"Just get me out of this!"

"You're scaring the baby." The woman turned mulish. She patted the baby on the back, which only made her cry harder. "If I remove the sheet, it'll disturb your wounds. I don't want to do anything to hinder your recovery. You've been very ill. . . ."

Beau interrupted, making a conscious effort to lower his voice and speak calmly. "Just get me out of this. I'll help with the baby."

Evidently those were the magic words. He'd figured she'd do anything to stop the baby's crying and he'd been right. She grabbed the scissors and started snipping away at the sheet. The baby lay on the bed beside Beau, kicking and bellowing at the top of her lungs.

"Your bandages need changing." Beau sucked in his breath when she lifted the fabric Little Fawn and Laughing Waters had carefully laid over the tender wounds.

"Ow! That *hurts.* Take it easy!"

"I can't help it; I'm trying to be gentle." She gingerly peeled away another layer. "You don't have to be so cranky."

"You let a wolf gnaw on you for supper and see how full of brotherly love you are. Ouch! Look out; that hurts!"

There was a time when he would apologize for yelling at a female, but much had happened to change him in the past year. He gritted his teeth in renewed agony when cold air hit his wounds.

"There, now . . . one more . . ." She removed the last bandage and he sagged with relief.

Raising himself up, he sucked in his breath at the pain and closed his eyes until the room stopped spinning. He didn't know a man could hurt like this. Foul-smelling mud encased his body; the odor made him sick.

The woman sat down in a nearby chair and rocked the baby. "You remember the wolf?" She stared at him as if she was afraid he'd keel over.

"I try not to." He winced when the baby's howls continued. "Hand her to me."

She glanced at him in surprise. "You feel like holding her?"

"I can hold her better than I can stand to listen to her."

She hurriedly gathered the baby in her

arms and carefully handed her to him. Beau caught his breath when one tiny flailing fist hit one of his wounds.

"I'm so sorry!" She started to take the infant, but Beau shrugged her away and eased the tiny bundle into the crook of his arm. He laid his head back on the pillow, feeling as limp as a piece of worn-out rope. A fine sheen of sweat stood on his forehead. To his relief, the baby promptly ceased crying and snuggled deep into his side.

The room became quite peaceful. Beau gazed down at the infant in his arms. "You know, little one, you're picking up some bad habits," he said softly. "Some man's going to have to take that fire out of you someday if you don't control that nasty temper."

The baby hiccuped, then stuck her fist in her mouth and sucked loudly.

"She's hungry," he said.

"I know she is, but she refuses to take her milk."

"Give me the cloth."

The woman fetched the cloth and gave it to him. In moments the baby was sucking contentedly.

"How did you do that?" She seemed awed by the way he handled the child.

The tiny baby girl settled snugly next to his large frame, her big amber eyes drooping with exhaustion.

"I've always been good with kids. I have a nephew I used to visit every day. We got along real well."

Beau refused to think about the child he'd lost.

He held the baby until she slowly dropped into a peaceful slumber. She nestled trustfully against him, and somehow the pain in his heart began to ease. The image of Betsy, heavy with child, drifted into his thoughts. *Oh, God, not now, please.* He didn't want to think about Betsy . . . didn't want to remember it could have been his child tucked against his side. . . . He could feel the aching sadness creep back to overwhelm him.

"Would you like me to move her?" the woman asked.

Beau tucked the baby's blanket snugly around her. "She'll be fine right here."

"I need to put clean bandages on your wounds."

"In a while." He lay back, exhausted. As

soon as he got his strength he was getting out of this madhouse. Toothless women torturing him, a squalling baby, and this woman who watched him like a hawk. Did she think he was going somewhere? In his condition? From what he could tell, she was still young. Small and slender with hair the color of a raven's wing, nice green eyes, and a wide, generous mouth—certainly nothing about her appearance to turn a man away. He realized he hadn't noticed a woman in a very long time, and he didn't plan to start now. There would never be another Betsy in his life. Not ever.

Charity tried not to stare, but her eyes wandered back to the bare expanse of masculine chest. She remembered how protected, how wonderful she'd felt when he'd held her, even if he had thought she was his Betsy.

She suddenly realized that she missed having her own man, missed being held and kissed and loved.

She didn't think of Ferrand as often, but

then she hadn't thought of him any less. Having this man in her house was improper, but surely God would condone compassion. Human compassion of which the apostle Paul spoke so eloquently.

After her husband's death she'd sworn she'd never love another man, never again risk the hurt he'd caused her by going off and getting himself killed in that senseless war.

It occurred to Charity that she'd been angry at Ferrand for a long time. Now she could feel that anger subsiding. For the first time since his death she found herself thinking that maybe it would be possible to love again. To feel again.

She longed to have her own child. Mary Kathleen was precious, but she wasn't hers. Taking care of Letty's baby only reminded her of the emptiness in her heart, the void. If only she'd had Ferrand's child the last few years she wouldn't have been so lonely. Her gaze drifted wistfully back to the stranger and she wondered anew why she found him so attractive. His hair was shaggy, he hadn't shaved in weeks, and his large frame was whipcord thin. The two large wounds across his middle were covered with a thick, sticky poultice. His ribs were poking through his skin. Still, she found him extremely . . . interesting.

Charity found the admission disturbing. Would her growing feelings for this stranger only serve to bring her new heartbreak?

"I guess we should introduce ourselves." She willed herself to take one step at a time. She drew her palm across her dress to dry the moisture from it and extended her hand. "I'm Charity Burk. I shot the wolf. This is my cabin."

The man glanced at her extended hand but made no effort to take it. "You shouldn't have bothered."

"Oh . . . no bother." Charity faltered. She thought he'd be immensely grateful that she'd saved his life. She paused, waiting for a thank you, but when "God bless you" didn't come, she dropped her hand to her side.

"What did you say your name was?" He hadn't said, but she thought it only decent he supply some sort of information about himself.

"Claxton."

Charity smiled. "Just . . . Claxton?"

"Beau. Beau Claxton."

"That's nice. I'll bet your mother chose that name." Charity noticed he was losing interest in the conversation. "Well, Beau, I must admit, there were times when I thought I'd never know who you were." She watched his eyes droop with fatigue. "Are you from around here?"

"No." His voice sounded weaker than before.

"I'm sorry I had to leave, but Letty—the baby's mother—she needed my help. I'm so thankful Laughing Waters and Little Fawn happened along when they did."

"I'm not sure I'm all that thankful, but I'm too tired to think about it. How long have I been like this?"

"Nearly a week, but you're getting better." It was a relief to see his wounds starting to improve. He still had many weeks before he was healed.

He was silent for a moment. "You said the child's mother died?"

"Yes, I'm afraid she did."

"That's too bad. A baby should have its mother."

"Would you like some broth? I see that Laughing Waters and Little Fawn left some on the stove for you."

"I'm not hungry. Just tired. Bone tired."

"Rest a spell. We can talk later." Charity leaned to tuck the sheet around him and the sleeping infant. The two made a fetching sight. His eyes drifted shut. She stood and gazed fondly from the baby to him. In moments they were sound asleep, his large arm wrapped protectively around Mary Kathleen's tiny shoulders.

I hope there's no Betsy waiting for you to come home. Charity found herself appalled by her thoughts. Startled by her wistful thinking, she realized how selfish she sounded.

If he was married, she would write and inform his wife of her husband's injuries straight away. And yet . . . She reached to brush a lock of golden hair from his forehead and sighed.

Maybe . . . just maybe Betsy was his sister. But no, he wouldn't kiss a sister the way he'd kissed her. Could Betsy be an acquaintance? The possibility sent a pang of jealousy through her. Jealousy? Now where had that come from? Beau Claxton was a stranger. But she couldn't forget the way he looked, lying there helpless, and she couldn't forget those blue eyes. Anyone could tell from the way he acted he'd been brought up a gentleman.

Well, no matter who Betsy was, Beau Claxton was a fine man. If there wasn't a legal Mrs. Claxton, there'd be one soon—if she had anything to say about it.

CHAPTER 5

The smell of corn bread baking in the oven woke Beau next. He had no concept of time. The tempting aroma filled the cabin, and his empty stomach knotted with hunger. How long had it been since he'd last eaten?

He glanced down at the small bundle snuggled against his side, and a smile touched the corners of his mouth. The baby was sleeping peacefully.

Without disturbing the infant, he shifted to ease his stiff joints. The movement hurt, but not as much as before.

Settled more comfortably, he let his gaze drift toward the window, where he noticed the last rays of sunshine glistening on the pane. *It must be late afternoon,* he thought, realizing this was the first time he'd been able to distinguish the hour of day. His head felt clearer, more alert. How long had he been drifting in and out of darkness that had threatened to sweep him away forever?

His gaze moved on, roaming aimlessly around the room. The bright gingham curtain hanging at the window looked freshly washed and ironed. A buffalo rug covered the floor. Everything was tidy.

The room had a woman's touch. The colorful red-and-blue patchwork quilt draped across the foot of the bed reflected long hours spent on the intricate rows of tiny stitches. He didn't know much about such womanly pursuits, but he'd watched his mother sit beside the lamp in her parlor, working late into the night on a coverlet much like the one he saw now. Bets had brightened their home with pretty things. His chest tightened when he remembered the home he had built with such high hopes. He'd planned to grow old there, raise a fine family of Claxton men and women. When Betsy died, taking their child with her, he'd lost everything: his home, his will to live— even his trust in God. He felt ashamed at the way he had acted. Just walked away from the people who loved him, away from the values he'd been taught; he sure hadn't been living the way a Claxton had been taught to live.

He'd been drifting for a long time, bitter, angry, and not caring if he lived or died, but now it seemed God had decided that he'd live. He guessed you couldn't run far enough or long enough to get away from God. Beau knew it wouldn't be easy, but he was going to have to make a life for himself again. Life went on, whether a man wanted it to or not, and the time had come for him to bury Betsy and let her go. He had to get up and go home, back to Missouri. Maybe he'd talk Ma and their housekeeper, Willa, into coming to live with him. The women could tend the house while he worked the fields. It wouldn't be the rich, full life he'd had with Betsy, but it would be livable.

The sound of a voice humming "Dixie" distracted him. His head slowly pivoted on the pillow, seeking the source of the clear, sweet tones.

He saw a young woman standing at the stove, stirring a large pot with a wooden spoon. Instead of the foul-smelling brew the pot had formerly sent off, a delicious aroma of meat and vegetables rose from the steam.

Who was this girl? Beau searched his memory for her name. Charita? Cherry? He couldn't remember.

"Well, hello. You're finally awake." Charity's voice interrupted his thoughts. She set the spoon aside and wiped her hands on her apron. "Dinner will be ready soon. I hope you feel up to eating a bite."

His gaze drifted back to the pot on the stove. The smell of stew simmering piqued his interest. "I believe I could eat."

"Well, good!" Charity brought her hands together enthusiastically. "That's the most encouraging sign of recovery so far." She ladled the thick stew onto a plate, adding a piping hot wedge of corn bread and slab of freshly churned butter, then arranged everything on a tray along with a large glass of milk.

The baby was beginning to stir when she approached, so she set the tray on the small table beside the bed and gently scooped Mary Kathleen into her arms. "Best you eat slow," she cautioned. "It's been a long time since you've had solid food. Too much taken too fast might upset your stomach."

"Aren't you going to eat?" His eyes were on the corn bread, thick and crusty—just the way Ma used to make it.

"I'll feed the baby first." Charity returned to the stove and removed the bottle of milk she'd warmed, pouring some in the dish she'd used earlier. She tied a knot in the end of a square of cheesecloth and dipped it in the milk. "You and Mary Kathleen had a nice long nap."

Beau picked up the piece of corn bread and took a cautious bite. The exquisite flavor burst in his mouth. It'd been a long time since he'd tasted anything so good.

"Looks like snow to the west." Charity sat down in the rocker and held the baby, who was eagerly sucking from the cloth. "Sure could use a good soaking. It's been real dry."

Beau took another bite of the corn bread and chewed it slowly. "What time of the year is this?"

"Late November." Charity cocked her head to one side. "Why?"

November? He'd been wandering for over a year? The thought astounded him, and he felt a pang of remorse. His family must be sick with worry. "Exactly where am I?"

"Kansas, why?"

"No reason." Beau picked up the spoon and brought a bite of stew to his mouth.

"This is my home . . . mine and my husband's until he died."

"I'm in Kansas? I'm not in Missouri?"

Charity laughed warmly. "You're in Kansas. Not far from a town called Cherry Grove."

"Kansas?"

"Kansas," she repeated. "What part of Missouri are you from?"

Kansas? How had he ended up so far from home? Ma must be nearly out of her mind with worry. Lilly Claxton was a mother hen, never happy until all of her sons were safe beneath her wings.

"I . . . River Run . . . I think."

Charity thought his answer was odd. Had the sickness affected his memory? In a way, it would be to her advantage if he couldn't remember his past. If he couldn't remember who he was, then he might be more easily persuaded to stay and help her. She decided to face her biggest obstacle first.

"Who's Betsy?"

He met her inquiring gaze, and a defensive light came into his eyes. "Who?"

"Betsy. You kept calling for her while you were unconscious." Charity bit her lower lip, praying Betsy would be *anyone* but his wife.

Beau pushed his plate away though he'd barely touched it.

"You're finished already?" Her tone rang with disappointment.

"I've had enough."

"But you barely touched your food."

"I lost my appetite."

Charity hated to hear that. If he didn't eat properly, she knew he'd be slow to regain his strength. "I'll put your plate in the warming oven; you'll feel like eating more later."

He seemed to ignore the suggestion. He settled back on the pillow and closed his eyes.

Charity felt like crying. They had been getting along so well until she mentioned Betsy. She hated to ask him again, but she had to know. If he had a wife, then she'd nurse him to recovery and then send him on his way. She sighed. Maybe she should give up and go back home. Her family would welcome her.

No. She had to stay and fight. Ferrand had worked too hard for her to turn her back on this land and walk away.

When Mary Kathleen finished the milk, Charity lifted her up to her shoulder and patted her back gently, savoring the sweet fragrance of the baby's skin. Once more her thoughts turned to the baby's father and where he could be. All afternoon she had been expecting him to return for his daughter, but it was getting dark and she feared he wasn't coming.

If he didn't come tomorrow, she wasn't sure what she'd do. Send someone to fetch him? She didn't know who it could be. And it would be impossible to leave Beau and the baby alone. You'd think Ansel would be hungry for the sight of this precious child. Mary Kathleen was all he had left of Letty, and she needed her father. Maybe he was making arrangements for someone to help him care for his child.

Grief had rendered Ansel temporarily forgetful, she reasoned. It was the only explanation she could come up with to explain his puzzling behavior. Surely tomorrow he would come for his daughter. She needed milk bottles not cheesecloth to drink from.

Returning to the present, Charity remembered that Beau hadn't answered her question about Betsy. Was it an oversight, or had he deliberately avoided the subject? There was only one way to find out. She could be what Ferrand had always called downright nosy. She decided to chance it.

"You never answered me about Betsy."

This time, she was sure he was deliberately avoiding her question. He lay on the bed, eyes closed, hands folded peacefully across his chest. Ignoring her.

The baby burped loudly, filling the silence that had suddenly crowded the room. Beau remained silent.

"Well?" Charity prompted. She wasn't going to give up until he answered her.

Finally he drew a deep breath and opened his eyes. He met her gaze across the room, his face twisted into a pained expression. "Betsy is my wife."

Disappointment ricocheted like heat lightning through Charity's heart. She'd known it was a possibility that he was married, hadn't she? Hadn't she warned herself not to get her hopes up? But nothing could dull the dismal feeling of frustration closing in on her.

"Oh . . . I—I thought maybe that's who she might be." Her voice sounded high and hollow even to her own ears.

Well, Charity, you've no one to blame but yourself for getting the foolish idea in your head that he was sent to you as a personal gift. It was plain he wouldn't be any use to her now. He had a wife, Betsy, waiting for him when he recovered. She recalled the love in his eyes when he had been so terribly sick and mistaken her for Betsy. He wouldn't stay. She couldn't expect him to.

She sighed and squared her shoulders. "First thing tomorrow morning, I'll write your wife a letter informing her about what's happened and where you are."

Beau stared at the ceiling for a moment with expressionless blue eyes. Charity thought she detected a veiled sadness creeping into them. "Yeah, you can do that, but I don't see how you're going to have it delivered," he said softly.

"Shouldn't be too hard. It's about time to go into town for the mail. I'll send the letter then. It will take a few weeks to reach your wife, but—"

Beau interrupted. "You can't do that. Bets is dead."

Charity's gaze lifted to his, witnessing the grief in his eyes. She ached for his loss, but she couldn't smother the faint glimmer of hope for what this might mean to her.

"I'm so sorry."

Dead. Betsy was dead! Relief filled her, and she was instantly ashamed for being so heartless and selfish. It was plain to see that his wife's death had nearly destroyed him.

"Yeah." He took a deep, ragged breath. "So am I."

"How long ago?"

"Over a year. She was carrying our baby, and a rattler . . . bit her."

Charity knew this couldn't be easy for him. Memories of Ferrand's death flooded back. She listened to Beau speak about his wife's accident in quiet, almost reverent tones. She had a feeling he didn't talk much about Betsy. The way he said her name, the flickering pain in his eyes, told her this was something too private to share with many people. She felt honored he was opening up with her.

"It didn't take long. . . ." His voice broke momentarily, and then he cleared his throat. Charity was surprised to see him reach for his plate again. He calmly picked up the spoon and ladled a bite of vegetables into his mouth. He chewed for a moment, absently, like he didn't taste the stew. When he glanced back at her it was almost as if he'd forgotten she was there. "I loved my wife very much."

"I'm sure you did," Charity said softly, feeling his pain as deeply as she'd felt her husband's loss. "It's hard to get over something like that. I lost my husband four years ago."

"Oh?" He looked surprised, and she realized he hadn't given a thought to why she was living here alone in the middle of Kansas. He'd been too wrapped up in his memories to care about anyone else. She could understand that. Been there herself.

"The war?" he asked.

She nodded. "Ferrand was riding with Sterling Price's Confederate raiders in the fall of sixty-four. When the Confederacy made its last offensive west of the Mississippi, Curtis Steward, with the help of Alfred Pleasonton's cavalry, whipped the Confederates and drove them back into Arkansas. Ferrand was killed near Westport, Missouri."

"The Confederacy?" Beau glanced up. "Your husband fought for the South?"

"His decision was very difficult—especially for me. But I understood his reasons. There was a lot of talk. You must remember, in the Civil War Kansas sent a larger number of Union soldiers to the field, in proportion to its population, than any other state. But my husband and I came from Virginia, and your upbringing is hard to forget. Our families still live there. Ferrand was torn at first, but when it came right down to it, he felt he had to fight for what he believed in. Of course, all he did was go and get himself killed."

"It must have been hard on you."

"Still is," she confessed. "We had barely started homesteading this piece of land when Ferrand decided to join up. For a long time after his death I didn't know what I should do. My family wanted me to move back to Richmond, and that would probably have been wise. But my husband said I was as stubborn as a stuck door when it came to holding on to what's important to me.

After all the hard work we'd put into this cabin, I couldn't just walk away and leave it for someone else."

"You have been trying to work the land by yourself?" It was a question, but she could see the knowledge in his eyes. And behind the knowledge lay understanding. The war had left a lot of widows. Women forced to do work they'd never had to do before and for which they were ill suited. She was just one of many.

He shook his head. "I'm having trouble seeing someone your size driving a team of oxen and building fences."

"I've been doing a miserable job of it," Charity admitted. She wasn't too proud to confess. "The fences are mostly down, I haven't had a decent crop in two years, and I haven't begun to make the improvements the state requires to grant me a title." She looked down at the baby. "I must admit, I was near my wits' end when you happened along."

Beau finished the stew and corn bread and drained the glass of milk. She took the tray from him. "I hope the food's setting easy in your stomach. You need to eat if you're going to get your strength back." He couldn't drive posts while he was weak as newborn calf.

His eyes narrowed. "Why haven't you re-married?"

She shrugged. "We have a real shortage of men out here, Mr. Claxton. Besides, other than my husband, I've never met one I'd want." She looked at his blue eyes, the gold of his hair, the way he was built and knew she had just told a bald-faced lie. She'd met one all right. She couldn't believe she was feeling this way about a man who was more stranger than friend. She suddenly felt bashful. "Never met one I'd want to have underfoot all the time," she corrected.

He smiled, a nice, soft gesture. "I know the feeling. Since Bets died, I haven't been interested in a woman. Doesn't matter, I guess, because I'm never going to marry again."

Charity arched her brow slightly. "Oh?"

"I loved Bets. No one could come close to taking her place."

She overlooked his pessimism. "Do you have family in Missouri? I can write and tell them about your accident."

"I have family, but you don't need to bother getting in touch with them. I've been wandering around ever since Bets died." He paused for a moment before continuing. "I'll write them and let them know where I am, soon as I'm up and around."

"You've been drifting all this time?" She wondered what that would be like. Shut the door on everything she owned and ride away. Some days she'd been in a mood to do just that, but she guessed it was different with women. Some women, like her, needed a home, a permanent place . . . roots.

"Yeah, just drifting."

"Didn't you ever think about home?"

"I don't believe I thought about much of anything. Just trying to outrun the memories."

"You can't run far enough to leave the memories behind," she confided.

"*I* couldn't. Tried, but I couldn't." He glanced at Mary Kathleen asleep on Charity's shoulder and changed the subject. "Where's the baby's father?"

"I'm not sure. Ansel brought me home yesterday, then up and disappeared."

"Disappeared?"

"I don't know what to make of his strange behavior. Ansel's wife, Letty, died giving birth to the baby a few days ago. Now he seems so lost—not like himself at all. When he brought me home yesterday, I thought naturally he'd take the baby with him, but he didn't. He climbed back in the buckboard and drove off." Charity shook her head, still puzzled by Ansel's peculiar behavior. "I figure once he comes to terms with his grief, he'll be back."

She rose and walked over to lay Mary Kathleen at the foot of his bed, her mind going back to what he had said about no other woman ever replacing his wife. She didn't know why that bothered her. It was only natural for him to feel that way. She wouldn't be asking for his love. All she needed was his strength and stamina for the next few months. To clear land and set fences.

It was just as likely that no other man would ever replace Ferrand in her heart. What she felt for Beau Claxton was an attraction, due to the fact she hadn't seen a good-looking, unattached male since she became a widow. This marriage—should she convince him to stay—would be strictly a business proposition. If he'd agree to marry her, they'd be starting out even. And she supposed she shouldn't be beating around the bush about her intentions either. Now was as good a time as any to tell him about the plan.

"Mr. Claxton," she began in a formal tone.

"Call me Beau." He'd closed his eyes again now, looking relaxed and comfortable. Well, she was getting ready to wake him up.

"I understand how you feel about the loss of your wife, and I can sympathize with your feelings about not wanting to marry again. I loved Ferrand with all my heart, but I've discovered that sometimes you have to put personal feelings aside and go on with life. . . ." Her voice trailed off.

"That's what they say."

Trying to gather enough courage to proceed with the conversation wasn't easy. Like pulling hen's teeth. She wasn't an aggressive woman. Asking this man to marry her was going to be one of the most brazen things she'd ever undertaken, but she'd never before faced losing everything either.

Necessity overrode her fear in this instance. She knew she had him at a certain disadvantage. He was still too weak to walk out on her if he didn't take to the idea right away. If he did balk—and she was fully braced for that possibility—she would at least have a few days to make him change his mind.

"You're wondering about what?" he asked.

She took a deep breath and shut her eyes. There was no easy way to do it. She'd simply have to be blunt and forthright before her courage failed her again.

"I was wondering . . . would you marry me?" Her voice suddenly sounded downright meek. And brazen. Definitely brazen.

For a moment it appeared her words had failed to register. His eyes remained shut, his head nestled deep within the pillow.

"Ordinarily I'd never be so blunt," she rushed on, determined that he wouldn't think her a sinful, immoral woman. "But I'm afraid I'm in a terrible quandary." Her voice picked up tempo when she interpreted his continued silence to be a hopeful sign. "You see, if I don't make the required land improvements within a year, I can't claim title to my homestead. To be candid, Mr. Claxton, I need a man. That's why I think it was God's care—you know, the way I found you in my stream. I dragged you back to the cabin and worked day and night to save your life—though I suppose most of the credit should go to God, then to Little Fawn and Laughing Waters. Regardless, I worked just as hard, and if it hadn't been for Letty desperately needing my help, I would never have *dreamed* of leaving you here . . . to die . . . alone." She paused. "But, of course, you didn't die, and I'm tremendously grateful that you didn't. Now—" she paused again for air, preparing to make her next recitation in one long breath—"you'll find I work hard, cook decently, bathe regularly, and make a good companion." She hurried to the side of the bed and sat down, enthusiasm growing as she explained the plan. "I figure if you'd be so kind as to marry me, then at the end of the year, I can claim my land and you can be on your way."

Beau's eyes remained closed. She prayed he hadn't fallen asleep during the discussion. "Of course, I realize I'm asking you to spend the whole winter here, but I think it will take many months for you to fully regain your strength. In the meantime we can make the needed improvements on my land, weather permitting. Naturally, I'm prepared to pay you well for your time and effort," she promised. "I'm not a rich woman, but I do have a small nest egg, and I can assure you I'll see that your generosity is handsomely rewarded." She paused, bending closer to see if he was listening. She couldn't tell. "It wouldn't take very long, and I'd be most grateful for your assistance."

Beau's left eye slowly opened.

Charity held her breath. If he refused, she wasn't sure what she'd do next.

Both eyes opened wide, staring at her in disbelief. "*Marry* you?"

Her smile wilted. She might have been a bit hasty in revealing her plan. Maybe she should have waited a few days, let him get to know her better. . . .

"I realize this may have come as a bit of a shock, but you see, Beau—"

"Mr. Claxton," he interrupted curtly.

Her chin tilted stubbornly and she ignored his frosty attitude. She understood this might be disconcerting for him. She *was* a stranger. "Mr. Claxton, I'm afraid my unfortunate circumstances have forced me to come directly to the point, though to be honest, I don't know any other way to be. I've been truthful by telling you why I'd make such an unusual suggestion, and while I can't fault you for being shocked, I don't think you have a right to act like I've escaped from an asylum for the insane. I'm . . . desperate." Her tone switched from meek to pleading.

Beau stared at her, looking like he found the sudden turn of conversation incredible. "Let me understand . . . you're *seriously* asking me—a man you know nothing about—to marry you? For all you know, I could be a worthless drifter, a debaucher, a hired killer, and there you sit offering to be my wife—and *pay me* for the privilege?"

"I am indeed," Charity stated firmly. "I need a man."

He shook his head, frowning "Lady, this is—"

"I need a man's strength. Someone to help me work the land, meet the requirements so I can keep what Ferrand and I have invested our lives in." She felt her face color. This was so embarrassing. What would her husband think if he could see her now? The heat intensified at the thought.

"Why in the world would you ask a stranger to marry you? Are you addle-brained?" His tone was less than charming. "A woman should never ask a man to marry her, regardless of the circumstances."

"I'm not addlebrained, and I told you *why,*" she said. "I don't want to lose my land, and I'm going to unless I come up with a man soon."

"So you propose marriage to the first man you meet?"

"You're not the first man I've met. You're just the first *available* man I've met," she corrected.

The baby started to fret. Charity rose to pick her up. "Besides, you're not a stranger—not really. In fact, I feel rather close to you." Caring for him had brought an intimacy much like she'd known with Ferrand. He didn't know it, but he'd kissed her, even if he'd thought she was someone else. "I know your name is Beau Claxton; I know that once you've recovered from your accident, you'll be a strong, healthy man— healthy enough to clear land, set fence posts, and drive a team of oxen. I know you come from Missouri, you're widowed, and because of your injuries, you're going to be laid up here for a good long while." Charity turned and smiled at him. "That's all I need to know, Mr. Claxton."

"You must be addlebrained," Beau muttered. "You don't know a thing about me, and I told you, I don't plan on ever marrying again."

"Are you refusing my offer?" She had the sinking feeling that he was.

He glared at her again, disbelief reflected in his blue eyes. "Of course I am."

"You won't at least think about it?"

He shut his eyes again and it appeared he was praying for patience. "I feel obligated to you for saving my life, but not enough to marry you."

Silence fell between them for a moment. Charity tried to digest his words. He wasn't going to marry her; that was plain as the nose on her face. Well, she hadn't wanted to take advantage of the situation, but he was leaving her little choice. The silence had grown thick and dark.

He glanced over at the rocker, and from the expression on his face, his temper was starting to simmer. He took a deep breath. "If you're so desperate for a husband what about Mary Kathleen's father? Seems to me he could use a wife right about now, and the two of you know each other."

"Ansel?" Charity looked up in surprise. She had never considered him. He'd be the logical choice she supposed, but it would be months before he could think of taking another wife. She quickly discarded the idea. Ansel was out of the question. She needed a man right now if she hoped to save the land.

"Ansel isn't my answer." Charity hated to resort to underhanded tactics, but it seemed clear she'd have to force Beau's hand, however unpleasant.

"Then I'm afraid you're up a creek without a paddle," Beau said.

"Maybe, but you're in the same boat."

He glared at her. "How do you figure that?"

She shrugged. "If you won't at least consider my idea, I'll have little choice but to turn you over to Little Fawn and Laughing Waters."

Beau's eyes widened. "Those two squaws—"

"The lovely women who took care of you in my absence." She felt almost shameful for being so mean. But not quite. "They're very enamored of you, you know. I had a terrible time convincing them that you're my man. They feel they have a certain claim to you since they played a large part in saving your life."

Beau's chin jutted stubbornly. "No one has a claim on me." But his tone of voice said he wasn't all that sure. She didn't blame him; Little Fawn and Laughing Waters were rather formidable.

"I know it's disconcerting." Her tone turned soothing, but she could be as heartless as he if he wouldn't cooperate. "I'm afraid if you don't marry me, then I'll have no alternative but to give you to them. They're coming back Sunday. I'll tell them you're not my man after all. They'll take you to their camp, nurse you back to full health, and then—" Charity's eyes narrowed, and her tone turned venomous— "you'll be on your own, Mr. Claxton, because they *both* want you." All traces of pleasantness were gone. She straightened, smiling. "Of course, if you'd prefer Laughing Waters and Little Fawn over staying here and helping me save my land, then I suppose there's no point in our talking."

"You know what? I'm getting out of here. Missouri is looking better to me all the time. If those two women come back . . ." Beau struggled to the side of the bed and sat up, grabbing the edge of the table. He groaned and lay back on the pillow.

Charity watched, feeling vindicated. He was too weak to outrun Little Fawn and Laughing Waters, even though they were too big and clumsy to run very fast themselves. She had no intention of turning him over to the squaws, but he had no way of knowing that. She felt a little bit sorry for him, realizing how hard it must be for him to be cornered by a woman half his size.

"I could still die," he threatened.

"I don't think so. You've already missed your chance. Besides, I can't understand why you find marrying me so offensive. You obviously don't have anything else to do; you said so yourself."

"This is blackmail." The pillow muffled his voice. "You're crazy if you think I'm going to let you get away with it!"

"Suit yourself." Charity walked to the rocker and sat down, gently rocking the baby back and forth, humming "Dixie."

She knew she had him. He was sensible enough to know when he was bested. When he'd had time to think about it, he'd choose marriage to her over facing an uncertain fate with Laughing Waters and Little Fawn. Who wouldn't? The room was warm and comfortable compared to the tent they lived in. And she hoped she wasn't completely unappealing to him.

"I mean it." Beau eyed her sternly. He was sitting up now, his head bobbing weakly back and forth. "I'm *not* marrying anyone, least of all two crazy squaws or an addle-brained girl."

"We'll see. Do you know what day it is, Mr. Claxton?"

"No."

"Saturday." Charity sent him a smug look. She should be ashamed of herself; he was still very sick and could do little about the circumstances facing him. But she was desperate, and desperation turned nice people into monsters.

"So?" he sneered.

"Big Father's Day is tomorrow." She hummed softly.

"Big Father's Day?" Beau slumped back on the pillow, and Charity knew her words had just sunk in. He would remember the two women saying they'd be back on "Big Father's Day."

He looked back at her with dawning horror in his eyes. "Tomorrow is Sunday?"

She nodded, smiling.

He glared at her. "You can threaten all you

want, but you can't make me marry you.
You're bluffing. Just bluffing, and I'm not
about to fall for it."

Charity kept rocking. And humming.

She felt sorry for him.

CHAPTER 6

The sun rose earlier than Beau would have liked. He'd been awake most of the night, trying to figure a way out of his entrapment. Sleep would have been impossible anyway: the baby had screamed the entire night. He lay on his side of the curtain Charity had rigged across the room to provide privacy and thought about where he had ended up and how he had gotten there. Kansas was a long way from home. For the first time in a long time he had a yearning to go back.

Beau had to admit he felt sorry for Charity. He'd heard her pacing the floor, trying everything she could think of to quiet the baby. Nothing had worked. The infant had only stiffened in anger and cried all the harder, throwing a real temper fit.

The sun was coming up when Mary Kathleen finally dropped into an exhausted slumber. Charity had placed the infant in the small crib she'd fashioned from a drawer and tiptoed to the rocker, dropped into it, and fallen into a sound sleep.

Beau lay quietly thinking about Charity and her demand. Marriage? Over his dead body. He was grateful to her for saving his life, and he wouldn't mind fixing a little fence if it would help her out. There wasn't any denying he was beholden to her, and a Claxton always paid his debts; Cole had drummed that into him early on.

He knew he'd left some unpaid bills back in Missouri when he'd walked out, and he fully intended to make them right if Cole and Cass hadn't already done so. But what he owed Charity couldn't be paid with money. It was a debt of honor.

That didn't mean he had to marry her though.

He didn't plan on getting married again, but if he ever did, *he'd* do the asking. Still, he couldn't say he didn't feel sympathy for her predicament. There were a lot of women facing the same situation—husband a casualty of war.

This woman was stranded on the Kansas frontier with a seriously injured man and a baby who wasn't hers. Didn't seem rightly fair. With her tending his needs, and the baby's, she'd barely had time for chores. No wonder she looked like she was worn to a frazzle. She was too small, too delicate to have to work like this. If she had any sense she would pack up and go back home to her family in Richmond. She wasn't cut out to be a pioneer wife. Ferrand should have taken better care of her. Beau felt downright indignant at the thought. Running off to the war when he had a wife to see about.

Not only did he sympathize with her, he was starting to feel guilty because he'd let her sleep in the rocker the past two nights, allowing him the luxury of the soft, straw-filled mattress. Truth be told, neither of them had gotten any rest, what with the baby crying. It was amazing how one little girl could make so much noise.

He heard Charity awaken and begin to move around in the small quarters. It was unjust that so much misery could fall on one woman, but he wasn't about to let compassion overrule common sense. Marriage was out of the question. He could see where it would benefit her, but what could he gain from it? Saddled with a woman he barely knew. While it was easy enough for her to say he could ride away at the end of the arrangement, he knew he wasn't the kind to take vows and then walk out. Once he gave his name, he was duty bound to make good on it.

He shook his head. While he could pity her plight, he wouldn't let himself become part of it. As far as her threatening him with Indian squaws was concerned, she was downright crazy if she believed she could *scare* him into marrying her. He didn't scare easy, but if he had been the kind to scare, those squaws would do it. Little Fawn had a gleam in her eyes he fully distrusted.

Charity might be flighty, but she wouldn't actually make good on her threat and he knew it. No one would be that callous. He was a sick man, helpless to defend himself. She wouldn't do that to him. Or would she? No telling what a woman, particularly this woman, might do. He needed to concentrate on getting well. Then he would be in a better position to defend himself. A man too sick to get out of bed was helpless.

He shook his head, thinking of all that had happened to him since that day at the stream when the wolf had attacked him. Two Indian women determined to cart him off, Charity talking marriage when she didn't know a thing about him. As soon as he was able, he was going to leave here and head for Missouri. At least the women back there were sane.

Charity pushed the curtain aside and brought his breakfast. They both carefully avoided the subject of marriage. Still, he kept one ear tuned to the door, listening for signs of Laughing Waters and Little Fawn. When they hadn't come by midmorning, he relaxed, figuring Charity was running a bluff. They couldn't kidnap him in broad daylight. He agreed to keep an eye on the baby while she went to the stream for fresh water.

She returned with the full buckets and set out to gather chunks of dried dung left by grazing cattle and buffalo, along with dry twigs, tufts of grass, hay twists, woody sunflower stalks, and anything else she could find to burn.

Later, while Mary Kathleen napped, Charity built a fire outside the cabin and set a large black kettle filled with water from the spring over it. Beau watched out the window as she used a bar of lye soap and a washboard, scrubbing the baby's diapers and hanging them to dry. The weather had turned unseasonably warm.

When she came in the house he asked, "What day is this?"

"Sunday."

Actually, he'd known the day. "That's what I thought. Most of the women I know don't wash on Sunday."

It wasn't right. Sunday was supposed to be a day of rest.

Her face reddened, but when she spoke she sounded civil enough. "Normally I don't wash on Sunday, but I have very few diapers for Mary Kathleen, and the baby's needs come first. God will understand."

"Well, yes." Beau allowed that she did have a point.

"Remember that verse about getting the ox out of the ditch?"

He did.

"This isn't my ox and I didn't drive it in the ditch, but the baby needs diapers and I'm the only one who can wash them." This time her words carried a bite.

Beau figured it would be a good time to take a nap. He didn't want to rile her any more than he had. He was still dependent on her for basic needs. He shut his eyes and pretended to doze.

By the time Charity had finished the wash, the baby was awake and demanding to be fed again.

"I'll do that," Beau offered. Charity warmed the milk, carrying the baby in one arm to still her hungry cries.

She glanced at him. Her hair hung in limp strands around her face. "Are you sure you feel up to it?"

"I'll manage."

He figured it was the least he could do. He didn't suppose she felt much better than he did after the morning she'd put in.

When Charity placed the baby in his arms, Mary Kathleen quieted down immediately. She handed him the cheesecloth and warm milk and tucked the baby's blankets snugly around her. "She seems to like you."

"You're going to squeeze the life out of her," Beau said. "Give her room to breathe." He loosened the blanket, and Mary Kathleen made a funny little sound, like she was heaving a sigh of relief.

"I don't want her to catch a chill."

"She won't. Babies don't need so much mollycoddling." When Beau put the cloth in Mary Kathleen's mouth, she began nursing hungrily. "Soon as I can I'll rig up a bottle. She'll get more milk."

"She's real cute, don't you think?" Charity bent over his shoulder and peered at the baby, looking flushed with maternal pride. And the baby wasn't even hers. He could imagine how she would be with her own child. He closed his eyes.

She smelled fresh and lemony. It had been a long time since he'd noticed how a woman smelled. When he opened his eyes he studied Mary Kathleen's wrinkled, reddish face and decided it reminded him of a scarlet prune. He answered the question. "Not really . . . but she might be, given a few more weeks."

"Oh, what would you know about babies?" Charity moved to the stove and slid the skillet on the fire.

"My brother Cole and his wife, Wynne, have a baby. Jeremy must be getting nigh onto three years old now." He felt an unexpected tenderness when he talked about his family. He'd never realized how much he missed them until he woke up in this little cabin in Kansas. He needed to let them know he was all right.

"Do they live in Missouri?"

"They have a piece of land not far from my place."

"Is your brother taking care of your farm while you're gone?"

"He said he would." He gazed thoughtfully down at Mary Kathleen. "Don't you think someone should see about getting this baby's daddy to assume his responsibility?"

Beau didn't think it was fair for Mary Kathleen's father to have waltzed off and left the baby with Charity, even if he was grieving over his wife. If his and Betsy's baby had lived, he was certain he'd have seen to its care. Couldn't imagine leaving a cute little bug like Mary Kathleen for someone else to take care of.

"I thought Ansel would be here by now." She sank down wearily in a chair by the kitchen table and began peeling potatoes. "I'll ride over to his place this afternoon while the baby's napping—"

There was a sudden knock at the door, and both Charity and Beau looked up.

"That's him now." Charity hurried to the door, and Beau held his breath, praying it wouldn't be Laughing Waters and Little Fawn. He didn't want a run-in with those two anytime soon.

When Charity found Ansel on her doorstep, hat in hand, a pleasant smile on his face, she gave a cry of relief. "Where in the world have you been?" Her voice sounded more critical than she'd intended, but she was bone tired and he'd been downright irresponsible.

"Miss Charity. I hope I'm not disturbing you?"

"You're not disturbing me," Charity said curtly. "I've been worried sick about you. Where have you been?"

"Worried about me?" He stared vacantly at her. "Why?"

"Why? Because you rode off and left Mary Kathleen with me."

"Who?"

"Mary Kath—oh, never mind. Come in." Charity ushered the baby's father into the house and closed the door.

He stopped in his tracks when he saw Beau lying in the bed and glanced back at Charity with a puzzled look. "Didn't know you had company."

"Company?" Charity looked at him, bewildered. "I don't have company."

His gaze switched to Beau. "Who is he?"

Charity glanced at Beau, then back to Ansel. "The man I found in the stream." She was more confused than ever by her neighbor's odd behavior. What was wrong with the man? It was as if he'd forgotten all about the stranger. "You know—the one the wolf attacked?" *And the one you left ME to bury,* she wanted to add but didn't.

Ansel walked to the table and sat down, seeming to dismiss Beau for the moment. "It's right pleasant out this morning."

Charity was surprised by the almost immediate change of subject. "Ansel, are you all right?" She moved to the table and knelt beside his chair. "I've been so worried. Where have you been?" she asked for the third time.

"Been? Why, I've been at home. Why?"

"Home . . . well, I've wondered. . . . Are you sure you're all right?" He didn't act all right. If she didn't know him so well, she'd think he'd been drinking. But Ansel and Letty had never allowed alcohol in their home. Ferrand hadn't held with serious drinking either, but he did keep a bottle on hand for medicinal purposes. Ansel had refused even that.

He looked up and smiled. "Yes, Letty, I'm just fine. How are you today?"

"I'm good." Charity frowned. He had called her Letty. Was that a slip of the tongue? "And the baby's fine. Would you like to hold your daughter?"

Ansel's face brightened. "Why, yes, I think that would be nice."

Now that was encouraging. This was the first time the man had shown any sign of wanting to hold his little girl or even remembering that he had a daughter. She hurried to the bed to retrieve Mary Kathleen from Beau's arms. Of course he'd want to hold her. Why else would he be here except to claim his precious daughter?

Charity introduced Ansel to Beau, who'd been watching the exchange. "I know you'll be glad to hear Mr. Claxton is doing fine now. When I got back, I discovered he was being nursed by Little Fawn and Laughing Waters—I think I've mentioned them to you before. The two women stopped by to visit and found Mr. Claxton and knew exactly what to do."

Ansel didn't look much like he cared one way or the other. Charity glanced at Beau and shrugged her shoulders, dismayed by her neighbor's apparent bad manners. Ansel did have a lot on his mind. A body had to make allowances.

Charity settled Mary Kathleen in his arms. "There now, isn't she beautiful?"

He gazed down at the tiny bundle, his face growing tender with emotion. "Oh, she's real pretty."

"She truly is."

Mary Kathleen opened her eyes and stared angelically at her father. He returned her smile and hesitantly reached to trace his forefinger around each rosy cheek. "She looks like you, Letty. Just like you," he whispered softly.

Charity wasn't sure if he was speaking to her or his deceased wife. Would he talk to Letty out loud like that? It didn't seem right.

Still, she knew enough about grief to allow him some leeway. He was still lost.

"She does look exactly like Letty. She has the same eyes, the same color of hair. She would be proud," Charity acknowledged softly.

"Yes, yes, she would." Then, as quickly as he'd accepted the baby, Ansel handed Mary Kathleen back to Charity and stood up. "Well, I mustn't overstay my welcome. My chores need tending."

Charity blinked at his sudden change of attitude. But she guessed he'd be wanting to get the baby settled. Still, his departure did seem a trifle abrupt. She began gathering the baby's belongings, keeping up a running line of chatter. "You're always welcome, Ansel, but I understand your wanting to get back home. Mary Kathleen's a sweet baby to care for. She's a bit fussy at night, but I think you'll get along fine. I don't have a bottle and nipple; I've been giving her milk through cheesecloth. She's been eating about every two—"

The sound of the front door closing made her whirl in disbelief. The room was empty, except for Beau and herself—and Mary

Kathleen. Charity faced Beau. "Where'd he go?"

He shrugged. "Said he was going home."

Charity raced to the door and yanked it open in time to see Ansel's buckboard rattling out of the yard. "What in *tarnation* is wrong with that man?" She slammed the door shut. The baby jumped with fright, puckered up like a thundercloud, and started squalling. Wonderful! Just what she needed. As if her nerves weren't stretched to the limit.

Beau tried to quiet the baby while Charity stormed around the cabin, mumbling under her breath about the injustices of life. She slammed the iron skillet on the stove and angrily spooned lard from a can and flung it into the pan.

"I *can't* imagine *who* he thinks he is to leave me with his baby! I *can't* take care of a baby and fix fences and drive oxen and— Letty was my *friend,* but there's a point where friendship ends. I can't take on any more responsibility!" Charity irritably questioned Ansel's sanity—and her own—as she chopped potatoes and onions and dropped them into the sizzling fat. She had her limit and Ansel Latimer had just gone past it.

Beau managed to calm Mary Kathleen but left Charity alone. He figured only a fool would try to talk to her now. And he hadn't been raised to be a fool. He had no idea what was going on, but it was plain to him that Ansel wasn't in full control of his faculties. The realization did little to calm him. Maybe because he'd been in a similar situation and he hadn't been all that much in control either. He could still remember the fog that had blanketed his mind. Couldn't think, couldn't do much of anything except ride away. A man wasn't responsible for his actions at a time like that. Still, Ansel had a child; he needed to pull himself together for Mary Kathleen's sake.

If Ansel Latimer had gone off the deep end because of his wife's death, he was going to be left as the only candidate to help Charity save her land, and that grim prospect made him even more uneasy. He felt like he was in a deep canyon and the walls were closing in on him.

He wasn't a man who liked change. He and Bets had been building a good life together, and in one short afternoon, it was all gone. He'd stood beside his wife's grave, knowing his plans and dreams for the future had died with her. Beau Claxton was an empty shell of a man with nothing left to give. He'd always heard almighty God could bring good out of bad, but he couldn't imagine any good coming out of losing Betsy. Now here was Charity wanting to marry him so she could hang on to her homestead, and he had a feeling she wasn't the kind to take no for an answer.

As if she understood his turmoil, Mary Kathleen burst into tears.

Charity slammed a bowl on the table and began mixing a batch of corn bread, still mumbling heatedly under her breath.

"I know how you feel," he confided to the baby. "It's a mess, isn't it?"

Monday morning Beau drained the last of his coffee. The front door burst open, and he mutely stared at the dark outline of the two squaws silhouetted starkly against a noonday sun. They were back.

Both women's arms were piled high with stove fuel. Stories of people being burned at the stake flashed through his mind. They didn't still do that, did they?

The memory of Charity's earlier threat closed in on him: *"If you won't marry me, I'll have no other choice but to hand you over to Laughing Waters and Little Fawn. . . . They both want you for their husband."*

Husband? To both of them? Was that legal? How could he explain that to God? Let alone try to explain it to Bets if he ever did make it to heaven, which was looking more doubtful every day. Bigamy, that's what it was, and he didn't plan to partake.

"Laughing Waters! Little Fawn! How nice to see you." Charity stood at the table washing dishes. She cast a pointed look at Beau and then wiped her sudsy hands on her apron. She stepped forward to greet the two visitors.

"We come see Gold Hair." Little Fawn stated their purpose, and Laughing Waters's stern, austere expression reinforced it. Well, Gold Hair didn't want to see them. How could he get out of this? There was only one answer: Charity had to help him, but she was looking far too happy to suit him.

"Well, how nice. Please come in. I know he's been anxious to see you." Charity smiled pleasantly at Beau and reached for her shawl hanging on the hook beside the door.

Beau shot her a warning look, but she ignored it. Was she out of her mind? Did he look *pleased*?

"I'll feed the chickens and gather the wash while you three visit."

"Charity!" he snapped.

"Yes?" Charity turned to face him with a look of wide-eyed innocence that was as crooked as a barrel of fish hooks. He'd get even with her for this. She'd rue the day she tried to threaten him.

"You have company. It's not proper for you to leave." Though he kept his voice firm, he knew she could hear desperation. "Besides, the baby will be waking up anytime now."

"Little Fawn and Laughing Waters aren't here to see *me*." She paused to tie the string on her bonnet. "They've come to visit you, Gold Hair. Don't worry; I'll listen for the baby. You go right ahead and enjoy your visit." She sent a gracious smile at the two women. "Make yourselves at home, ladies."

Charity reached for the egg basket. Little Fawn and Laughing Waters set their bundles of chips by the doorstep and silently walked into the cabin.

"The fuel is a nice gift," Charity said. "I'll see that Gold Hair is warmed by it."

Beau couldn't believe she would be callous enough to desert him! "Charity . . . now, hold on a minute!"

"Papoose asleep?" Laughing Waters asked.

"She's sleeping soundly. Would you like to see her?" Charity invited. She sent another pointed look his way.

The squaws edged toward the table where Charity had placed the baby's drawer crib. The women's dark eyes intently surveyed the infant until their curiosity was satisfied. They slipped back to stand quietly at the doorway.

"Well, I'd best get to my chores," Charity announced.

How could she walk away like this? Did she save him from the wolf to abandon him to an even worse fate?

Laughing Waters nodded, and Charity

hung the egg basket over her arm and slipped out the door. Little Fawn stretched her mouth in a wide grin and began creeping toward the bed.

Beau froze. Charity Burk had thrown him back to the wolves.

"Gold Hair heap better," Little Fawn said. "No longer pale. Look healthier now, and handsomer and stronger than any other warrior." Her dark eyes moved to Beau's hair. He noticed her fingers wiggling like she was itching to get hold of him. Scalps? Did the Kaw do scalping? He had no idea. He looked around the bed searching for a weapon, anything to defend himself, but the only thing his groping fingers found was the edge of his pillow. Somehow a pillow fight seemed lame.

They were fixated on his hair. He'd been around enough Indians to know that while the men of other tribes let their hair grow long, Kaw men shaved their heads, leaving only a well-curved tuft on the crown where they wore warriors' eagle feathers.

Only when grieving a death would a Kaw allow his hair to grow, proof of his inconsolable sorrow.

Little Fawn's eyes glittered. "My heart

beat faster just looking at you. Soon, Swift Buck with Tall Antlers will be mine, and I give thanks to Wa-kun-dah, the All Powerful, for sending me such a fine, strong brave."

Beau recognized the possessive light in her eyes and drew back defensively into his pillow. He didn't know who this Swift Buck with Tall Antlers was, but he was welcome to Little Fawn. If she already had her eyes on a man, why was she looking at him? He'd seen a cat eye a baby rabbit like this once. The rabbit didn't have a chance. This woman with her wide, toothless grin made him uneasy.

"Now, don't you go messing with my hair," he warned in a voice that he hoped sounded like it brooked no nonsense.

"Gold Hair speak! See! Gold Hair speak!" Laughing Waters quickly joined Little Fawn at Beau's bedside, and the two smiled down at him. Where was Charity!

"Ohhhh, Gold Hair heap better," Laughing Waters said. "I take Brave Horse with Many Wounds back to camp," she exclaimed. "White Sister claim Gold Hair, but we have more right. We save his life."

Little Fawn frowned. "Swift Buck with Tall Antlers go with *me*."

Laughing Waters waved a dismissing hand. "We settle this later. No time now."

After a minute Little Fawn nodded. "White Sister come back soon. We must hurry."

Beau shifted restlessly. They were planning to take him with them. "I'm not going anywhere. You two ladies forget all this nonsense." He had a good, solid name; he didn't plan on being called some outlandish name like Swift Buck . . . or Wounded Horse?

Laughing Waters shook her head. "You come. We been alone too long. Speckled Eye, Little Fawn's husband, die of smallpox last winter. My husband, Handsome Bird, rode off on buffalo hunt three years ago." She held up three fingers. "No come back."

Beau shook his head. Considering Laughing Waters's lack of charm, he would have kept going too. A man could ride a fair piece in three years, and if he ever got free from Charity Burk, he was going to do the same.

Little Fawn frowned. "You belong to us. We save life. Not let White Sister keep you. We have a plan."

Laughing Waters giggled. "Very good plan. Almost work once before. Will work this time. Can't fail."

Beau sighed. A new stubborn look, one he didn't like, had entered Little Fawn's expression.

"The plan won't work," he said. "I'm not going with you or any other woman. Do you understand that?"

Laughing Waters shook her head. "We not speak English. Not good. Not understand."

"We bring you gift," Little Fawn announced.

Beau knew he had to put a stop to this conversation and fast, or he could find himself running around half naked, hunting buffalo for the rest of his life. "I don't want to hurt your feelings, but—"

Laughing Waters slyly withdrew a bottle from beneath her red blanket and handed it to him. "We bring *pi-ge-ne.* Make you heap better!"

Beau cautiously took the bottle of amber liquid and examined it closely. "What's this?"

Little Fawn proudly displayed another toothless grin. "*Pi-ge-ne*—firewater!"

"Whiskey?"

Laughing Waters and Little Fawn's heads bobbed enthusiastically.

"Where'd you get this?"

"Trade pony and two buffalo robes," replied Little Fawn.

He couldn't take their whiskey. He'd sworn off whiskey when he became a Christian, and Betsy had been dead set against alcohol of any kind. He quickly handed the bottle back to Little Fawn. "I appreciate the thought, but I can't drink this."

Their faces fell. "You no like *pi-ge-ne*?" Little Fawn asked.

Beau shook his head. "I can't accept your gift."

"White Sister no like *pi-ge-ne*?" Laughing Waters prodded.

"That's it. White Sister no like *pi-ge-ne*." Pin the blame on Charity, he decided. If it hadn't been for her, he wouldn't be in this mess. She wasn't around to hear, so what could it hurt? He figured if he let the squaws think he belonged to "White Sister," they'd be on their way and out of his hair, literally.

Little Fawn turned to Laughing Waters, her eyes openly puzzled. "Gold Hair no want *pi-ge-ne*."

The squaws were noticeably upset by his lack of gratitude. Despite their infatuation with him, he had to admit that if it hadn't been for their dedicated care, he'd probably be dead right now. They'd been good enough to stay with him in Charity's absence, applying the healing poultices to his wounds, stoking the fire, and here he was, treating them unsociably.

"I appreciate all you've done for me, but we might as well get it straight. I'm not going to marry either one of you."

The women exchanged frank looks. Little Fawn whispered sharply to Laughing Waters.

Dark eyes suddenly riveted on Beau. Laughing Waters immediately turned sullen. "Gold Hair no be husband to Little Fawn and Laughing Waters?"

"No," Beau said. "I'm beholden to both of you for saving my life, but as soon as I'm able, I'll be moving on. I'm not going to marry anyone."

"No be husband to White Sister?" Little Fawn asked.

"No, no be husband to White Sister," Beau confirmed, noticing the squaws' faces swiftly light with renewed expectation. "*No be husband to anyone*," he stated. "I'm not the marrying kind."

They looked puzzled. "No like gift?"

"Nice gift," he agreed. "But I don't drink whiskey."

"We trade pony and two buffalo robes," Laughing Waters said. "You belong to us!"

"No, I belong to no woman. You get that through your head." Talking to these two was like spitting in the wind. Useless.

"Okay, no marry," Little Fawn said.

Laughing Waters nodded. "Gold Hair has spoken."

Beau relaxed. That was more like it. About time they started showing some sense. He glanced out the window and saw Charity throwing corn to the chickens.

He felt smug when he thought how shocked she was going to be when she discovered how easily he'd outfoxed her and the two squaws. She thought she'd backed him to the wall with her threats of "marry me or else." He smirked. Once more, he'd proved you couldn't tangle with Beau Claxton. At least, not a puny little woman like Charity Burk.

Little Fawn reached out a tentative finger,

grinning at him. "Swift Buck with Tall Antlers have pretty hair."

Beau drew back. He thought they had that settled. How many times did he have to say it? He tried to be diplomatic. "Don't touch my hair, ladies. We'll get along better if you leave my hair alone."

Laughing Waters grinned. "Never see warrior with hair like yours. We be envy of tribe. Brave Horse with Many Wounds handsome warrior. Make strong papooses."

Beau's grin felt a bit uneven. "Brave Horse do no such thing."

She could get that thought right out of her head. Well, all right, maybe he *hadn't* gotten through to them as well as he thought. He'd try again. "Look, ladies, I do appreciate all you've done for me, and when I can, I'll reimburse you for the pony and buffalo robes, but I'm not going with you. Subject closed."

Little Fawn looked cross. "No go with us?"

Beau shook his head. "No go anywhere with anyone. That's final."

Laughing Waters bit her underlip. She nudged her sister. "We have powwow."

Beau felt his temper rising. "There is nothing to talk over. I've said my piece. Now you go on along about your business and leave me alone." He stared out the window. Charity was taking her sweet time feeding the stock.

Lord, You got to help me out here. They're not taking no for an answer.

The two women stepped to a corner of the cabin and engaged in a furious Kaw exchange. Little Fawn kept shaking her head no. Beau watched the argument, wondering what they had in mind now. They eventually reached an agreement because they approached the bed, marching in quickstep. He instinctively drew back against the pillows, wishing Charity would get in here.

Laughing Waters grinned. "We give up Gold Hair. Let White Sister have you."

Beau didn't like the sound of that. They wouldn't give up this easily. They'd hatched another plot. "I don't think so, ladies."

"We want to help."

Or trick him; he wasn't a fool.

Little Fawn reached out to touch his hair, and he jerked back. "None of that now. I don't want you messing with my hair."

Little Fawn grinned. "We glad Gold Hair feeling better."

Laughing Waters nodded. "You need to get strength back now."

"That would be nice." It couldn't happen fast enough for Beau. He wished God would speed up the healing process. The minute he was strong enough, he wouldn't let his shirttail hit his back until he was on his horse and headed back to Missouri, where the people were normal.

Laughing Waters said, "You want to get strong fast?"

Beau sighed. "That would make me very happy."

She nodded. "I fix tea."

"Now hold on here," he said. "What kind of tea?"

"Good tea. Make you very strong," Little Fawn said. "We fix."

"I don't know," Beau said. "Charity might not want you in her kitchen."

"White Sister no care," Laughing Waters assured him. "She say to make ourselves at home."

She had said that, Beau reflected. So let them make the tea and leave. He didn't have to drink it.

Laughing Waters was at the stove pouring hot water over something. He watched her with a jaundiced eye. She approached, holding out a cup. "Gold Hair drink. Make strong."

He took the cup, sniffing the contents. "What is it?"

"Tea, made from plant. Good plant. Not know name, but just what Gold Hair need to get well." She grinned. "Trust me."

Trust her? Beau wanted to laugh. Still, they had saved his life. They had used herbs then. Evil-smelling things that had sucked the poison out of his body and made him breathe whether he wanted to or not. Maybe the tea would work.

He sipped the hot liquid and found it not all that unpleasant. Sweetened with honey, mild tasting. He drank again and Laughing Waters beamed at him. "That right. Drink it all. Make much better."

He finished the tea and leaned back against his pillow. The two women stood at his bedside, waiting. A white fog crept slowly through his mind, swirling peacefully, lightly. The two sisters suddenly blurred. He fought to keep his eyes open, but his eyelids were too heavy. He felt giddy. Someone giggled, and to his horror, he realized it was him.

Tricked. He'd been *tricked* and fallen for it. Someone was running their fingers through his hair. He tried to tell them to stop it, but all he could do was laugh. What the Sam Hill had they given him? Whatever it was, it had made him as helpless as a newborn calf.

CHAPTER 7

Guilt was starting to set in. Charity felt bad about leaving Beau alone with the squaws. She was desperate for a man's help, but her conscience told her it hadn't been right to leave him to the mercy of Little Fawn and Laughing Waters. They'd scare him half to death. They were so big, bigger than a lot of men, and determined too. He was still weak as a kitten.

Her hand dipped into the corn bucket, and she scattered kernels on the hardened ground for the flock of chattering hens. She'd been heartless to threaten to turn him over to Laughing Waters and Little Fawn if he didn't marry her. It hadn't done a bit of good and more than likely had made him

more stubborn. She'd never been able to
bluff Ferrand, not once.

He would have been ashamed of such
underhanded tactics. He'd always said a
person was only as good as he was honest.
Charity had to face it: she'd seriously jeop-
ardized her integrity lately. She didn't see
another choice, though. She couldn't lose
the land and all the work that had gone into
the place.

Something else troubled her. She'd lied
and tried to trick a man into marrying her.
Lying and dishonest dealing were sins.
Her Bible said so, plain and simple. There
wasn't any way to justify what she'd done,
and now that she'd had time to think about
it her conscience hurt her something fierce.
She stopped scattering corn and stood
looking up at the sky, talking to God in her
heart.

*Lord, I'm sorry. I knew better; it's just that
I'm so tired of trying to do it all by myself. I
don't have the know-how or the strength to
improve this place, and now there's a sick
man and a baby to take care of, and I'm
worn-out.* She didn't know if God would accept her excuses, but it was the gospel

truth, and He'd know that. Life had sort of caved in on her right now.

She'd do her best to make things right, apologize to Beau for behaving so badly, and furthermore, she'd assure him that she wouldn't hinder his return to Missouri once he'd recovered. It would be hard to keep that promise, but she'd do it. Come hell or high water.

She would consider asking Ansel Latimer to marry her. She knew him to be strong and kind. After he weathered the initial shock of losing Letty, he'd need someone to help him raise Mary Kathleen, and Charity would love the child as dearly as if she were her own. She already did.

But in truth, she knew marriage to Ansel would be disappointing. He'd never make her stomach flutter the way Ferrand had. No one would ever give her that delicious, giddy feeling again, and she might as well accept it. He could smile a certain way, and her pulse would race with heady anticipation.

There wouldn't be any surprises with Ansel. What you saw was what you got— quiet, dependable, but he was also a trifle boring. He had been right for Letty, but he wouldn't be right for her. On the other hand, Ansel would never mistreat her, and she knew Letty would be proud to know Charity was raising her daughter.

She heard the door open, breaking into her thoughts. Her jaw dropped when she saw Laughing Waters and Little Fawn haul Beau out of the cabin, spread-eagled between them. His backside dragged the ground, and he had a silly, stupefied grin on his face. *What* did they think they were doing, and what was the matter with Beau Claxton? Why would he let them manhandle him like a sack of grain?

She dropped the corn pail, spilling the contents, and sprinted toward the cabin, trying to catch up. The two women weren't wasting any time. Their legs pumped and their flat feet thundered over the crusty ground.

"Hold it!" Charity shouted. "You bring him right back here. Now!"

At the sound of her voice both women glanced her way but made no effort to slow their rapid departure up the hillside.

Beau grinned and waved. "'Lo, Mrs. Burk!"

"Hey! I said *wait* a minute!" Charity broke

into a run when she realized the two women had no intention of stopping. She couldn't imagine what was going on. Did they really think they could just carry him off like that? She'd been fully aware that Little Fawn and Laughing Waters were smitten with Beau, but she'd had no idea they'd take their whimsy to this appalling extent!

And Beau! He not only appeared indifferent to his abduction, but it looked to Charity as if he was a willing participant. It hadn't been half an hour ago when he was begging her not to leave him alone with them. What had happened while her back was turned? She should have known she couldn't trust that man.

Well, she had found him first. Beau Claxton belonged to her, and she wasn't in the mood to share.

"We go, White Sister," Little Fawn puffed over her shoulder when Charity gained on them. "One sleep, come back."

Beau looked like he had passed out; he was oblivious to the flight. The women carried him swiftly along with his backside bumping the ground every third step.

Charity finally got close enough to grab Laughing Waters's shoulder, jerking her to a sudden halt. She paused for a minute to catch her breath before taking them to task. "Now see *here*! You *can't* just come into my house and tote this man away like a sack of flour!"

"Gold Hair no care." Laughing Waters stubbornly planted her solid frame in front of Charity, keeping a firm hold on Beau's bare feet. Charity was relieved to see that the women at least had the forethought to put trousers on him.

"Well, we'll ask Gold Hair if he minds or not." She leaned over Beau's limp body. He opened an eye and grinned up at her.

"Hallo there, Mizzz Burk. Didja feed all them chickens?"

"What is *wrong* with you?" He looked and acted like he was *drunk*. She bent over him, sniffing for whiskey, but she couldn't smell anything. "What have you been drinking?"

"Had a little tea party with these two fine women. You know Laugh . . . Little . . ." He frowned, waving his hand in a dismissing manner. "Whatever . . . *Fine* ladies."

"What kind of tea?"

He shook his head. "Jus' tea. Had a little cuppa tea. Feel better already."

"I can't believe this!" Charity confronted

the two squaws, her anger flaring. "You carry him back to the house—immediately!"

She could see Laughing Waters and Little Fawn had no intention of obliging, and their stoic expressions proved it. So now what did she do?

"Gold Hair come with us," Laughing Waters announced, lifting Beau's feet—a signal to Little Fawn to move on.

"Hold on." Charity stepped around to block their path. "He can't go with you. I thought I made it clear: Gold Hair is *mine.*"

Little Fawn looked to Laughing Waters for direction.

"Gold Hair say he no marry White Sister," Laughing Waters argued.

"But he no marry Laughing Waters or Little Fawn either."

"Ladieees, ladieees, don't fight. I no marry any of you," Beau informed them.

Charity gritted her teeth. If he couldn't help the situation, she wished he would keep quiet. This was serious business. These two women had their hearts set on having Beau, and she knew he was in no condition to save himself. If he was to be delivered from this, it would be solely up to her. She frantically searched her memory for a bartering tool. She had so little left.

The brooch. Ferrand's grandmother's emerald brooch. It had been his gift to Charity on their wedding day. Little Fawn and Laughing Waters had admired it extensively since the first day they had discovered it in the tin box she kept under the bed. The brooch was her greatest treasure, but she couldn't stand by idly and let Beau be abducted.

She held up one hand, trying to gain their attention. "Let's hold on a minute. Surely we can reach a satisfactory solution."

Laughing Waters and Little Fawn held their ground, watching her with suspicious eyes.

"What White Sister mean?" Little Fawn finally offered.

"I agree you helped save Gold Hair's life, and I suppose you could argue that he is partly yours." She didn't want to go too far down that road. After all, possession was nine-tenths of the law, and they definitely were in possession.

Laughing Waters eyed Beau. She wasn't following the logic. "We save Gold Hair. We like. We take."

"I saved Gold Hair too."

"You leave Gold Hair to meet Wa-kun-dah, alone."

"I had a good reason. I was called away to help the papoose's mother, remember? She was very ill too."

From their stoic expressions she could see they remembered, but it was also clear they didn't care.

"Gold Hair heap good man. We want," Laughing Waters repeated sullenly.

"True; that's why I'm prepared to make you a trade."

Little Fawn hurriedly shook her head. "Gold Hair make good papooses. We keep."

Charity glanced at Beau, who had fallen back to sleep. "I'm sure he would . . . but I'm prepared to offer you my brooch. The one in the tin box. Remember how much you liked those pretty green stones? You said they sparkled like morning dew on the grass."

Laughing Waters exchanged a dubious look with Little Fawn but then curtly nod-ded.

Charity felt faint with relief. Ferrand had given her the brooch, thinking the heirloom would remain in his family. She pressed her lips together tightly, ready to do whatever was necessary to save Beau Claxton once again. "I will trade you my emerald brooch for Gold Hair."

Laughing Waters's eyes immediately lit up. "Green Rocks for Gold Hair?"

Charity knew the woman was completely taken when it came to bright, shiny things. Laughing Waters had wanted the emerald brooch from the first time she had seen it. Surely she would accept the trade. Little Fawn might be harder to convince.

Drawing a deep breath, Charity closed her eyes and repeated before she lost her nerve, "The brooch for Gold Hair."

The squaws looked at each other.

"We talk. White Sister stay," Laughing Waters said.

They dropped Beau's limp body in the dust, where he landed with a resounding thud, bringing him wide awake.

He sat up, looking dazed. "What's going on?"

"Serves you right," Charity snapped. "Because of your foolishness, I have to give up Ferrand's grandmother's brooch."

"Whose what?" He sounded befuddled. "My head's spinning like a wheel."

"Ferrand's grandmother's . . . oh, never mind." Charity knew he couldn't possibly understand anything in his sorry state. "You'd better hope they accept the trade or you're in serious trouble, Beau Claxton!"

Beau looked around him in a daze. "What? I wish somebody would make some sense. What am I doing sitting in the middle of the road? It's hot, and . . . I'm sick."

His bid for sympathy, if that's what he meant it to be, was wasted on Charity. She had too much on her mind to stand here and chat. He didn't look all that alert either, even though he talked more sensible and he wasn't slurring his words as much.

"I'm not interested in how you feel," she said curtly.

Beau looked hurt and eased back down.

Charity dismissed him, watching Laughing Waters and Little Fawn still conferring in hushed tones. Their prolonged conversation worried her. She had thought they would be happy to change a sick man for an emerald brooch that sparkled like sunlight on water. Occasionally, one would raise her voice, and the other would shake her head and angrily wag her finger. Clearly the discussion was getting a bit heated.

Charity decided to go over their heads. *Lord, I need help here. I can't let them take him; that wouldn't be right. I'm sorry I threatened to let them have him. I wouldn't have done that; You know I wouldn't. Please convince them to take the brooch. I don't have anything else to offer.*

She watched the two women, wondering what she would do if they refused to give up their claim on Beau. She was outnumbered and they could run faster. She was winded after the short chase, and Mary Kathleen was alone in the cabin and probably squalling her head off. Beau Claxton, that miserable lout, had gone back to sleep in the middle of the road. She had a good notion to boot him.

Charity slanted a look heavenward. "Sorry again, Lord. It's just that he makes me so *mad*."

The tense conversation went on for a full ten minutes. Charity was beginning to despair. If they refused the brooch, she didn't know how she'd prevent them from taking Beau away. She took another look at him and wondered why she cared.

He lay curled up in the road, sound asleep and blissfully ignorant of what was taking place. Charity wondered if he was really worth a brooch. Seemed like she was always having to rescue him, and as far as she could see, she wasn't getting anything out of the effort but extra trouble.

Finally, Little Fawn raised her arms, shook her hands in the air in exasperation, and stalked off. With a satisfied smile, Laughing Waters scurried back to Charity. "We trade Gold Hair for roach."

"Brooch."

Laughing Waters grinned. "Yes. Roach."

Charity heaved a sigh of relief. "Good. And Little Fawn? Does she agree?"

"She no care."

Charity seriously doubted that. "Now, when we make our trade," she warned, "it's final. You must leave Gold Hair alone, for he will be mine."

"Laughing Waters no see Gold Hair again?"

"That's right. Little Fawn must agree to relinquish her claim as well."

Laughing Waters thought for a moment and then shrugged agreeably. "Me tell Little

Fawn. Gold Hair White Sister's. We no take."

"Very well."

They reached down in unison, and Charity picked up Beau's feet and Laughing Waters carried his hands.

"We make good trade," Laughing Waters said proudly as they carried Beau's limp body back to the cabin.

Charity nodded glumly but truthfully. She had just grabbed the short end of the stick. She had given away her prized brooch, and she wasn't one inch nearer to saving her land.

But at least her integrity was intact, and for that she was grateful.

The old rooster stretched, flapped his wings, and loudly crowed in a new day. Rays of dappled winter sunlight spilled through the cabin windows, spreading a golden path across the wooden floor.

Charity groaned and stirred on her pallet, reluctant to face the new morning. Mary Kathleen had cried most of the night. Finally the baby had quieted down, and she had fallen into a deep sleep.

She got up and peeked around the curtain that separated the bed from the rest of the room. Beau was still sleeping soundly. He was lying on his stomach, his golden hair tousled appealingly like a small boy's, face burrowed into the pillow, arms wrapped snugly around it. Tight bunches of corded muscles stood out in his forearms.

He looked young and innocent. Charity wanted to brush the hair off his forehead and kiss him awake. She knotted her hands into fists in an effort to control her wayward fingers that itched to bury themselves in those loose waves.

Since it was still early and she felt lazy this morning, she stretched out on her pallet again. It would be sheer tomfoolery to become physically attracted to Beau; still, she couldn't deny that she found him more fascinating every day. He had recovered from the tea the squaws had given him with no long-lasting effects. She had found the dregs of herbs in her teapot, but she had no idea what they were—a mixture known only to the Kaw.

Beau had described the effect as wanting

to sleep, but also everything had been funny. Embarrassed, he'd admitted that he'd giggled, which seemed to bother him more than the attempted kidnapping. The memory of him sleeping in the road while she bartered with Laughing Waters and Little Fawn over him brought a flush to her face. She, Charity Burk, *bartering* for a man. How low would she go?

The days had passed without incident since that afternoon four weeks ago. The two women had stayed away from the cabin, and Beau was slowly regaining his strength. With proper food and plenty of rest, he had begun to shed his pitiful gauntness, and his body grew strong and sinewy again. She glowed with pride when she remembered the way he looked that day in the stream, half frozen, thin as a reed.

Every day he seemed more thoughtful. He helped with Mary Kathleen as much as his condition allowed. She realized how thankful she was to have him around. Trading her emerald brooch had been a small sacrifice for a large reward.

A smile curved her mouth. She rolled over and hugged her pillow tightly against her, remembering how grateful Beau had been when he'd learned Charity had intervened and saved him a second time.

He'd been too overcome by the tea to know he'd been captured or how Charity had accomplished his release. He couldn't remember anything beyond the first few swallows of the hot liquid Laughing Waters had talked him into drinking.

She thought of how sick he'd been afterward. He'd suffered a splitting headache for three days, but she figured it only served him right. He should have known better than to trust the two squaws, but then, she shouldn't have left him alone with them. It was her fault too. They wouldn't have given him the tea if she'd been there.

She sighed. She couldn't blame Laughing Waters and Little Fawn for their infatuation with Beau Claxton. He was bathed, clean shaven, and breathtakingly handsome now.

One truly exceptional man.

He was up and about more now. His tall, imposing frame loomed over her small one as they moved within the confines of the cabin. Although she warned herself not to, she had started feeling content and secure again, the way she'd felt when Ferrand had been close by.

At times she caught Beau's blue eyes studying her as if he felt the same sort of contentment—or maybe that was only wishful thinking on her part. Regardless, he was polite and a joy to be around. They'd talk for hours on end, passing Mary Kathleen back and forth between their laps when she became fussy.

It was then that Beau would confide in her how he was looking forward to returning to his family in Missouri. He spoke fondly of his brothers, Cole and Cass, and told her of the stunts they'd pulled together on Willa, the family housekeeper.

He talked about his ma's biscuits and Willa's chicken and dumplings, and how much he loved them both. One evening he asked Charity to help him write a letter to his family, informing them of his injury, yet assuring them he was healing properly. They moved to the table where the light was better, and while Beau talked, Charity penned the letter in her neat, legible hand. The following day, she made the long ride into Cherry Grove and mailed the missive for him, although she had been terrified that his family would come looking for him and take him home. Away from her.

She sighed, recalling how she had felt unusually lonely on her ride to town and back.
With Beau safely sleeping behind the divid-
ing curtain, she'd slipped outside and sat
for a while, listening to the lonely wind on
the prairie, broken occasionally by the howl
of a coyote or the gentle whish of the tall
grass and realized how empty her life would
be without him.

Even now, she found herself thinking
about it and sinking ever lower into self-pity
when she reviewed her own gloomy circumstances. She missed her mother and father
unbearably, and she thought it would be
sheer heaven to curl up on her old feather
bed beside her sisters, Jenny and Sue, and
pour her heart out to people who really
cared. Then, after a visit with her family, and
a good long cry, it would be good to return
to her homestead and find a man like Beau
waiting for her.

She closed her eyes and fought the
yearning stirring inside her. She wished
Beau would forget about going back to Missouri. She hadn't mentioned marriage to
him again, but it still seemed like a good arrangement to her.

They might not ever love each other the

way they'd loved Ferrand and Betsy, but it wouldn't be hard for her to adjust to living with a man like Beau, with his kind ways and gentle nature. In time, she felt sure their mutual respect could bring them a union that would be, if not passionate, at least comfortable.

Her eyes flew open and she wondered why she was thinking such nonsense. The very best she could hope for from Beau Claxton would be an act of mercy in her behalf, not love and undying devotion, with a passel of golden-haired babies thrown in.

Still, she knew that once he was gone, there'd be a large void in her life. Maybe even larger than the one Ferrand had left. He had been gone so long it was sometimes hard to remember how much she had loved him.

The sun went behind a cloud, and the room suddenly turned a dreary gray, as gray and sad as Charity felt this morning. She found herself deliberately dawdling as her mind turned to another weighty problem, one that only served to drag her sagging spirits even lower.

Something had to be done about Ansel. For the past week he'd visited the cabin daily, and on each visit his behavior had been more irrational. Though she hated to admit it, she'd concluded that Letty's death had left Ansel temporarily unstable.

At times he acted as though Charity were Letty. On other occasions he was totally at a loss as to where his wife had gone. He still paid little attention to Mary Kathleen, sometimes behaving as if he resented the child.

His continuing confusion worried Charity, but she didn't know what to do about it. Beau said it was natural; he hadn't known up from down for months after Betsy died. Time. Ansel needed time to come to grips with his situation.

Charity wasn't so sure. Once, she'd thought about asking Ansel to stay with her so she could take care of him until he could cope again, but she knew that would be improper; besides, the house couldn't hold another person. It was full now with her and Beau and the baby.

On top of everything else, Beau's suggestion that she marry Ansel to get the help she needed with her land kept popping into her mind. Apparently that was her only alternative. Once he returned to his old self, she would ask him to marry her. She realized

she was trying desperately to persuade herself that it was the only solution left, but the
thought left her cold.

Ansel was a reasonably young and vital
man, and once he got past the shock of losing his wife, he would be a good provider,
but right now he wasn't ready to take a wife,
and she wasn't ready to take on a man who
didn't seem to know who she was most of
the time.

Ferrand surfaced in her mind. She had
loved him desperately. The weeks and
months after his death had run together into
one dark blur, but he was gone and she
was left to go on. If her husband had lived,
she would never be having these thoughts
of another man, wouldn't have needed or
wanted anyone else. However, times had
changed, and a woman did what she had to
in order to survive. She needed a man to
help with the work, and the only way she
could get one in an acceptable manner was
to marry him.

She tried to visualize what it would be like
to be Beau Claxton's woman. He would
take good care of his wife. Look at the way
he mourned for Betsy. If she had to choose

between Ansel and Beau, she knew which one she'd pick.

She shouldn't be thinking of Beau this way—surely it was sinful, and disrespectful to her late husband's memory, but her mind seemed bent on tormenting her.

If there had been close neighbors there would surely be talk about a man living here, but Beau was still basically incapable of impropriety, which would be the last thought on his mind. He was a gentleman through and through.

What if he knew what she was thinking? She would be so ashamed. Decent women didn't have thoughts like that, did they? She couldn't help her thoughts, but she didn't have to linger over them.

A brisk rap on the door interrupted her musings. Charity bolted upright and pulled the blanket up around her shoulders.

She heard Beau stirring. "Someone's banging on the door," he mumbled after the second loud knock.

"I can't imagine who's calling this early."

"Better answer it before they wake the baby." She heard him roll to a sitting position.

The rap came again, and Beau called, "You want me to get it?"

Charity sprang to her feet, pulling on a thick wrapper.

She scampered barefoot across the floor, pushing the heavy mass of dark hair over her shoulder. She pulled the door open a crack. Her mouth dropped when she saw Reverend Olson and his wife standing on her doorstep, smiling warmly at her.

"Good morning, my dear. I hope we're not disturbing you." Reverend Olson's kind face reminded Charity of her father, and she was always glad when the reverend and his wife stopped by for a visit.

But not today.

This morning she wanted to shut the door in their faces. She was reluctant to reveal Beau's presence. Once the neighbors found out that he was staying with her, gossip would be inevitable. As far as she knew, only Ansel knew about him, and she preferred to keep it that way. She was aware of the mussed pallet on the floor, of Beau, half dressed and sitting on the edge of the bed behind his curtain, of Mary Kathleen sleeping in her makeshift crib.

What had seemed so natural now

seemed tawdry. She had a man living in her house. A man who had been seriously injured, but would they understand? These were good, caring people, and she couldn't bear to disappoint them. Well, the secret would be out now, and there was nothing she could do except brace herself and brazen it out.

Cherry Grove was a tight community, and its residents were unyieldingly straitlaced. For them, right was right and wrong was wrong, and there was no middle ground even if a man had nearly died.

Deep down she knew her neighbors wouldn't judge her harshly for nursing an injured stranger, but she knew there would still be some who'd argue that it wasn't proper for a man and woman to live under the same roof without the sanctity of marriage, especially when the woman happened to be a young widow like Charity Burk and the man was a handsome widower.

It wasn't like they were misbehaving. Beau had been a complete gentleman, and she had been careful to keep the curtain in place during the evening hours. Since he no longer needed daily care, she didn't see him lying on the bed. They were living under the same roof, but in different worlds. Would the good reverend and his wife understand the forced arrangement?

"Reverend Olson . . . Mrs. Olson. How nice to see you." Charity swallowed. Her fingers nervously plucked at the collar of her wrapper. "You must forgive me; I'm afraid I've overslept this morning."

"We heard you've been quite busy, dear." Mrs. Olson leaned forward, her blue eyes twinkling. She spoke in a soft, compassionate tone. "Has your unexpected visitor been keeping you awake nights?"

Charity smiled lamely. They knew about Beau. "Yes . . . some . . . but I don't mind."

Reverend Olson looked hopeful. "Well, may we come in to see her?"

"Her?" Charity vacantly stared at him.

"The Latimer babe. We understand you're caring for Ansel's child." Reverend Olson inclined his head. "We were wondering if we might see the little cherub."

When she realized they'd come to see Mary Kathleen, Charity felt limp with relief. "Oh . . . of course! But she's still sleeping— perhaps you could stop by another time?"

Reverend Olson glanced from his wife to

Charity with a benevolent expression. "I'm afraid that would be most inconvenient, dear. We plan to make several calls today. But I promise we won't take up much of your time, just a few minutes."

"I'm not dressed."

"We'll wait in the buggy while you get yourself together," Mrs. Olson suggested brightly. The elderly couple would not be easily deterred.

"Yes, well, I'll only be a moment." Charity gave them a hesitant smile; then, closing the door, she sank to the floor in despair.

Now what was she going to do? Reverend Olson and his wife would know she was caring for a man in her house and then brows would lift. "Who is it?" Beau asked. His voice drifted across the room, breaking into her frantic thoughts.

"It's Reverend Olson and his wife!"

The fire in the stove had died, and Charity felt goose bumps rising on her arms. She hurriedly crossed the room to stoke the embers into a rosy glow.

"What do they want?"

"They want to come in and see Mary Kathleen. I don't know how they found out I have her, but they did."

Beau poked his head around the curtain, unshaven, hair on end. "Should I hide?"

She added more fuel to the fire and turned back to face him. She knew she couldn't complain about the incriminating position she found herself in. It wasn't his fault, and nothing could be done to correct it now. She would just have to tell the truth and pray that Reverend and Mrs. Olson would understand. "Where could you go? We'd better get dressed. They're waiting."

Ten minutes later Charity opened the door and smiled cheerfully at the reverend and his wife, who were waiting patiently in their buggy. "You may come in."

For the occasion Charity had put on her best yellow wool and tied a matching ribbon in her hair.

Reverend Olson helped his wife off the seat, and they hurried inside.

Rebecca Olson was engaged in lively chatter when they entered. Shrugging out of heavy coats, the couple made for the cheery fire, warming their hands. They stamped their booted feet, trying to thaw out. The cold winter day promised snow by evening.

Charity clasped her hands tightly and

braced herself. Rebecca stopped in mid-sentence when she caught sight of Beau.

He stepped around the curtain wearing a pair of Ferrand's faded denim overalls and a dark cotton work shirt. To Charity he looked unusually tall and handsome this morning. She suddenly wished he looked fifty years older and six inches shorter, with eyes that were as pale and nondescript as Ansel's.

It would make her explanation much more believable.

"Why . . . hello." Rebecca smiled hesitantly and offered her small, gloved hand to Beau. "You didn't mention you had company, Charity." The reprimand in her soft voice was unmistakable.

"How thoughtless of me," Charity apologized.

"Good morning, ma'am." Beau stepped forward and took Rebecca's hand. "Such a cold day to be out." His voice dripped charm like molasses off hot biscuits.

Rebecca glanced at her husband. "It won't be long before travel will cease until spring."

Charity drew a deep breath, unclasped her hands, and stepped forward.

"Reverend Olson, Rebecca, this is Beau

Claxton. He's—he's been my guest for the past few weeks."

"Oh?" Rebecca's smile slowly faded. "Your guest, dear?"

"Beau had the misfortune of meeting up with a wounded wolf in the stream, and as a result, he was gravely injured. I've been looking after him until his injuries heal." Charity tried to sound breezy and carefree, and as if it were the most natural thing in the world for a single woman to care for a stranger in her home.

Rebecca glanced at her husband. "Oh . . ."

"Why, that must have been a terrible experience. It's a miracle you survived, young man." Reverend Olson reached to clasp Beau's hand. "I guess that explains the bandages."

"I'm afraid without Mrs. Burk's excellent care, I wouldn't be here today," Beau admitted.

"Oh, dear." Rebecca's eyes anxiously studied the angry welts still visible on Beau's face. "I do hope you're feeling better, Mr. Claxton."

He flashed her a melting smile. "Please. Call me Beau."

The pastor's wife colored; her face turned three shades of rose. "Beau. What a lovely Southern name. Are you from the South?"

"No, ma'am. I'm from Missouri."

"Missouri? I have a sister in Kansas City." Although the elderly couple was trying to be cordial, Charity saw the wary glances Rebecca sent her husband. She knew they were unnerved by Beau's presence and didn't know what to make of the situation.

"Well, my, my, why don't we all sit down and have a cup of coffee?" Charity invited, hoping to smooth over the awkward situation.

"Coffee would be nice," Reverend Olson agreed. "But we can't stay too long, Rebecca. We do have other calls to make, and it looks like weather will be moving in soon."

"Yes, dear. We'll only stay a minute." Rebecca turned back to Beau. "Exactly where in Missouri do you hail from, Mr. Claxton?"

"It's a small town, River Run—not far from Springfield." Beau held a kitchen chair for Rebecca, and she slipped into it gracefully.

"Now, we'll only stay a minute," Rebecca reiterated. Charity began to pour coffee. "Claxton . . . Claxton—you wouldn't happen to be kin to the Claxtons of Savannah, would you?"

"As a matter of fact, I am." Beau smiled. "My father's family is from Savannah."

"They are?" Rebecca glanced at the reverend expectantly. "Did you hear that, Reverend? He's a Savannah Claxton."

Rebecca's minute proceeded to drag into an hour, then two, and before Charity realized it, suppertime was drawing near.

Rebecca had become enamored of Beau. Throughout the afternoon he'd entertained her with exciting war tales about his brother and himself and stories of the Savannah Claxtons. Charity and the reverend shared Mary Kathleen, periodically changing diapers and warming milk.

While Charity prepared the evening meal, Reverend Olson gave up on an early departure and dozed peacefully in the chair before the fire. The morning sunshine had turned to clouds, and outside a cold rain pelted the windowpanes.

During supper the conversation was cordial, but Charity occasionally caught a renewed note of disapproval about Beau's remaining at the Burk cabin while he recovered.

"The reverend and I would be happy for you to stay with us until you're well. Isn't that right, Reverend?" Rebecca prodded.

"Hummph . . . uh . . . well, of course, dear." Reverend Olson cleared his throat and reached for a third biscuit. "Mr. Claxton would be most welcome to share our home."

"I do appreciate your offer, Rebecca," Beau said. "But I'd like to stay here awhile longer. I notice Mrs. Burk has a few fences down, and I thought before I went home, I'd help out a bit to repay her for my keep."

Charity glanced up from her plate in surprise. Their eyes met and held for a moment, and she tried to convey her gratitude. Why would he do this? Did it mean he actually planned to stay on and help her with the land, or was he only trying to pacify the reverend and Rebecca? Charity felt her pulse trip. She smiled at him, and he smiled back.

"But, Beau, dear, you're not going to be able to mend fences for weeks." Rebecca was clearly appalled that he'd consider remaining at the house.

"I'm doing better every day, ma'am, but I thank you for your concern." Beau's gaze slid easily away from Charity's and returned to the food on his plate. "Another week or two and I should be up and able to work. If this mild weather holds, I'll start on that fence. Winter isn't a good time, but I'll do what I can."

Charity decided a change of subject was in order and promptly mentioned Ansel Latimer, inquiring whether the Olsons had noticed Ansel's odd behavior since Letty's death.

They agreed they had, and Charity discovered Ansel had told the Olsons of Mary Kathleen's whereabouts. She was relieved when they devoted the remainder of the supper conversation to that topic.

It was late when the reverend and his wife finally prepared to take their leave. Charity held an umbrella over their heads and walked them to the buggy, while Beau put Mary Kathleen down for the night.

"He's a perfect gentleman," Rebecca said. "So tragic about his young wife."

"He loved Betsy very much."

Reverend Olson helped his wife into the conveyance, tucked a warm fleece robe over her legs, and then ambled around to check the rigging while the two women continued to chat. The rain had slackened to a cold, fine mist.

Charity wrapped her shawl tighter and smiled. "I'm so glad you stopped by, Rebecca."

She laughed. "We didn't intend to take up your whole day."

"We didn't mind at all." Charity was surprised how easily she'd begun to include Beau in her statements.

Mrs. Olson glanced toward the front of the buggy. The reverend was busy adjusting the harness. She turned back to Charity. "Dear, I don't know how to say this . . . but I feel that I must."

"Say what's in your heart, Rebecca."

At that moment Reverend Olson walked back to the buggy. "All ready, dear?"

"Well." Rebecca paused. "I was about to remind Charity that while I find Mr. Claxton a perfectly delightful man, there will most assuredly be others in the congregation who'll question the propriety of this—this unusual arrangement. Don't you agree, Papa?"

"Hummph . . . well, yes, dear, as a matter of fact, I've been thinking the same thing," he admitted. He turned to Charity, his faded eyes growing tender with concern. "Now, mind you, I'm not judging, but I'm sure you're aware it isn't proper for two . . . uh . . . single adults to share the same roof, no matter how innocent the arrangement may be." He cleared his throat nervously. "Once the town hears a man is living with you, there will be talk, Charity, and I'm afraid it will be unkind, my dear. Mrs. Olson and I don't want to see that happen."

Charity's chin rose, and she knew she looked stubborn. "Talk doesn't bother me, Reverend. And he isn't *living* with me. He's staying here until he's strong enough to move on." Surely even the most judgmental couldn't fault an act of kindness.

"I'm aware of that, dear, but we must protect your reputation."

"We're not alone," Charity argued. "I'm taking care of Letty's baby until Ansel returns, and Beau is a sick man. Where is the impropriety?"

Reverend Olson shook his head. "I'm afraid that's beside the point. There *will* be talk, so I'd like to suggest Mr. Claxton reconsider our offer to stay with us until his recuperation is complete."

Charity lifted her chin a notch higher, determined that gossips wouldn't control her life. "Are you saying you and Rebecca will inform the town about my houseguest?"

"Certainly not!" Rebecca objected, clearly horrified that they'd be accused of such betrayal. "But you know a thing like this will eventually leak out. We're only thinking of you, Charity. We don't want to see your reputation harmed."

Charity's face crumpled like a child's and her brave facade faded. "I know . . . but it's so unfair. We aren't doing anything immoral," she insisted.

"We know that, but other people won't be so understanding," Reverend Olson predicted. "I want you to promise me you'll talk to Mr. Claxton about moving to our place, soon as possible. I'm sure your secret will be safe for a few more days, but after that . . ."

Charity looked deeply into his eyes and understood he wasn't being self-righteous. He was genuinely concerned for her welfare, and he was right. There would be talk, and it wouldn't be pretty.

"Promise us you'll at least think about it, dear," Rebecca coaxed. "I'll take excellent care of your young man. Soon the snow will be so deep we won't be able to take him home with us."

Charity swiped at the tears starting to roll down her cheeks, wondering when she'd become such a crying ninny. "I'll speak with Beau about your offer," she conceded.

Reverend Olson patted her shoulder, then reached into his pocket for a handkerchief. "I think you'll see that it's for the best, dear."

But Charity didn't see it that way. When Beau left, she would be alone.

Just her and Mary Kathleen to face the long winter.

Beau watched from the cabin window as Charity chatted with the Olsons. Judging from her solemn face, he had a hunch he knew the subject of their conversation. Him. He hadn't thought of it before, mainly because at first he had been too sick to care, and then because it had seemed so natural, but his staying here would cause talk. About Charity. He couldn't have that. It would be a sorry way to repay her for all her kindness.

The Olsons disappeared into the swirling

mist, and Charity walked slowly back to the house. She opened the door and stepped inside, her expression subdued. Beau waited for her to speak, and when she didn't, he figured he'd better.

"The Olsons get away all right?"

She looked startled. "Oh, yes, they're gone."

"Nice people, especially Rebecca."

She fingered her apron, her gaze distant as if her mind was a hundred miles away. More likely just down the road—to the community. "They are very nice. Surprising that she knew your relatives."

"Yeah. Guess the world's not as big as it feels."

She gave him a weak smile and started to pick up her pallet. Beau took the bedding from her. "Let me do that. You have other things to take care of."

She stiffened as if he had reprimanded her. "I can do it."

"I know you can, but I want to help." She was one stubborn woman. He studied her flushed face. "Mrs. Reverend giving you a hard time over me?"

She looked up and then glanced away, but not before he saw the gathering tears.

"Hey, don't cry." He ached with the desire to take her in his arms and wipe her tears away.

Mary Kathleen whimpered, and she moved away to see to the baby's needs. Beau watched her, wishing he could do something to make her feel better. He was only too aware of what the talk would be like if the people in town found out about him.

He would have to leave. He knew it as surely as he knew his own name.

CHAPTER 8

After supper Charity slipped off to catch a breath of fresh air. It had been a worrisome day. The Olsons arriving so early and catching her still in her nightclothes had been bad enough, but Beau's presence had really upset the applecart. Fortunately, Rebecca had liked Beau, but it hadn't been difficult to see what she was thinking. Never had Charity felt so embarrassed, and the thing that upset her the most was that nothing improper had happened between her and Beau, but she knew enough about the way people's minds worked to realize no one would believe that.

Reverend Olson's advice drifted in and out of her thoughts. Moving Beau to the

Olsons' residence would be the sensible thing to do. But could she let him go? She felt an inner peace when he was near, one that had been sadly lacking in her life since Ferrand's death. And if she wasn't mistaken, Beau felt that same harmony. If he left now it wouldn't stop the talk. Maybe make it worse. She could just hear people claiming the Olsons had forced her to give him up. Either way she would be considered a scarlet woman. It wasn't fair.

Should two lonely people—each in need of the other—be denied friendship merely to appease those who had nothing better to do than find fault where there was none? It seemed unjust to Charity that anyone should take this precious gift away from her. She and Beau weren't hurting anybody, so why should they be denied the pleasure of each other's company for the remaining few weeks before he returned home?

An hour later she was still seated on a bale of hay, staring up at the stars. Beau came out of the house and paused to enjoy the night. "Mind if I join you?"

She smiled, scooting over to give him room, grateful to have him—for right now, anyway. She wondered what he thought about the Olsons' visit. He had offered to hide, so he must have realized the impropriety their situation posed. Although where he thought she could find a place to hide a man his size baffled her. A one-room cabin didn't offer much in the way of hiding places. He could have sat behind his curtain while the Olsons were here, but she had her doubts that would have worked either.

Besides, it would have been dishonest.

He sat down beside her, wincing as he slowly eased his injured leg into place. "Seems like you can see more stars on the prairie than anywhere else."

"Is your leg bothering you today?"

"It stiffens up when I don't move around enough."

"But you're doing much better." Charity wrapped her shawl snugly around her shoulders. "It's so cold."

"I never liked cold weather," he said. "Old Man Winter is seldom friendly."

An involuntary shiver trickled down her spine at the thought of another winter alone.

Winters in Kansas were long and harsh, bringing numbing temperatures and unbelievable snowstorms. Charity knew a Kansas blizzard could be a terrifying spectacle. Without warning, dark, billowing clouds would roll across the sky, unleashing blinding bursts of snow. Wind and snow could sweep across the plains with the force of a cyclone, taking a heavy toll on livestock and people. Communication with the outside world could be cut off for weeks at a time, and travel was impossible. Nothing moved until hundreds of men could dig openings through the drifts. In early fall Charity stored a winter supply of stove fuel and stocked up on canned goods, flour, sugar, and salt. She had moved the livestock closer in so she could care for them in bad weather.

She rubbed her hands down her arms to warm them and turned her thoughts to a more immediate concern. "Is the baby still sleeping?" Mary Kathleen had dozed off in Beau's arms while Charity cleaned up after their evening meal.

"I think the reverend and his wife wore her out." Beau chuckled and added solemnly, "Thank goodness."

Charity laughed at his open candor. "I thought you liked children."

"I do, but I was under the impression they slept once in a while."

"I think most of them do, but Mary Kathleen seems to be a bit confused about when she should be doing her sleeping—day or night. But with all the excitement today, we should be able to get a good night's sleep for a change."

Silence stretched between them. She sensed Beau studying her beneath lowered lashes. "What are we going to do about that situation?" he asked.

"The baby?"

"I don't mean to criticize, but it appears to me that Ansel is a sick man. Doesn't look to me like he's going to be able to take care of a baby for a long time . . . if ever."

Charity sighed. "He's troubled, all right." If anything, he slipped more out of touch with every passing day.

"What are you going to do? Keep the child indefinitely?"

"I promised Letty I'd take care of her. Ansel's a fine man. Given time, he'll accept her death. It was so sudden for him." She only wished she were as confident as she sounded.

"I'm not sure that's wise, Charity. You're getting mighty attached to the baby.

Wouldn't it be better if he hired someone to care for Mary Kathleen until he's better?"

Charity turned to him with mock surprise. "*I'm* getting attached? I've noticed she has *you* wrapped snugly around her little finger."

Beau's laugh was guilty as sin. "She's a charmer, all right."

"She's more than a charmer, and I wouldn't feel right about anyone else taking care of Letty's child. I love caring for her." He was right, of course. Giving up Mary Kathleen would be like tearing out her heart, but she knew eventually it would come to that. As much as she loved the baby, Ansel had first rights.

"Seems like a lot of work on top of everything else you have to do."

"I don't mind." She really didn't. The baby *was* a lot of work, but she was so precious. Letty lived on in her daughter. Mary Kathleen's hair, the color of her eyes, even her smile reminded her of the sweet-natured young woman Charity had called friend.

They sat in silence for a while, studying the star-studded sky, sharing a contentment that neither of them questioned.

"You're quiet this evening," Beau finally remarked.

"Am I? I guess I'm just thinking."

"Must be serious," he teased. "Usually you're a real chatterbox."

Charity shrugged. "Nothing profound."

"Your thoughts wouldn't have anything to do with the reverend and his wife, would they?"

Charity glanced up, surprised by his astute perception. "What makes you say that?"

"I noticed they weren't any too happy about me staying here with you."

"I expected their disapproval." Or she would have if she'd thought about it, but expecting and coming up against it weren't exactly the same thing. The Olsons' disapproval would be mild compared to the way others would feel. Beau would leave when he was able, but she would have to live here knowing how the people in town felt about her. She would always be the woman who'd had a man living with her without marriage vows.

Still, if Beau would stay, she would gladly face the gossip for the privilege of having him here. *Lord, does that make me a bad woman?* She had been lonely for so long;

she couldn't bear the thought of being alone again.

"It bothers you, doesn't it?"

Charity refused to look at him. "Well, surely Kansas isn't all that different from Missouri when it comes to morality."

"Morality? No, but we've done nothing to be ashamed about."

She finally met his gaze. "I see their point, Beau. I might think the worst if I were in their place and didn't know the true situation."

"Now that they know I'm staying here, Reverend Olson will explain the circumstances. They're God-fearing folk. Any one of them would likely do what you did."

She shook her head. "I'm not worried. I know I'm not doing anything wrong, and Ferrand always said that's all that counts. I sleep with a clear conscience." She wouldn't let idle talk dirty her feelings for Beau.

They sat in silence until he straightened his leg. "I guess I should give serious thought about taking the Olsons up on their offer to move in with them."

Charity closed her eyes and bit her lower lip, forcing herself to answer. "I suppose that would be the proper thing to do."

Beau stood up and lifted his gaze to the sky. A pale moon washed the landscape with light. "You always for doing the proper thing?"

The question surprised her. "Well, most of the time I try to do what's right, but I guess I've gone astray a few times." Her mother had said she was the most stubborn and contrary of her three daughters, but she'd never done anything really bad before. Not evil bad. "I'll wager you usually did what was right."

"Don't tell my ma, but I've slipped up a few times too. It's best to do what you think is right, but what you think is right and what other people think is right is often a different story."

She glanced up, her breath leaving a frosty vapor. "You think this is one of those times?"

He lifted his shoulders. "Could be."

She sighed and turned her attention back to the night sky. "The situation isn't exactly proper. I suppose we'll be faulted for it whatever we do, so if you want to go I'll understand, but you're welcome to stay."

He fell silent. Then, "I suppose we could

just sit tight for a while and see what happens."

Charity felt her heart leap with expectation. It was the closest he'd come to agreeing to stay. "There will be talk, but the Lord sees the true story."

He bent over, his features solemn in the moonlight. "If you don't have any objections, I'd like to stick around for a while longer. I'd leave at first light if I thought it was best for you, but I'd worry about you and the baby if I rode away now. I've been doing some thinking since the reverend left." His voice softened in what she accepted as an attempt to spare her feelings. "I can't marry you, not that you wouldn't make a fine wife, but I guess Bets was sort of it for me . . . you know."

"I wasn't expecting you to offer me your love, Beau." Her voice quivered and she tried to hold it steady. "I know how much you loved your wife."

His tone dropped. "I wouldn't marry any woman without giving her my all. It wouldn't be proper. Marriage is sacred and not to be taken lightly. A man and woman should be committed to one another before they enter into such an arrangement."

"But sometimes it doesn't work out that way," she said softly.

"I know it doesn't, but it should, and just because I can't marry you don't mean that I can't see that you're in a real bind. I'd like to help you out. Since I'm going to be laid up another few months, I could lend you a hand. I know I've never said it in so many words, but I'm beholden to you for saving my life, Charity. I'd like the opportunity to pay you back, if you'll let me."

"It wasn't all me," she reminded him.

"I know Laughing Waters and Little Fawn helped, but you're the one who took me in and sewed me up and sat up nights with me." He laid his hand over hers. His touch was warm, even though the night was icy. "I won't be forgetting what you've done. You're a good woman, and I'd be proud if you'd let me repay your kindness. There's no reason I can't stay till spring. By then I should have your land in good enough shape that you can claim your title. I'd be glad to do that for you, if you'd let me."

At another time in her life Charity might have refused his offer, pointing out that she neither wanted nor needed his sympathy. She didn't want him to stay because he felt beholden to her, but she guessed it was better than nothing. Sometimes you had to settle for what you could get. She'd discovered the hard way that no man—or woman, for that matter—could make it on the prairie alone.

She would've preferred he stay because he wanted her companionship. Nevertheless, she'd accept Beau Claxton on any terms.

Her hand gently closed around his. The touch was like nothing she'd previously known. "If you want to stay, I'll be grateful to have you."

"There's bound to be ugly talk when the town finds out I'm here. Soon as I'm able, I'll be headed to town for wire to string fences. If they don't know about me by then, they'll be finding out."

"Talk doesn't bother me long as I know it's not true."

His hand gently squeezed hers. "I say we see this thing through together. I could stay in the lean-to, if that would help any."

"You'd freeze to death with no heat. And it wouldn't stop gossip because you're here whether you're in the lean-to or sleeping behind a curtain in the house where it's warm.

I've never let anyone freeze yet, and I don't plan to start now."

He still held her hand. "I wouldn't do anything to hurt you. I want you to know that. I respect you too much."

She smiled and clung to his hand, unable to speak over the large lump in her throat. He wanted to stay, if he was sure it was all right with her. It was more than all right with her. It was wonderful.

She wouldn't have to face another winter alone.

They started back to the house, and Beau wondered if he was doing the right thing. He knew all too well how vicious gossip could be. People who prided themselves on high standards expected everyone else to live by their rules. He knew how it would look to the people of Cherry Grove, him living out here in the same house with a young widow. For that matter, he knew how Ma and Willa would feel about it. Cole and Cass would understand, but understanding didn't always mean approval.

Usually he would ignore troublemakers, but this was different. He couldn't stand by and let Charity be judged unfairly. But if he gave in to gossipmongers and moved to the Olsons', he'd have to leave her and Mary Kathleen alone. That wouldn't be right either. On top of trying to run her homestead without a man's help, she'd been good enough to take him in and nurse him back to health and care for a newborn child that wasn't hers. And now the town would be down on her for what she'd done, when in fact she'd been the Good Samaritan.

What kind of a man could walk off and leave a woman to face the severity of a Kansas winter alone? She didn't have enough buffalo chips to last more than a couple of weeks, and he knew exactly how little food she had on hand. She'd tried to stock enough for winter, but him being here had used up most of her provisions, and keeping the cabin warm while he had been so sick had taken a toll on the stove fuel.

He glanced down at her in the moonlight, noticing the curve of her lips, the contours of her face. Funny, lately when he dreamed of Betsy he had trouble remembering her features. It was Charity's face that haunted the late-night hours. He didn't want it to be that way. No one could ever take Betsy's place in his heart, no one.

Her hand touched his as gentle as a butterfly caress. "Don't worry. I know I'm safe with you here. It means a lot that you'd offer to stay. No matter what people say, God knows we're innocent and that's what really counts."

Beau swallowed hard, surprised at the wave of tenderness that threatened to seize him. "That's right. God knows."

His hand gently squeezed hers, and he struggled against the need to take her in his arms. He was surprised to discover he wanted to, and he might have, if thoughts of Betsy hadn't surfaced, reminding him it wouldn't be loyal to her memory.

All he had left of Betsy were his memories, and he figured if he let those go, Betsy would be gone. Forever.

But if he left Charity here to fight the elements alone, she'd be gone too. Seemed like God had laid out a pretty tough choice. Regardless, the course was set. He'd stay and face whatever the consequences.

Lately he'd been doing some thinking about God, and his thoughts had shamed

him. He knew enough about the Bible to
know God hadn't walked away from him.
I will never forsake you. He knew those
words by heart, knew what they meant. He
couldn't run far enough to get away from
his Creator. Beau Claxton might have shut
God out, but that didn't mean God had forgotten Beau Claxton. All the time he had
stumbled around in a fog, not knowing or
caring where he went, God had watched
over him, even directed his steps. Had God
brought him to Charity? He was beginning
to think so.

Heavy snow fell off and on the next two
weeks. As the fine white flakes mounded
around the cabin, the predicted trouble arrived, but in a form Beau least expected.

He was feeding Mary Kathleen her first
milk of the morning. Charity bustled around
the kitchen fixing breakfast.

The smell of fresh coffee, buttermilk biscuits baking in the oven, and bacon sizzling
in the cast-iron skillet filled the room.

Fire burned brightly in the stove. The relentless wind whistling across the frozen landscape made little difference to the occupants nestled inside the warm room. Outside, dwarfed by endless sky and sweeping plains, the Burk homestead seemed hardly more than a snow-covered mound on the prairie.

Charity stood on tiptoe and looked out the window at the swirling flakes of pristine white. "I love snow, and I suspect we'll be getting more than our share this year." She rubbed the steam from the glass with her elbow.

"I thought you hated winter." Beau set the baby's milk aside, then tipped Mary Kathleen over his shoulder and gently patted her back.

Charity caught the paternal act out of the corner of her eye. Beau performed the task so naturally now that he seemed to enjoy taking care of the baby. Though he said Mary Kathleen was growing like a ragweed, the infant looked tiny draped over his broad shoulder. And he had no room to talk. He was filling out rapidly these days, becoming an impressive man in his own right.

Charity couldn't help but feel a strong surge of pride at the way her small family thrived under her care. She had to remind herself every day that they weren't really her family, only temporary gifts the good Lord had sent to see her through another long winter.

She didn't know when Ansel would come to his senses and show up to claim Mary Kathleen. She didn't like to think about losing the infant, but she'd learned long ago to live for the day and let tomorrow take care of itself. Trust in God one day at a time. Whatever happened, she knew He'd see her through.

"I don't mind snow so much, but I hate the wind and cold."

"Well, if it makes you feel that good, maybe you ought to come out and help me today," Beau teased. "No sense sitting in the house and missing all the fun."

Though Charity had argued that he wasn't strong enough yet to work, Beau had already begun taking over chores. The day before, he'd fed the cow and cleaned out the chicken roost. This morning, he said he wanted to make some much-needed repairs on the lean-to. She worried he'd use up his hard-won strength, but she was learning Beau Claxton didn't take orders.

He was definitely his own man—and stubborn to boot.

Charity moved away from the window and returned to the stove to check on the bacon. "I'd be happy to help you out," she said, "but I must insist that you let me do the hard part."

He winked. "If you *insist.*"

Charity knew he was teasing. He wasn't a man to stand by and let a woman do his work, even though his injuries still pained him. But she was certain she could do more than he allowed her to. Yesterday they'd had a discussion over workload. She couldn't wield a heavy sledgehammer to drive the posts into the hard-packed ground, but she could lift the posts from the wagon and have them waiting in place.

Beau wouldn't hear of it. He said she had enough to do taking care of the baby and keeping meals on the table. While he was around, he'd do the heavy work. Charity winced when she recalled another incident where they'd gotten downright snappish with each other.

Beau had been gathering chips, slowly and cautiously, while the pile beside the house had steadily mounted. Charity was sure that he was overdoing it, so she'd bolted outside four or five times to caution him to slow down.

Each time she'd appeared to give him advice, Beau had promptly, but politely, sent her back into the house. "Go bake bread or something," he'd said. When she'd kept popping out the door to repeat the same warning again and again, he had finally lost patience with her.

"I used to help Ferrand all the time," she complained.

He'd lowered the ax, leaned on the handle in disgust, and fixed his blue eyes on her till the pupils had looked like pinpoints. "Well, I'm not Ferrand. And I'd sure appreciate it if you'd march right back in the house and nail your feet to the floor so I can get my work done."

Nail her feet to the floor! Why, that stubborn pain in the neck! Willing her voice to remain calm, she'd replied in a strained but pleasant tone, "You don't have to remind *me* you're not Ferrand. *He* would never have spoken to me in that tone. Besides, I was only thinking of your comfort. You're a fool to work this hard so soon after your accident."

"I feel fine. I want you to quit acting like a mother hen, constantly clucking over me. I'm going to gather fuel until I get enough to last us for a few days, and I don't want to hear that back door flapping every five minutes like a broken shutter in a windstorm. Do I make myself clear?"

Charity took a deep breath and squared her shoulders, her temper blazing hotter than a blacksmith's iron. "I'll see that you're not disturbed again." She tossed her head, marched back into the cabin, and slammed the door loudly enough to send Mary Kathleen into a startled howl.

They hadn't spoken to each other the rest of the day. By the following morning, they'd both concluded they were living too close in their tiny quarters to remain silent indefinitely, so they resumed communication.

Charity snapped out of her reverie and reminded Beau that breakfast was on the table.

He laid Mary Kathleen back in her bed, then washed his hands. Charity took the pan of biscuits out of the oven and poured their coffee.

"Smells good," he complimented, and she realized he always had something nice to say about her cooking. He was a delight to cook for, liked anything she set before him. Since he was feeling better, he ate like a harvest hand at every meal.

"Thank you. I hope you're hungry."

He grinned. "I'm always hungry for your cooking."

She smiled back, relishing the compliment.

They sat down to eat and someone knocked at the door.

Charity glanced up from her plate with a curious frown. "Now who could that be?"

"I'll get it." He winked at her solemnly and pushed away from the table, sending her pulse thumping.

When Beau opened the door, she saw his expression change from amused to baffled. Charity peered past him to see Ansel standing in the doorway. He wasn't wearing a coat or hat, only dirty overalls and a thin cotton work shirt. His shoulders were covered with a thick dusting of snow. His body shivered uncontrollably, and his teeth chattered so badly he could hardly form words.

"I-I-I want to se-e my ba-b-by."

"My word, man. Where's your coat?"

Beau reached out and pulled Ansel inside the shelter. Charity hurried to assist him.

"What's happened to you?" Charity had never seen him looking so disreputable—so unkempt. He was filthy, and his clothes looked as though they hadn't been washed in weeks. He'd lost so much weight his overalls and shirt hung loosely over his skeletal frame. She wrinkled her nose at the rank, offensive odor accompanying him. His unusually long hair was dirty and hung in matted strands around his face. Charity found it hard to believe that this was the same Ansel Latimer she'd known so well. He'd always been so clean, so careful about his appearance. Letty used to laugh about how often he used to change his clothes, and he'd had his hair cut every two weeks on the dot.

"I co-me to se-e my ba-b-y," Ansel repeated, his voice almost belligerent now.

"Of course you can see Mary Kathleen—"

"Who?"

"Mary Kathleen," Charity repeated. "That's what we've been calling her, Ansel. It's the name Letty wanted. I hope you like it."

Ansel seemed to momentarily forget the topic. His gaze quickly shifted, his eyes

roaming insolently over Beau's tall frame.
"Who's this man?"

"Why, it's Beau. The man who was injured. Don't you remember?"

"I don't know him." He dismissed Beau
abruptly. He glanced around the room.

Charity sent Beau a curious look. If he
hadn't been here Ansel's strange behavior
would have frightened her.

"Where's my baby?" Ansel's voice rose a
notch. "I want to see my baby!"

"Let's get you warmed up first," Beau
said. "Come over to the fire, man. We can't
have you getting sick."

Charity realized he was worse. Much
worse. He was acting crazy, and she was
afraid he'd suffered a complete breakdown.
"Let's sit down and have a cup of coffee.
You must be nearly frozen."

She reached to take his arm, but he
jerked away as if her touch burned him. He
looked her up and down with the same contemptuous glance he'd given Beau earlier.
"You Jezebel," he accused hotly, his voice
edged with hate.

Charity stared in stunned disbelief.
"What?"

"You're a shameless woman, Charity

Burk . . . shameless!" he repeated, his eyes filled with rage.

"Wait a minute." Beau reached over and pulled Charity protectively to his side. "You have no right to speak to her in that tone."

"She ain't nothing but trash!"

"Ansel—" Charity managed to find her voice—"what's *wrong* with you!" She was shocked by more than his language. What had prompted him to come with such outrageous accusations? They'd been friends for years. Why would he turn against her like this?

He eyed her with disgust. "Don't try to lie to me. I've heard the talk. You're living in sin with this man, and you've got my baby daughter in your viper's nest," he sneered. "Well, I'm here to deliver her from the hands of Lucifer."

"Oh, Ansel." Charity sagged weakly against Beau. "I don't know what you've heard, but it isn't true—"

"Lies! Nothing but lies!" Ansel stepped back, his eyes flaring wildly. "They say this man's been living out here for weeks. Can you deny it?"

"He has been, Ansel, but we're not living together—not the way those people are implying." She'd expected repercussions, but not like this. Ansel knew she'd done all she could to save Letty. She'd taken care of his daughter while he'd not even bothered to come and see if she was all right. He knew about Beau, had expected him to die from the wolf attack. Now he acted like he'd never seen the man lying pale and unconscious right here in this room.

He glared at her, hatred filling his eyes. "Lies! Nothing but dirty, filthy lies, you sister of Satan!" He spat the words as if they'd left a bitter taste in his mouth.

"All right, I think that's about enough, Ansel." Beau stepped forward, his fingers curling into fists. "I want you out of here, or I'll throw you out."

Charity reached to stop him from carrying out his threat. "No, Beau. He's ill—"

"I know he is, but he's not going to talk to you that way," Beau stated, his eyes hard. "Not after all you've done for him."

"I come to get my baby," Ansel said calmly. Suddenly all trace of emotion disappeared. "It's time I be taking her home."

Charity glanced urgently at Beau. "No . . . he mustn't take her."

She knew Beau understood and agreed.

He nodded, stalling for time. "You can't take your baby today. The weather's too bad. It would be better if you came back for her after the storm clears."

Ansel's chin jutted out and he turned belligerent again. "I can take my baby any time I want!"

Beau shook his head. "You're a sick man—you need help. Let me take you into town and—"

Ansel started backing toward the doorway, his eyes wild. Charity held her breath when he paused beside Mary Kathleen's bed. He glanced down and saw the sleeping baby, and his face suddenly took on the plaintive look of a small child's. "Ohhh . . . Letty . . . she looks like Letty."

"Ansel . . ." Charity eased forward, hoping to divert his attention so Beau could remove the baby from harm's way. "Let me fix you a cup of coffee, and then you can hold her and see how pretty her eyes are. They're amber—like Letty's."

He looked up. "I can hold her?"

"Of course you may hold her."

He reverted back to normalcy. He straightened his stance and moved with somber grace to sit quietly in a kitchen chair. Charity drew a breath of relief. She poured the coffee and fixed him a plate of food. Poor man; he looked like he hadn't had a decent meal in weeks. He drank the coffee Charity set before him and chatted amicably with Beau about the weather and spring crops.

After a while Beau nodded to Charity and she brought Mary Kathleen, placing the baby in her father's arms. Tears sprang into the father's eyes as he gazed down at his baby daughter. "She does look like my wife." His voice held a reverent awe as he brushed one finger lightly over the baby's cheek. Mary Kathleen laughed and waved her fists.

He looked at Charity, his eyes filled with wonder. "She's real pretty, isn't she?"

"Yes," Charity said softly. "She's a beautiful baby." It broke her heart to think Letty would never see her precious daughter.

He kissed the baby's forehead and smiled at Charity and Beau. "I know I've been acting real strange, Charity, but I think seeing my baby has helped me understand that Letty's gone," he admitted. "Maybe as soon as I have a few weeks to get my life back in order, I'll be able to take my daughter home and be a proper pa to her." His eyes misted again. "She would've wanted that, wouldn't she?"

"Yes, she would."

"Losing Letty . . . well, I can't tell you what it's done to me."

"I know. You don't have to explain, Ansel." Charity patted his shoulder consolingly. People handled grief in different ways. She hoped Ansel had the worst behind him. Maybe he could start to heal now.

"Do you think I can take the baby outside?" he asked. "The snow's so pretty. I feel like Letty would be there with us too. I'd like my daughter to experience snowfall with me. That would be all right, wouldn't it?"

Charity was touched by the earnestness in his eyes. What would it hurt to let him take her out for a minute? "It's cold out there. You can only keep her out for a short time."

He nodded. "I wouldn't want her to take a chill. I'll be careful with her, I promise."

Charity hurriedly went about gathering the baby's blankets to comply with his request.

While Ansel cooed and talked to Mary

Kathleen, Beau followed her across the room, whispering out of the side of his mouth, "I don't like the way he's acting."

Surprised, she paused to glance up. "Why? He seems like his old self, Beau."

"That's my point. He was crazy as a loon a few minutes ago."

"I've been concerned about him too, but I think seeing his baby has finally helped him to come to grips with Letty's death."

"What about the way he was talking to you?"

"He must realize he was mistaken. He'll apologize before he leaves; you wait and see. He's acting like the Ansel I've always known. I think with a little time, he'll be back to normal. You heard him. He's even planning on taking the baby home in a few weeks."

Beau remained skeptical. "I guess you know him better than I do. I hope you're not being foolish. I don't want you or the baby getting hurt."

She reached out and touched his arm, deeply moved by his concern. "I can't deny Mary Kathleen's father the right to be with her, and it will do him a world of good."

"I'll abide by whatever you decide," Beau

conceded. "I just hope you're not making a mistake."

She squeezed his hand. "Thank you." How could it be a mistake to let Ansel spend time with his daughter? A baby had a way of changing things. Only good could come from this poor man being with his baby girl.

She shook her head at the irony, thinking of Beau's concern. If she was going to be hurt, it wouldn't necessarily be Mary Kathleen who'd break her heart. Come spring, Beau would be leaving. . . . She shook off the thought and hurried to bundle the baby properly for the brief outing.

"I'll only keep her outside a moment," Ansel promised, worriedly tucking in Mary Kathleen's little hand that persistently poked its way out of the blanket.

"A little fresh air won't hurt her, but she shouldn't be out long," Charity cautioned a second time. "The wind's sharp today."

"I'll be careful with her."

Beau opened the door and Ansel stepped outside, still talking to his baby in low, soothing tones.

"I might as well fill the fuel box," Beau offered, reaching for his coat. Charity began to clear the table.

"It is getting low." She knew Beau wanted to keep a close eye on Ansel and Mary Kathleen. If it made him feel easier, she wouldn't object. "Would you mind throwing these potato peels to the chickens?"

Beau crossed the room to take the small bucket out of her hand. Their fingers touched; their eyes met unexpectedly. Charity felt her breath quicken when she looked into his warm blue eyes. For an instant she found herself envying Betsy.

Strange, she thought, to envy a dead woman. But Charity realized that she'd gladly trade places with his deceased wife if, for only one second, for one brief second, Beau would look at her with the same love he had so fiercely reserved for Betsy. She knew it could never be, but it didn't keep her from wishing.

"This all you want me to take?" His voice was strained, and Charity thought his eyes looked vaguely troubled.

"Yes . . . that's all."

He nodded. "I'd best see about Ansel." He started to walk away, but she saw him hesitate. He turned and faced her, his face lined with worry. "I suppose gossip about us living together has started. That's what Ansel meant about hearing talk."

"It wouldn't surprise me."

"I don't like folks thinking that."

"We agreed we didn't care," she reminded him.

He acted as if he wanted to say more, but changed his mind. "I'd better check on Ansel."

Charity watched him walk to the door and open it. He adjusted his hat low on his forehead and then smiled at her. The door closed behind him and she turned back to clearing the table.

Suddenly, the door flew open, and Beau stood in the doorway, his features tight with fury. "That lying, thieving scum is gone."

"What?" Charity's hand flew to her throat.

Beau stepped into the room, removed his hat, and angrily shook off the snow. "He's gone, Charity. There's not a sign of him anywhere."

Her hand covered her mouth. "Oh, dear God . . . the baby! He took the baby?"

Beau nodded curtly. "I'll saddle the horse and go after him, but I don't know. . . . The snow's coming down heavier now."

Charity crossed the room in a daze, trying to make sense of his words. "Beau . . . Mary Kathleen . . ."

"You don't need to remind me, Charity. He's taken her!"

Charity's composure crumbled, and as naturally as if it happened every day, she moved into the haven of his arms. She knew she had taken him by surprise. He held her stiffly at first, until she began to cry. Then his arms folded around her, and he pulled her closely to him.

His arms felt unbelievably good. He smelled of soap and smoke and fresh outdoors. There were still traces of snow on his shoulder, cold and wet against her cheek. She buried her face in the warmth of his neck and cried harder. It was all her fault. She'd been a fool to let Ansel take the child, and now Mary Kathleen would pay the price of her misplaced trust.

"There's no call to start crying," Beau whispered tenderly, smoothing her hair with one large hand. "He couldn't have gotten far. I'll find him and the baby before any harm's done."

"It's my fault," Charity sobbed.

"No, it's mine. I should never have taken my eyes off him."

"I want to go with you."

He grasped her shoulders and held her gently away from him. His blue eyes locked gravely with hers. "You should stay here in case he decides to come back."

"Oh . . . yes . . . he might come to his senses and bring her back." It was a hope to cling to, but she was so frightened. Mary Kathleen out there in this weather? She was so tiny, so helpless. And Ansel . . . *Oh, God, be with them, please.*

The blue in Beau's eyes deepened to cobalt. "I'll ride out and see what I can find. Will you be all right?"

"I'll be fine." She dabbed her eyes with the corner of her apron. "Hurry, Beau. It's so cold out there."

Beau smiled reassuringly. "The baby's bundled tight. She'll be fine."

Though Charity tried to muster a weak smile in return, fresh tears rolled from the corners of her eyes.

Beau reached out and caught the two tears with his thumbs, tenderly brushing the dampness away. "I have to go."

Charity nodded, too overcome by emotion to speak.

He looked at her for a moment; then very slowly he pulled her face to his and touched her lips briefly with his own. Just as quickly, he stepped away, almost as if he had done something he shouldn't. "I'll be back soon as I can."

He turned, placed his hat back on his head, and opened the door. "Be careful if Ansel comes back. I don't think he'd hurt you, but you keep the gun close—and don't hesitate to use it if you need to."

Charity nodded, her knees threatening to buckle from his unexpected kiss.

He went out the door, closing it firmly behind him. Her hand came up to reverently touch her mouth, where his taste still lingered. The kiss was only his way of reassuring her that everything would be all right.

She knew that.

But it was the most wonderful kiss she'd ever experienced, and she'd hold it forever within her heart.

The wind-driven snow lashed Beau's face. Heavy white flakes settled on his eyelashes, almost blinding him. He waded through deep snow to the lean-to where the horses had taken shelter from the storm. The wind howled while he saddled the bay stallion with fingers numb and clumsy with cold. *Father, I don't have any idea which way to go. Help me find them before it's too late.* Latimer could be anywhere out there. Did he have a horse or was he in a wagon? Surely he wouldn't be on foot. No one could survive a Kansas blizzard without shelter.

Beau swung into the saddle and rode away from the cabin, peering through the heavy curtain of snow, trying to locate tracks. His thoughts turned to Charity, knowing she would be pacing from the window to the door, praying for Ansel and Mary Kathleen and for him.

He thought about the way she had fussed over him the other day while he was gathering buffalo chips. She sure was cute when she got all flustered that way. It had been the first time he'd ever seen her lose her temper, and he'd discovered he rather liked her spunky nature.

The way she'd felt in his arms a moment

ago . . . she'd fit just right. She always had that pleasant lemony smell, and her hair had been like silk under his hand. She had felt so small, so sweet it almost took his breath away. Charity Burk was a special woman, and someday she'd make some man real happy. He regretted it couldn't be him.

He turned the horse to face the wind, praying he'd find Latimer and the baby in time.

He had to find them. Charity was depending on him.

CHAPTER 9

Lamps were burning when Beau returned.

Charity had spent the day alternately pacing the floor, praying, and wringing her hands in frustration. When she heard the horse approaching, she rushed outside without bothering to put on her coat.

Snow was still falling heavily, blanketing the ground with deep layers that made it difficult for her to walk. Beau was dismounting when Charity waded through deep drifts to meet him. Her gaze desperately searched his arms for a small bundle. When she saw there wasn't one, tears sprang to her eyes. "You didn't find her?"

"No." Beau quickly led the horse into the lean-to. Charity trailed behind.

"There wasn't a sign of him or the baby?"

He released the cinch and lifted the saddle, glancing at her. "You shouldn't be out here without a coat."

Charity clasped her hands around her shoulders, trying to keep her teeth from chattering. The wind whipped snow around the corners of the lean-to. They had to shout in order to be heard.

"Get back in the house!" Beau ordered.

She refused to leave. "What are we going to do about the baby?"

Beau put the saddle away, slipped the bridle off, and pitched a forkful of hay to the horse. Without a word he drew Charity under the shelter of his arm and propelled her toward the house. Heavy snowflakes mixed with sleet stung her face. Wind buffeted them. Charity stumbled and would have fallen without his supporting arm.

Beau forced open the door and they struggled inside. Heat wrapped around them like a warm blanket. Charity caught her breath, stunned by the sudden relief from the gale-force winds and bitter cold.

Once inside, he gripped her shoulders and turned her to face him. "I managed to pick up Latimer's tracks about a mile out, but it started snowing heavier and I lost them."

"Oh, Beau!"

"He's taken shelter somewhere along the way. He knows the baby can't survive in this storm," he consoled her.

"But he isn't thinking straight."

"He proved he can have lucid moments this morning. He's found shelter, and he and the baby are all right." Her eyes searched his, and she had a feeling he wasn't as confident as he sounded.

He released her, dusted off his hat, and stomped the snow from his boots. She quietly crossed the room to stoke the fire. He was half frozen and worn to the bone. It would be hard for him to accept defeat.

When she turned around, she noted the way worry and fatigue deeply etched his face, and she longed to go to him to offer comfort. She knew he'd grown as fond of the baby as she; yet she also realized it wasn't her place to hold him.

He moved closer to the fire to warm his hands, and she noticed his stiff movements. The wounds were bothering him again.

"You must be exhausted." Charity helped him remove his snow-crusted coat. "Sit

down by the fire and I'll dish up your supper." She hung his coat on the peg by the
door and hurried to the stove. He sat in the
split-bottomed rocker warming his hands as
she went around filling a dish with stew and
pouring hot coffee.

"Supper's ready."

He got up and walked slowly to the table,
shambling a little out of weariness. She
ached with the desire to place her hands on
his shoulders and massage away the sore-
ness of overstressed muscles. Afraid her
ministrations wouldn't be welcome, she
turned away to hew thick slices of bread
from a fresh-baked loaf.

After he'd eaten and she'd cleared the
table, they sat before the stove. She let her
expression silently beg him for some morsel
of solace.

"We wait, Charity."

"For what?"

"We wait until we hear something . . . one
way or the other."

Mutely she stared back at him, crushed
by the finality in his voice and aware he
was no longer pretending that all would be
well. He was being brutally frank now. He

couldn't know any more than she what the next few hours would bring.

Wait. The hours ahead loomed over her with a foreboding as dark and wild as the storm raging outside her home.

She found comfort in the thought that she would not be alone during the wait. Beau would be with her and God was there. He'd take care of Mary Kathleen. She had to believe that.

She silently crept into Beau's arms, and they stood before the fire holding each other, trying to absorb each other's grief in the only way they knew how.

The night passed slowly. Charity found rest impossible. She lay awake staring into the darkness, seeing Mary Kathleen's precious face. She had promised Letty she'd take care of her baby. God forgive her, she had broken that promise. Not intentionally, but the result was the same.

Beau had recovered enough to move about now. He'd insisted Charity return to her bed; he'd taken the pallet before the fire. Tonight he tossed about on the makeshift bed, and she knew he was restless and unsettled.

She stirred and called softly to him, "Are you all right, Beau? Do you need anything?"

"I'm fine; don't worry about me."

Thirty minutes later, he got up and stirred the fire. Charity dressed and came out to join him. They rocked and drank coffee. Beau started talking. He reminisced about happier times, carefree boyhood days spent with his brothers. Charity told him about Ferrand, her sisters, and how she longed to see them all again. Ferrand on the other side.

The endless night dragged on, and they talked of many things. The wind howled and buffeted the small dwelling. Occasionally they heard the sound of sleet hitting the windowpane. The fire burned low, filling the room with a rosy warmth. Charity gazed up at Beau, knowing he was talking to ease her burden, trying to help her the only way he knew how, and she was grateful God had sent him to her. She couldn't imagine what this night would have been without him.

It occurred to her that neither she nor Beau had spoken much of Ferrand or Betsy tonight. The discovery encouraged her. Maybe they were both moving away from their pasts.

"How will he feed the baby?" Charity asked once, returning to the subject uppermost in their minds.

"He'll find a way. It's his child—a man takes care of his own."

A man like Beau Claxton would, she reflected, but Ansel Latimer was a sick man. She remembered his dirty, disheveled appearance, his lack of a coat or hat. He hadn't taken care of himself. Would he know enough to take care of his daughter?

By first light the knock they'd been praying for sounded at the door. Beau gently restrained Charity when she bolted forward. He went to answer it.

Reverend Olson stood on the doorstep. Snow dusted his shoulders, and his kindly features were lined with weariness. "I know you must be sick with worry."

"The child?" Beau asked.

"She's with Mrs. Olson. Ansel brought her by late last night."

Charity joined Beau at the door, and he put his arm around her supportively. "Is she . . . all right?"

"She was cold and hungry, but she'll be fine. Mrs. Olson is spoiling her outrageously right now."

Charity sagged against Beau's side. "I'll get dressed and we'll go get her—"

"Charity." Reverend Olson's expression changed. "May I step in, dear?"

"I'm so sorry. Of course. You must be half froze."

The reverend stepped inside. Snow was coming down in large, puffy flakes; the wind was bitter cold. Pale morning light revealed a forbidding landscape buried under a heavy load of ice and snow. Beau closed the door.

"I'll fix you something warm to drink," Charity said.

Reverend Olson nodded, his expression grateful. He held his hands out to the stove, the heat sending steam rising from his damp overcoat. Charity brought mugs filled with hot coffee, and he cradled the cup in his hands, standing in silence for a moment.

While they drank coffee, Reverend Olson told them how Ansel had suddenly appeared on his doorstep the night before, cradling the baby in his arms, talking wildly.

"He was talking about Beau and me, wasn't he?" Charity held his level gaze.

"I'm afraid he is very ill. Somehow he finally comprehended Beau was staying here, and he was convinced the two of you are living in sin."

When Charity started to protest, Reverend Olson stopped her with an uplifted hand. "Surely you must know what the town is saying, dear. We discussed this at great lengths during my last visit, and if you recall, this is precisely what Mrs. Olson and I feared would happen. Apparently you preferred to take the risk. Beau has remained in your care rather than moving to our home for safekeeping."

Charity's eyes dropped, but Beau straightforwardly met the reverend's gaze. "We've committed no sin."

Reverend Olson's expression, kinder now, still held condemnation. "I know, my son, but surely you must see the impropriety of your situation. People are narrow-minded at times, and their tongues will continue to wag as long as you remain here with this young woman."

"Narrow-minded people find fault where there is none, Reverend. Charity needs my help. Soon as I have her land in proper order, I'll be moving on—and not a day sooner."

Beau watched the preacher's eyes grow cold. He knew how his being there must look to outsiders, but they hadn't done anything wrong, and he wasn't going to act like they had. Charity Burk was a lady. Circumstances had brought him into her life, but it hadn't been her choice, and she had committed no sin.

"You're making a grave mistake, young man." Reverend Olson shook his head. "What you're doing will remain to haunt Charity long after you've taken your leave. You must consider that as well."

"Charity and I are in full agreement on what we're doing." Reverend Olson was right in what he said, but he could not walk away from this woman. She needed help. It could have been Bets out here alone. He would have wanted someone to help her, however improper the arrangement appeared.

"Then I must warn you," said Reverend Olson, his tone solemn, "the child cannot be returned to your care."

A low cry of protest escaped Charity. "Oh . . . please, no . . ."

"Ansel has left the child with me, and I cannot, in good faith, return her to this situation."

"Exactly where is Latimer?" Beau demanded. "He has no right to steal the child and give her to you! Charity has been the only mother Mary Kathleen has known. You have no *authority* to take her away from here."

"I don't know where Ansel is, but he has every right to place the child where he feels she will be properly cared for. He is Mary Kathleen's father."

"He's insane." Beau slapped his hand on his thigh.

"I pray that isn't the case. I prefer to think he's a very troubled man, but regardless, we have a search party looking for him at this moment. He was barely lucid when he left the child last night. He wasn't wearing a coat. The townsfolk are concerned he won't survive the storm unless we find him soon."

"You have no right to keep that child. No one could give her any better care," Beau maintained.

"If Charity were married, there'd be no

question," the reverend reiterated. "Or if Ansel sees fit to return the child to her, then I suppose there would be nothing I could say. We'll simply have to find Ansel and try to ascertain what is best for both him and the child at this point."

Charity glanced helplessly at Beau. He set his jaw in a hard line and crossed the room to put on his coat. "I'll be riding back to town with you, Reverend." He was going to find Ansel and bring that baby home if it was the last thing he ever did.

"Oh, Beau." Charity followed him to the door. "You can't go out in this again. You were out all day yesterday—"

"I'm going." Beau cut her protest short, and she watched silently as the two men prepared to leave.

"I don't want you worrying. We'll be all right." Beau faced her when they stood in the doorway a few minutes later. She handed him a sack of food she'd hurriedly assembled.

He looked down at her, seeing the fear in her eyes. She was worried about him. And there was something else, something he'd seen only in Betsy's eyes. He swallowed and looked away.

"You be careful." She gave him a warm red woolen scarf she'd been wearing. One she'd knitted and given Ferrand on his birthday. "Be sure to wear this. The wind is terrible."

Beau smiled and winked at her, hoping his eyes silently conveyed his appreciation for her concern. "Thanks. You take care too."

He tucked the sack under his arm, pulled his hat low on his forehead, and nodded to the reverend. "I'm ready if you are, sir."

The search parties had split off into small groups. Beau and Reverend Olson met up with two of the men as they rode into the outskirts of Cherry Grove.

All four riders reined their horses to a halt. Lanterns burned brightly in the blowing snow. "Gentlemen, this is Beau Claxton," the reverend introduced them. Their horses pranced restlessly, their breath blowing frosty plumes in the cold night air.

The two men assessed Beau silently, their expressions easily discernible. "You the one living with the Burk woman?" Jim Blanchard finally ventured.

"Mrs. Burk was kind enough to care for me while I was ill," Beau returned evenly. "And I sleep and take my meals there, but I don't 'live' with her." Though Beau spoke quietly, there was an underlying edge of steel in his tone.

Jim Blanchard shot Troy Mulligan a knowing grin. Beau noted the snide exchange, and he eased forward in his saddle, casually resting his gloved hands on the horn. "I'd be mighty grateful if you gentlemen would be so kind as to pass the word along. I'd not take kindly to anyone who'd say otherwise."

His smooth voice had such an ominous tone it promptly wiped the smirks from both men's faces.

"Gentlemen, we're wasting time," Reverend Olson reminded patiently. "There's a sick man out there somewhere who needs our help."

The men agreed to search in opposite directions and meet back hourly to report any progress. Beau rode north; the reverend, south; Jim Blanchard, west; and Troy Mulligan headed east.

The wind continued to pick up. Icy pellets

fell from the leaden skies. Beau rode for over thirty minutes without one encouraging sign to indicate Ansel had gone that direction. He realized even if there had been tracks, the snow would quickly have covered the trail.

Sleet stung his face, and he paused once to tie the woolen scarf Charity had given him over his mouth. His hat brim sheltered his forehead. The faint smell of lemon lingered in the fabric, and Beau closed his eyes for a moment, drinking in her fragrance. The thought of her waiting and praying back at the cabin gave him the strength to push his horse forward in the ever-deepening drifts. He thought of Ansel out in the storm with no warm clothing to protect him and offered up a prayer for the poor lost soul. He'd been where Latimer was, everything lost and nothing left to hope for, and it was an awful place to be.

It was nearing dawn, and there was still no sign of the man. When Beau had reported back to the other men, he found that they too had been unable to shed any light on Ansel's whereabouts, but they'd all agreed to keep looking.

The storm had increased in intensity and

the men were exhausted, but no one was ready to give up. Beau headed back out again, knowing it would take a miracle to find anyone in this blizzard. His face felt numb, and he could no longer feel his hands in the fleece-lined gloves he wore. The drifts were nearly up to his horse's belly. Beau knew he was going to have to turn back soon.

The horse topped a small rise, and Beau reined him to a sudden halt. His eyes scanned the fields below him, and his heart sank.

On the ground, Ansel lay peacefully. Frozen to death.

Beau closed his eyes, despair washing over him. He sat atop his horse on that cold rise, looking at the new father. What an awful, lonely way to die. Why had he neglected to come in from the cold? But he knew the answer better than anyone. Ansel didn't care about living, not without Letty.

Did any man have the right to judge another? Beau slumped wearily over the saddle horn, staring at what once had been a vital, loving man. He searched his soul and found he couldn't condemn Ansel. Only God knew what this man had gone through, and only God had the right to judge. Beau couldn't help but feel Ansel had found a peace most folks would know nothing about.

He knew exactly how deeply Ansel had suffered. Hadn't he felt just as hopeless many, many times after Betsy's death? But through the grace of God and his mother's prayers, some inner strength had kept him going for another hour, another day, another week, always with the hope that the hurt would eventually ease. Like Ansel he'd had trouble accepting the change death had brought. But Latimer had been alone and Beau had family. It shamed him now that he'd run away from the people who loved him most. It also bothered him that he hadn't talked to Ansel. Maybe it would have helped if the grieving man knew someone else had walked through the same dark valley.

The only thing he could fault Ansel with was that, like himself, he had loved too deeply.

It only took a few minutes to ride to where Ansel lay. Beau gently lifted the lifeless body in his arms and carried him to his horse. He removed a blanket from his bedroll and wrapped it securely around the body, though he wasn't sure why. Maybe because Ansel looked so cold.

Before he secured the body to the back of the horse, he stood gazing down into the man's face, which looked surprisingly serene.

What had been his last thoughts? Beau wondered.

He was now beginning to believe that faith was a journey, not a destination. If only Ansel could have known the difference. The realization jarred Beau to his very core. He knew that if his life was to change, if he was ever to regain hope, he had to trust that though tomorrow would have its share of trouble, no man was asked to carry his burdens alone. That God's grace was sufficient for any need he might have.

Beau reached out and gently touched the cold cheek. "If it helps any, I understand. I'll do my best to see your daughter's cared for."

He wanted to say more, but he didn't know anything to add. Surely there had to be more profound words to speak at a time like this, but he guessed he'd have to leave those words to the wisdom of Reverend Olson.

He climbed onto his horse to take Ansel home.

A grave was never a pretty sight. Ansel couldn't be buried until a spring thaw, so folks had gathered around the Latimers' root cellar to say good-bye. Friends and neighbors had been called upon to bury the dead. In a matter of weeks circumstances had set aside these particular mourners to put to rest another victim of what seemed like a never-ending tragedy for the Latimer family.

Snow lay deep on the ground, and the small group huddled against the cold wind to listen to Reverend Olson talk about the "deeply troubled soul" of Ansel Latimer.

Beau stood beside Charity, solemnly listening to the minister's words. A weak sun slipped in and out of mushroom-shaped clouds, which promised neither rain nor shine. The icy wind whipped the mourners' coats about their legs, making the forced gathering more miserable than it already was.

Reverend Olson's voice sounded far away when he read from Isaiah. "'He giveth power to the faint; and to them that have no might he increaseth strength. Even the youths shall faint and be weary, and the young men shall utterly fall: But they that wait upon the Lord shall renew their strength; they shall mount up with wings as eagles; they shall run, and not be weary; and they shall walk, and not faint.'"

The reverend closed his Bible and wiped his eyes. "Ansel was weary; God gave him rest. Weep not for this good man, but hold tightly to the Word of God, our source of strength."

Our source of strength. Beau had not depended on God enough for that strength. He searched for a meaningful reason why so much heartbreak should come to one family, why so much misfortune should be thrust upon one innocent child. He could find none.

Mary Kathleen was alone now here on earth.

Who would see to her needs, rejoice over her first tooth, send her to school, or walk her down the aisle when she grew into a lovely woman? He realized, with a pang, how proud he'd be to do all those things for her.

Although Reverend Olson hadn't spoken again of the baby's welfare, Beau knew Mary Kathleen wouldn't be returned to Charity. And judging from the sadness on her face, Charity knew it too.

Beau had watched her going about her work the past two days with a quiet despondency. When he'd attempted to cheer her, she'd politely dismissed his overtures with a wan smile and a soft reprimand: "Don't worry about me."

The cabin was a forlorn place without the baby. He knew Ansel's death bothered Charity too. In times like this it was easy to wonder if something couldn't have been done or said to prevent the tragedy.

He knew Charity missed the baby. At night Beau had heard her crying into her pillow, and he'd wanted to go behind the curtain to comfort her. Instead, he'd lain staring at the ceiling, feeling her misery as deeply as his own, agonizing because he had no way of easing it.

Then the guilt had set in, keeping him

awake long after Charity had dropped into an exhausted sleep. A lot of the blame for her trouble rested on his shoulders. If he had gone to live at the Olsons' the way the reverend had wanted, Mary Kathleen would have been allowed to remain with Charity. His being there had brought this condemnation on her. Deep within his soul he knew a way to spare her this agony.

It would only take a brief marriage ceremony.

A seemingly simple solution, yet by offering to marry her, wouldn't he inadvertently be allowing her to exchange one anguish for another? Granted, the Olsons would be happy to return Mary Kathleen to Charity's care if she was properly wed, but Beau knew it would be unfair of him to marry her. While he certainly liked and respected Charity, he wasn't sure if he could ever love any woman again.

Betsy's death had changed him. He'd loved her with all his heart—but she was gone, and he had been left damaged and broken. The wound in his heart hadn't healed. Maybe it never would. Since both he and Charity had experienced good, loving marriages, would it be right for them to settle for security and companionship and never again know the depth of love they'd each shared with their deceased partners? It seemed to Beau that wouldn't make either one of them happy. There was always the chance Charity would meet someone she could love. Did he have the right to tie her to a loveless marriage? *Father, show me the right thing to do.*

He knew love came in many forms. He loved Wynne, Cole's wife, but not the way he had loved Betsy. If anything ever happened to Cole, Beau knew he would take care of Wynne and provide a good life for her and Cole's child. Maybe he could love Charity the same way he loved his sister-in-law, purely platonically.

Charity had been good to him, as good as any woman he'd ever known. He owed her his life. And since he was relatively sure no other woman could fill Betsy's void, why was he being so stubborn about marrying her?

He couldn't deny there was a strong attraction between them, but he was sure it grew from being so lonely for so long. Charity hadn't forgotten Ferrand any more than he had forgotten Betsy.

If he could save Charity's land by sacrificing a few months out of his life, why
shouldn't he? Once the land title was in her
hand, and he was assured she could take
care of herself, he could always go back to
Missouri. She would never try to hold him
against his will; he knew that. The day she
had asked him to marry her, she had promised to let him leave with no obligation the
moment she could claim her land.

Beau realized Reverend Olson had invited
the gathering to pray. They bowed their
heads and the minister's voice boomed encouragingly over the frozen countryside.
"'The Lord is my shepherd; I shall not
want. . . .'" The voices of the mourners
blended somberly together as they recited
the Twenty-third Psalm.

Beau saw tears seep from Charity's eyes.
He reached to clasp her hand and squeeze
it reassuringly as his deep voice joined with
hers in the moving recitation.

"'Yea, though I walk through the valley of
the shadow of death, I will fear no evil: for
thou art with me. . . .'"

Beau could see heads begin to lift when
Charity absently moved into the shelter of
his side. He knew tongues would wag anew,

but at the moment, she needed someone to lean on, and he had about made up his mind—like it or not—that he was the only one she could count on.

The top of her head barely reached his shoulder. The small feather on her black hat danced in the wind. She huddled against his coat, seeking shelter from the elements. She glanced up and their eyes met. Her gaze searched his imploringly, crying out for his quiet strength, and Beau was more than willing to give it to her.

The dreary day was suddenly obliterated when she smiled, and as if they were speaking only to each other, they recited the comforting thought: "'Surely goodness and mercy shall follow me all the days of my life: and I will dwell in the house of the Lord for ever.'"

Beau believed those weren't just words written a long time ago, but a firm promise a man could depend upon. His eyes lovingly brought the message home to her.

Maybe the words would make Ansel Latimer's death easier to bear. He knew she blamed herself for letting him take Mary Kathleen, but there was enough blame to go around. He should have known a man in Ansel's state of mind couldn't be trusted.

The service ended and the crowd wandered away.

Few chose to stop by the Burk sled to offer words of comfort after the service. Most of the mourners conveniently dispersed to the safety of their carriages for the return trip.

The reverend and Mrs. Olson paused briefly, clasping Charity's hand. Their eyes spoke of deep sympathy because they knew she'd lost another close friend, and their words were kind and reassuring. Beau noticed Charity holding tightly to Rebecca's hands, and he saw the older woman trying to comfort her. He'd also noticed the other women giving them a wide berth. They acted like they were too good to associate with Charity. It hurt him to see the look in her eyes when she experienced the women's behavior.

When the last of the mourners had gone, Beau and Charity sat in the sled staring at the closed cellar door. The Latimer homestead would go untended until better weather.

The sound of the wind rustling through

brittle branches was a lonely one. The sun had disappeared behind a cloud again, enveloping the earth in a shroud of gray that seemed fitting for the sad occasion.

"I hate death." Charity's voice sounded small and frightened in the cold air.

"It's as much a part of life as being born."

She turned to Beau, her face childlike now. The wind had whipped her cheeks red, and her moist eyes reminded him of pools of sparkling emeralds. He had never seen her look so pretty—or so lost. Since coming to the Kansas frontier, she'd seen more than her share of death, and he knew she needed to know there was more to life than this terrible, crushing sense of loss. "It hurts, Beau. It hurts." Her voice broke and tears slid down her cheeks.

"I know it does." He reached over gently and cupped her face in one large hand. His eyes held hers. "I wish I could make it easier for you."

"You do, just by being here."

She smiled through her tears, and the sun suddenly broke through the clouds in a splendid array of light, bathing the cellar and the small sleigh in a pool of ethereal warmth.

Or did it only seem that way because that's how Charity made him feel? When Beau glanced up, the clouds were as dark and dreary as they'd been before. He slapped the reins against the horse's rump and turned the sled toward town.

Charity had been aware that Beau had stared at her a very long time. It seemed as if he was struggling to say something but didn't know how.

She had waited patiently but felt disappointment when, after gently brushing her tears from her cheeks with his thumbs, he'd reached to pick up the reins. The horse slowly began to move over the rutted hillside.

Charity turned, staring over her shoulder as the Latimer homestead grew smaller and smaller in the distance.

"I hope he's with Letty," she whispered.

"Yeah, me too." Beau seemed preoccupied, and after a glance at him, she decided to leave him alone.

A stray flake of snow fell occasionally as

the sled wound its way back to Cherry Grove. Charity had mentioned earlier she needed a few supplies and would like to stop by Miller's Mercantile before they made the trip home.

Beau had readily agreed. He needed a new hammer, and he wanted to purchase a quantity of raisins.

"Raisins?" Charity's brows lifted when he mentioned the strange request.

"I'm partial to raisin pie. You know how to make one?"

"Why . . . I've never made one, but I'm sure I could."

"Then I'll get plenty."

She'd make him one for supper. She could make a pie, just had never tried her hand at making a raisin one. But if Beau wanted one, she'd try to comply.

But when the sled rolled into Cherry Grove, Beau drove right past Miller's Mercantile, the Havershams' restaurant, Dog Kelley's Saloon and Gambling House, the Parnell clothing store, the schoolhouse that served as the church on Sunday mornings, and the various other storefronts lining the almost-deserted Main Street.

A plume of white smoke puffed from the

chimney of Miller's Mercantile. Charity knew most of the townspeople who were brave enough to venture out on such a cold day would be huddled together around the old woodstove, exchanging tales of Ansel Latimer and, no doubt, the scandalous Charity Burk.

"You just passed the mercantile," Charity reminded him, thinking Beau had been lost in thought and missed his intended destination.

"I know."

The sled came around the corner, and the horse trotted at a brisk pace down Larimore Street. Charity leaned over to assist Beau in correcting the oversight, her breath making white wisps in the cold afternoon air. "Just follow Larimore around, and it will bring you right back to Main."

"I know where I am."

"You do?" His air of confidence assured her that he did, but she didn't understand. As far as she knew, Beau had only been in Cherry Grove one previous time to purchase nails and wire.

"How are you so well acquainted with the town?"

"I'm unusually bright for my age." He

winked at her and began to whistle a jaunty little tune, urging the horse to pick up its pace.

Charity sat back and enjoyed the ride, thinking how nice it was to get her mind off of the devastating events of the past few days. Beau seemed to be in an uncommonly good mood all of a sudden, and it made her own spirits lighter. She wasn't in any hurry to face the people gathered at the mercantile, although she knew she'd have to eventually. No one had said anything at the funeral, but their behavior had been cool. That hurt. The name of Burk had always stood for decency and integrity. She hated being the one to bring censure on Ferrand's name.

Beau pulled the horse to a halt in front of Reverend Olson's house a few minutes later, and Charity glanced at him, mystified.

"We're going to visit Mary Kathleen!" She tried to conceal the sudden excitement in her voice. She knew he missed the baby as badly as she did, and she didn't want to put a damper on his cheerful mood.

Beau set the brake and tied the reins to the handle. He got out of the sled and turned to lift her down. She put her hands on his shoulders and felt his strong grip on her waist when he lifted her from the seat. He held her gently for a moment before setting her feet on the ground.

Charity tried to keep up when he opened the gate on the white picket fence and ushered her up the walk. "Beau, I don't think we should drop in unannounced this way. The reverend may still be at the Latimers'."

"A minister shouldn't be surprised by unexpected company," Beau reminded. Before Charity could protest further, he rapped briskly on the parsonage door.

Rebecca answered the summons. Her face broke into a wreath of welcoming smiles when she recognized the visitors standing on her doorstep. "Land sake! Look who's here, Papa!"

"Who?" Reverend Olson poked his balding head around the doorway and broke into a smile when he saw the young couple. "Well, do come in, do come in!" he invited, swinging the door open cordially. "We just got home."

Charity noticed he had a cloth draped over his shoulder, and signs of Mary Kathleen's recent dribbling were in evidence.

"How very nice to see you!" Rebecca exclaimed. She bustled around collecting their coats and scarves. "I didn't expect to see you again so soon."

"Well, I had a few things to pick up at the mercantile," Charity offered lamely, never dreaming herself that she'd be standing in the reverend's parlor, enjoying the delicious smell of a fresh-baked apple pie on this of all days.

"You must stay to dinner," Rebecca insisted.

"I'm afraid we have to be getting back soon," Beau refused politely. "It's starting to snow again."

"It is? Oh, dear. I just hate winters, don't you?" Rebecca chattered. "Ansel's service went well, don't you think? So sad. So sad."

Charity nodded, wondering why they were here. She was sure Reverend Olson wouldn't change his mind about letting her have Mary Kathleen.

"You must be here to visit the baby, but I'm afraid she just went down for her nap," Reverend Olson apologized. "She didn't sleep well at all last night. . . ."

"Actually, she hasn't been sleeping well since she got here," Rebecca confessed.

Reverend Olson laughed. "I'm not sure

how many more nights I can walk the floor with a screaming baby and still retain a charitable attitude. The good Lord didn't mean for old people to have babies—with the exception of the biblical Sarah, of course."

Charity was about to say they understood and would be happy to return as soon as they completed their shopping when Beau interrupted. "We'd sure like to see the baby, but that's not what we're here for, Reverend."

Charity's gaze flew up to meet Beau's. "It isn't?"

"It isn't?" Reverend Olson parroted.

"It isn't?" Rebecca echoed.

"No, sir . . . I . . . me and Mrs. Burk want to—to get married."

"You do?"

"We *do*?"

"You *do*!" Rebecca clapped her hands together gleefully. "Wait just a minute! I need to straighten my hair."

"Beau!" Charity turned to him, dumbfounded, her heart beating like a trapped sparrow's. She suddenly felt light-headed. He was going to marry her? The least he could have done was *tell* her.

"Yes. You don't have any objections, do you?" His eyes radiated that stubborn blue she'd come to recognize, and yet they looked a bit sheepish too.

"No . . . I—I'm just surprised, that's all."

"Well, If we want to get Mary Kathleen back, it seems the only sensible thing to do." Beau took a deep breath and continued. "I figure since we're in town, we might as well get it taken care of."

"You—you don't mind?"

"Wouldn't be doing it if I minded," he said abruptly.

"But, Beau, are you *sure* you want to do this?" Charity had no idea what had changed his mind, but she didn't want him to do something he would regret in the morning.

"It's the only thing left to do."

"But is it what you want, Beau?" She desperately wished he would say something more reassuring—anything—but did she have a right to question his motives? If he was good enough to help her out, then shouldn't she accept his kindness and not worry? But "it's the only thing left to do" wasn't the most romantic proposal a woman ever heard.

"It's all right with me if it's what you want."

"I don't have any objections . . . if you don't." She didn't press her luck by asking him if their marriage would be a permanent commitment or only a temporary arrangement. At this point it seemed immaterial.

Beau took a deep breath and straightened his shoulders. "Then let's get on with it, Reverend."

Rebecca breathlessly returned, hair in place, and moments later the ceremony began.

Charity's hands trembled, and her voice could barely be heard when she nervously recited her vows. Beau's hands were steady as a rock, and though he repeated his words woodenly, his voice never wavered.

How vows were exchanged made little difference; for better, for worse, within a scant three minutes, Charity Burk and Beau Claxton had become man and wife.

"Do you have a ring to give your bride as a symbol of your vows?" Reverend Olson asked.

"I'm sorry, sir. I don't."

"No matter. A ring doesn't insure love." Reverend Olson's kindly gaze met Beau's.

"It will be up to you to cultivate love and make it grow, son."

"Thank you, sir."

"You're both good people. I wish you Godspeed." Reverend Olson firmly closed the Bible. "You may kiss the bride—and the baby needs changing."

CHAPTER 10

Fifteen minutes later, Beau and Charity were standing on the opposite side of the Olsons' front door with Mary Kathleen once again nestled snugly in Charity's arms.

"Did you get the impression Reverend Olson was anxious to hand the baby back to us?" Charity grinned, thinking of the older man's relieved expression when he gave Mary Kathleen to her.

Beau laughed. "Sure looked that way. Never saw anything like the way he hustled around gathering up her stuff."

"He barely gave Rebecca time to say good-bye."

"And he seemed awfully concerned we get an early start home," Beau added.

Charity giggled. "I'll bet he's already curled up in bed sound asleep."

"I wouldn't doubt it."

They stepped off the porch together and walked to the sled. Charity waited while Beau settled the baby comfortably on the seat, making sure she was well protected from the inclement weather. Then he turned to assist her.

He lifted her slight weight easily, his strong arms suspending her momentarily in midair as his eyes met hers. Charity grew a little breathless as she stared back at her handsome husband, and she suddenly found herself wishing the unexpected alliance between them could somehow be a permanent one. She knew she would do everything within her power to make it so. Was it possible she was falling deeply in love with Beau Claxton?

Whatever had caused him to change his mind about marriage, she was grateful. She would have welcomed his presence in her life regardless, but she would be a fool not to recognize the difference wearing his name would make to other people.

"Charity . . . about the ring . . ."

"Yes?"

"I'm sorry I didn't have one to give you."

"It's all right." As if she cared about a ring when she was Mrs. Beau Claxton.

"And . . . I'm sorry I didn't ask you proper . . . to marry me. I . . . well, this wasn't easy for me . . . or you. . . ."

"I understand." She smiled, hoping to assure him that it didn't really matter. Her mind vividly replayed the kiss he'd given her at Reverend Olson's request. It was brief, emotionless, nothing more than a polite ritual, but it had sent every nerve in her body singing.

"I've been giving the problem serious thought." His expression turned solemn, and she realized what he was trying to say was important to him. "I've lain awake more than once considering it, and I think we made the only reasonable choice."

She nodded, too busy wondering what it would feel like to touch his hair to pay much attention to his words. Would it feel soft or coarse and springy? And his mouth. Beautifully shaped, with full, clearly defined lips that looked warm and tender.

Her eyes widened with guilt when she realized that he was aware of the way she was shamelessly regarding him. A slow grin spread across his features, the devilish smile crinkling the corners of his eyes.

For a moment he looked as if he wanted to kiss her—really kiss her this time, and her heart stood still. But the moment passed, and before she knew it, he was quickly walking around the sled and taking his place beside her without further ado.

The stark white, frozen countryside looked different, filled with an ethereal beauty she knew had nothing to do with the lowering sky and everything to do with the brief ceremony that had bound them together as husband and wife. *Mrs. Beau Claxton.* She tried it out in her mind, liking the sound of it. Beau climbed into the sled beside her and turned the horse toward Main Street.

The stop by Miller's Mercantile was kept brief because of the worsening weather. The store was busy, and Beau offered to hold Mary Kathleen while Charity made her purchases. She noticed the sideways glances sent her way by the female population of Cherry Grove. The men seemed a shade too friendly, as if she had lost the right to be respected. She went about choosing her purchases with her head held high, well aware of the spots of color burning her cheeks.

Beau carried the infant around the store, acting very paternal, pointing out various articles to the child, which Mary Kathleen could not possibly understand or appreciate the meaning of. Charity watched when he paused and whispered conspiratorially about a certain rag doll Santa Claus might be persuaded to bring her next year, if she promised to get her outrageous sleeping schedule back in order. His endearing behavior warmed Charity's heart.

When her purchases were completed, the baby exchanged hands so Beau could shop. Charity browsed through the bolts of brightly colored yard goods.

Agnes Troxell, one of the town's busybodies, sidled up close to her. "My, Mr. Claxton's a right nice-looking man, isn't he?"

Charity tried to keep her expression serene as she met the inquisitive brown eyes. "Yes, he's a very handsome man."

"How long is he planning on staying out at your place?" Agnes's nose fairly quivered in her pursuit of juicy gossip she could repeat at the Ladies' Guild.

"Why, where else would a husband stay except with his wife?" Charity asked, pleased to note she sounded genuinely surprised.

Agnes's face fell. "Husband? You're married?" Her expression turned to skepticism. "Who performed the ceremony?" she demanded.

"Why, Reverend Olson, of course." This time Charity allowed herself to sound even more surprised that Agnes would ask.

Several other women had gathered around, listening to the exchange.

Agnes flushed an alarming red. "Well, just when did this wedding take place?"

Charity raised her eyebrows. "Why would you want to know?"

Bethany Dierckson's lips quirked in a barely suppressed smile. Mary Kathleen chose that moment to start fussing. Charity bounced her gently and inclined her head in a half bow. "It's good to see you ladies again, but if you'll excuse me, this youngster needs attention."

She walked away, knowing she had set a limit on the amount of poison Agnes Troxell could spew. Bethany was a good woman.

She would do what she could to put a stop to the gossip.

Beau wandered down to the hardware section.

"This is the finest one we have in stock," the proprietor, Edgar Miller, proclaimed. He handed Beau a heavy hammer. "The head is forged iron, and the handle is solid oak."

Beau examined the tool carefully. Assured it would serve his needs well, he agreed to buy it and turned his attention to the vast array of hoes, rakes, spades, ropes, and kegs of nails. When he'd satisfied his curiosity about all the shiny new farm implements, he moved on to examine the food staples behind the counter on long rows of shelves.

There were large containers of soda crackers, coffee, tea—black and Japanese—starch in bulk, bottles of catsup, cayenne, soda, and cream of tartar, often used in place of baking powder.

The floor of the mercantile was lined with barrels. There were two grades of flour—

white and middlings, as well as coarse meal, and buckwheat flour. Large barrels of Missouri apples, sacks of potatoes, turnips, pumpkins, and longneck squashes were in plentiful supply. There was more: salt pork in a crock under a big stone to keep the meat down in the brine; vinegar; salt; molasses; and three grades of sugar: fine white—twenty pounds for a dollar—light brown, and very dark.

The counters were brimming with baskets of eggs—three dozen for a quarter—and big jars of golden butter, selling for twelve and a half to fifteen cents a pound. There was cheese all the way from New York, maple syrup, and dried peaches and apples.

"Do you have any raisins?" Beau asked.

"Raisins?" Edgar scratched his head thoughtfully. "Afraid not . . . but I could probably get some from over in Hays."

"How long would it take to get them here?"

"Depends. If the weather cooperates, they should be here in a couple of weeks or so. They'll be right costly, though."

"I'll take four pounds."

"Four?"

Beau nodded. "Four should do it."

While Edgar wrote the order, Beau looked at the row of watches and rings displayed in a glass case beneath the counter. His attention was immediately drawn to an exquisite emerald brooch that lay nestled on a bed of royal blue velvet. Something about the brooch reminded Beau of Charity. The stones were elegant and the design intriguing. The delicate piece of jewelry seemed out of place among the large watches and gaudy baubles surrounding it.

"May I see the brooch, please?"

Edgar glanced up and smiled. "Lovely piece, isn't it?" He moved over to unlock the case and gently lifted the box containing the brooch, placing it on the counter for Beau's inspection.

"Just got it in a couple of days ago," Edgar volunteered.

"It's beautiful." Beau lifted the pin from the velvet box. The green stones caught the light, and it suddenly occurred to him why the piece of jewelry reminded him of Charity. The stones were the exact shade of her eyes.

"Yeah, a couple of Indian squaws come waltzing in here day before yesterday and offered the brooch in trade for three bottles of whiskey and a handful of peppermint sticks."

"You don't say." Beau turned the piece over and examined the craftsmanship closely. It was worth more than three bottles of whiskey and a handful of peppermint sticks.

"I'll make you a good deal," Edgar offered.

"How much?"

The price Edgar set was completely out of line, especially in view of the fact he'd just revealed what he'd given for the brooch. However, Beau knew the man would have no trouble finding someone who'd pay the exorbitant price.

"Thanks, but I'm afraid that's a little too steep." He regretfully placed the brooch back in the box. He'd gotten married today, and he didn't have anything to give his new bride. The brooch would have made a nice gift.

Edgar slid the box back into the case and Beau started to walk off. He suddenly turned and went back. "How much did you say those raisins would cost?"

Edgar repeated the price. The brooch would cost four times what the raisins would, but by not buying the raisins, he'd have the money to buy the brooch. He wanted Charity to have it.

"Then cancel the raisins, and I'll take the brooch," Beau said, grinning. He hadn't had a raisin pie in over a year; he guessed he could do without one a little longer.

Edgar smiled. "A gift for your lady?"

"Yes. I married Charity Burk about an hour ago. I think she'll enjoy the brooch more than I'd enjoy the raisins."

Beau's grin widened when he saw Edgar's jaw drop.

Charity was quiet on the way home. It was getting dark, and they still had several miles to go before they reached the cabin. The baby was sleeping and seemed unaffected by the night air. Beau urged the horse's steps to a faster trot.

"You cold?" he asked.

"A little." The weather was uncomfortable, but Charity didn't mind. She was still bathed in a warm glow from the unexpected turn of events. She barely noticed the discomfort. The baby was back in her arms and she'd just married Beau. She didn't see how she could complain about a little thing like bad weather. God had certainly blessed her this day.

"I'd hoped to make it back before dark," Beau apologized. "Guess I spent too much time browsing in the mercantile."

"I don't mind. I'm fine."

"You think the baby's cold?"

"She doesn't appear to be." Charity reached down and adjusted the heavy blanket surrounding Mary Kathleen like a cocoon.

They'd ridden in silence for a few minutes when Charity remembered. "Were you able to get the raisins?" She'd gladly bake him all the pies he wanted.

"No . . . Mr. Miller would've had to order them."

"Oh. How long would it have been before they'd arrived?"

"He said about a month."

Snow began to fall again. The horse briskly trotted down the road, pulling the sled containing the newly formed family.

Charity let her thoughts wander as the last vestige of twilight faded. The world around her became a fairyland of white. Snow sifted down in earnest now.

She longed to snuggle closer to her husband's large frame, but she wouldn't. He would surely think her forward, and just because they were married, she couldn't take such wifely liberties. It was still to be determined to what extent he intended to participate in the marriage.

Her gaze drifted shyly to him, and she found him immersed in his own thoughts. His hands deftly handled the reins while he drove the sled. She thought how nice it was to have a man perform that task for her. She'd never liked driving the prairie alone at night. It would be too easy to miss the road and get lost.

Would he expect a marriage bed? The thought jumped unexpectedly into her mind, startling her. It was shameful to be thinking such thoughts, but the prospect sent goose bumps skittering up and down her spine.

Would she object? The answer came more easily than the question: not at all. She was prepared to be his wife in every aspect. Even if he planned to leave her in the spring, it would not change her feelings. She would seek his comfort, tend his needs, and share his life for as long as he chose to remain with her.

And when the time came for him to leave, she would see him off with a smile and good wishes. She'd made herself that promise and she intended to keep it.

Charity shifted on the seat, adjusting the blanket more tightly around her. The darker it became, the colder it was.

"You might be warmer if we moved closer together." Beau's suggestion was spoken so casually that Charity wasn't sure if it was an invitation or request. "Slide the baby onto your lap. She'll probably be warmer there anyway."

"Oh . . . well, yes. Thank you." Charity carefully repositioned the infant and then edged closer to him until she felt her hip make contact with his solid thigh.

She was so aware of him, not only aware of his masculinity, but close enough now to note his distinct scent: a combination of soap, leather, wool, and the elements.

"Better?" Beau glanced at her and smiled.

"Yes, thank you."

They were closer than they'd ever been, and Charity felt her limbs getting weak.

Christmas had come and gone with little fuss but much warmth. Since she'd lost Ferrand, Charity had considered Christmas just another lonely day on the prairie. But with Beau here, the day had been as special as when she was a small child. He had shot a turkey, and she had made stuffing and baked a pumpkin pie.

Before they ate, he had reached for her hand. "I think I'd like to say grace—if you don't mind."

She nodded, bowing her head and closing her eyes. Mind? She was elated that his trust and hope in the Lord was gradually coming around.

"Lord," he began, "I want to give thanks to You today. For my life, for this woman who cared for me when I couldn't care for myself. Thank You for Mary Kathleen and what this little girl has brought into our lives—peace, joy, living proof that life goes on. When I look at this innocent baby I am reminded of Your love—a love that goes far beyond our understanding. Today we celebrate the gift of Your love: You gave Your Son, Jesus, for our sins. I couldn't have done the same, Lord. And I'm beholden to You. Amen."

"Amen." Charity blinked the wetness out of her eyes and passed the bowl of sweet potatoes.

She was brought back to the present when Beau finally broke the strained silence. "Seems like we should be saying something a little more meaningful, doesn't it?"

"Meaningful?"

"I mean, it is our wedding day. . . ."

"Seems we should have something to say, all right." Charity fondly recalled the day she and Ferrand had married. Birds had been singing, and the grass had been a rich, lush green carpet for her to tread upon. The church had overflowed with well-wishers, and there had been baskets of flowers and a large wedding cake.

"Was the weather nice the day you married Betsy?"

Until now Charity had been able to view and talk about Betsy in a charitable light. But now, the casual mention of her name sent streaks of jealousy shooting through her when she thought about the intimacy

Beau and his first wife must have shared on their wedding night.

"Yes, it was a warm fall day. The leaves on the trees were gold and yellow and brown. . . ." His eyes took on a faraway look, and Charity wished she hadn't brought up the subject.

"What was the date?" It shouldn't matter; yet, for some reason, she had to know.

"Second of October. What about you and Ferrand?"

"June second."

Silently each pondered the coincidence; it was the second of January—their wedding day.

"I—I was quite surprised when you asked Reverend Olson to marry us," Charity confessed. "But very thankful."

"The gossip was bothering you, wasn't it?"

"A little," she admitted. "But I would've seen it through." It hadn't been easy facing the accusing stares. The few times she'd ridden into town for supplies had been disconcerting, but having Beau remain with her had been worth it.

"No need for either one of us to be the

source of malicious gossip. Talk should quiet down now."

"I hope you don't mind, but I—I told several women at the mercantile we were married now."

"I don't mind. I mentioned it to Mr. Miller myself."

Charity grinned. "You did? Well, thank you."

"You should've seen Edgar Miller's jaw hit the floor."

"He's the biggest gossip of all."

"That's why I made sure he was the first to know about the marriage. His tongue will have a chance to cool down now."

Charity sighed. "I surely hope so."

"By spring I should have the land in good shape," Beau predicted. He urged the horse across Fire Creek and headed north.

"With the two of us working it shouldn't take long," Charity agreed.

She wanted to ask if he still planned to leave then, but selfishness stopped her. She wanted nothing to interfere with the happiness she was feeling.

"Charity . . . about our marriage . . ." Beau paused, apparently hesitant to broach the subject.

Charity felt the conversation was about to take a more personal turn. "Yes?"

"I know you must be wondering if I expect to claim my . . ." Beau's voice trailed off. She was sure if she could see his features clearly, he would be blushing!

Her lofty spirits plummeted. She braced herself; next he would tell her that he had no intention of claiming his husbandly rights because he didn't want to make love to anyone but Betsy.

Beau started again. "I . . . well, I think we would . . . of course, we both need to . . . well, we should talk about . . . but then it's not going to be exactly the same. . . ."

He appeared to be having a hard time making his point.

"Are you trying to say you don't plan to be my husband . . . not really?" Charity offered gently, hoping to help ease his dilemma.

Beau's gaze flew to meet hers. "No . . . I wasn't trying to say that."

"You weren't?" Charity's pulse jumped with his rather adamant denial.

"No . . . I didn't mean that at all. I meant it might be sort of . . . embarrassing at first. . . . Well, you know. . . . It might take us a while to get used to . . . get to know each other. . . ."

"You mean, you think we should give it time?" Charity agreed.

"Yes, that might be wise," he said.

She settled deeper into the blanket. A few moments later she scooted closer, pressing herself tightly against his side.

Beau was aware of her movements. He shifted his leg so it was resting more fully against hers. "I was thinking how nice it will be to get home," he remarked. The horse trotted along in the falling snow.

"It will be nice. The fire will feel exceptionally good this evening." She slipped her hand into his.

His hand tightened perceptibly on hers. He had no idea what was happening to him. He found himself thinking of Charity in a new way, as if the marriage vows had freed him from the chains of memory binding him to Betsy.

Well, why not? he argued, trying to still the faint twinge of conscience pulling at him. Betsy was gone. And he was still a young man, and the woman beside him now was his wife.

But you haven't given one single thought to whether you'll be staying with this woman come spring, his conscience reminded. *You went off half cocked and jumped into marriage without giving the future much thought.*

"I hope the baby decides to sleep tonight," Charity said softly.

"It won't hurt her to cry a little. I think we're spoiling her."

"No," she agreed. "It won't hurt to let her fret for a spell."

Charity's head had somehow drifted to his shoulder, and she turned and pressed her face into the warmth of his neck. He guessed she was feeling some of the same emotion that choked him.

"How much farther?" she whispered.

"Another mile."

He glanced down and caught his breath when he saw their mouths were only inches apart. "Don't go to sleep on me," he urged.

She looked up at him, her heart in her eyes. "Now you're being silly."

Charity, her heart overflowing with love, watched Beau carry the baby into the cabin. She loved him. Maybe not in the exact way she'd loved Ferrand, but it was very, very close. She gathered up the blanket and prepared to jump down from the sled when she saw him come to an abrupt halt. He glanced back over his shoulder and called to her, "Did you leave a lamp burning?"

Charity glanced toward the cabin window and frowned when she saw the warm, golden ray of light spilling out across the freshly fallen snow. "No."

He returned to the sled to grab his gun and hand the baby back to Charity before he turned toward the house again.

"You stay here until I see what's going on."

"Beau, wait. It may be dangerous!" Charity scrambled off the seat. Beau strode back and kicked open the door, gun drawn and positioned.

The young man sitting at the table looked momentarily startled at the hasty entrance.

Quickly recovering, he invited in a dry voice, "Well, hello. Do come in."

Charity quickly stepped behind her husband, her eyes widening when she saw the splendid, dark-haired man sitting at the kitchen table.

His boots were off, and his stocking feet were propped casually on the table. He had achingly familiar turquoise blue eyes and shamelessly long, thick black eyelashes. His hair was outrageously curly, and he looked as ornery as sin.

The man grinned, flashing a set of brilliant white teeth at her. "About time you and big brother were showing up."

CHAPTER 11

Beau shot an irritable scowl at his younger brother. "You always did have a way of being in the wrong place at the wrong time."

Cass Claxton flashed a roguish grin. "I've ridden for two weeks, through rain and snow and dark of night, just to see how my big brother is getting along, and he acts like I was some varmint come crawling out of the woods."

Cass was being melodramatic. The boy couldn't help it; it was in his nature. Still, it didn't make Beau any happier. How had he gotten here so soon?

"How'd you find me?" Beau pulled Charity into the room and closed the door. "Don't mind him," he said, nodding toward his younger brother before he crossed the room to lay Mary Kathleen down in her bed near the hearth. "It's my brother, Cass. He's harmless."

Charity smiled uncertainly. Her frozen fingers worked to untie the strings of her bonnet.

Cass grinned and pushed back from the table to get to his feet. A cocky, devil-may-care attitude stood out all over him, and Beau wanted to tell him to behave. "Well, hello, ma'am. You must be the lovely Widow Burk." He politely tipped his hat.

Charity grinned, not at all sure how to take his cavalier attitude. She glanced at Beau for guidance.

"She used to be Mrs. Burk," Beau said easily while busily removing the baby's warm bunting. "How'd you get here?" He hadn't seen an extra horse in the yard.

"I brought a sled from town. It's out back. I wasn't sure where to stable the horses." With undisguised curiosity Cass watched Beau settle the baby.

"How did you find me?" Beau turned his full attention to the guest.

"Your letter was pretty clear about where you were. When I reached Cherry Grove, I asked around. An old man gave me directions to the Burk cabin. When it started getting dark and you failed to show up, I began to wonder if I had the wrong place."

"We had business to tend to. Why'd you bring a sled?"

"You know Ma and Willa," Cass complained. "I had to bring half the root cellar, extra blankets, and medicine in case you weren't being properly looked after." Cass glanced at Charity and his grin widened. "All that worrying for nothing. Looks to me like you're being taken care of real well."

Beau frowned. He didn't like his brother's tone of voice, or the disrespectful tone. "Mrs. Burk has been good enough to take care of me while I was ill. I owe her a great deal, including my gratitude and respect."

Cass shook his head. "That's what I meant. We all appreciate what she's done for you."

So Cass had brought provisions. It was like his mother to think of everything. Beau gave Mary Kathleen a fatherly pat and walked over and warmly clasped his brother's hand. "Good to see you, Cass."

Charity looked from brother to brother, and Beau could see she felt left out. He could understand that. Cass might be spouting off, but you could look at him and see not only love but a deep respect shining in his eyes. The Claxton boys were knit tight with each other with an intangible bond that would be hard for an outsider to penetrate. Loyalty ran deep and strong among the brothers, and he thanked God for it.

Cass Claxton clasped Beau's hand tightly, his face turning somber. "You're looking a whole lot better than I'd expected."

Beau shrugged. "It was close, but, thank God, I'm on the mend."

"We've all been worried about you, Ma in particular. You've been gone a long time." There was an unspoken reproach in the statement.

Beau remembered Cass was the one who couldn't understand his need to leave. Now he shrugged, realizing there was no way to explain to his brother the unrelenting darkness that had invaded his heart when Betsy died. The need to get away from all that was familiar. "I'm sorry I haven't written sooner," he said. "I should have done better."

Cass nodded. "We understood, but we

couldn't help wondering if you were all right."

"The family all okay?" Beau asked.

Cass grinned. "Doing fine."

"Ma?"

"Strong as an ox."

"Cole?"

"Healthy as a horse."

"Wynne?"

"Pretty as a picture."

"Did your teachers ever mention anything about enlarging your vocabulary?" Beau asked.

"Nope."

Beau good-naturedly clapped his brother's shoulder. "Come here. I have someone I want you to meet."

The two men turned their attention to Charity, who was standing by the fire looking out of place. She smiled and Beau walked over and placed his arm around her waist. "Cass, this is my wife, Charity."

For a moment Cass was stunned by Beau's unexpected announcement, and his face showed it. But to his credit he managed to regain his composure quickly. "Your . . . wife! Well, how about that." He brushed his hand down the side of his tight-fitting denims and graciously extended it. "Welcome to the family, ma'am. You're sure going to be a lovely addition."

"Thank you, Cass. I'm so happy to meet you. Beau has spoken of you often."

"He exaggerates," Cass objected. "Once you get to know me, you'll find out I'm fairly decent."

Charity laughed. "I can assure you, it has all been very complimentary."

"Don't tell him that," Beau protested. "I won't be able to live with him." He watched in amazement as his younger brother poured on the charm. How did he do it? Cass and Cole both could be as sweet and as slick as warm honey. He'd never had the gift himself. He could be smooth enough with an older woman like Rebecca, but with one closer to his own age he wasn't so smooth. Maybe because he'd never practiced the art. Betsy had won his heart when they were both young, and he'd never looked at another woman.

"So, you've remarried." Cass's gaze drifted nonchalantly over to Mary Kathleen's crib. "Been . . . married long?"

Charity spoke up quickly. "Oh, no! Uh . . . the baby . . . she's not Beau's."

Beau looked at her with a stunned expression. "She isn't?" He turned to Cass. "Now is that anything for a bride to tell her husband?" he said in feigned disgust.

"Beau!" Charity looked horrified.

Beau sent her a roguish grin. He watched her face flush a bright scarlet. His arm tightened affectionately around her. "The baby's parents are dead, and Charity and I have been taking care of Mary Kathleen," he explained. "We're hoping we'll be given permanent custody of the child, once things settle down."

Cass had a strange expression on his face, like he wasn't sure that would be a good idea. Beau figured he was remembering the day his baby died with Betsy, but if that was what he had on his mind, he hid it well. Cass peered down at the sleeping Mary Kathleen. "You don't say? Been taking care of a new baby, huh? She's real cute."

"We think so," Beau said proudly.

While Cass filled them in on recent happenings, Charity cut thick slices of pie and made a pot of fresh coffee.

"Wait until you taste her pie," Beau bragged. He was proud of her cooking. She hurried around to wait on them, so pretty and flustered at having unexpected company. Charity Burk . . . Claxton was a woman any man would be proud to have carry his name.

Cass leaned back in his chair. "Makes good pies, huh?"

"Best I've ever eaten."

"Better than Ma's?"

"Almost as good."

The lamp had burned low when it was finally decided that they had more than one night to visit.

"I hope I'm not putting you out by staying a few days," Cass apologized.

"Not at all!" Charity said. "I'm thrilled to finally meet a part of Beau's family."

"Well—" Cass began to yank off his boots—"just tell me where to roll up. I'm so tired I could sleep on a thorn and not know it."

Beau watched his new wife, realizing that in all the excitement it hadn't occurred to either of them that their privacy was going to be affected by Cass's unexpected arrival.

"Well, I suppose you'll be sleeping . . ." Charity grappled awkwardly with the problem of where to put him.

"Outside," Beau interjected.

Cass's face fell. "In this kind of weather?"

Before Beau could answer, Cass glanced down and saw the neatly made pallet by the fire. A relieved smile replaced his earlier frown. "You always did like to pull my leg. I suppose I'll take the pallet. It's been a long day."

Charity smiled lamely. "Yes . . . well . . . good night."

Cass paused. "You're sure I'm not putting you out?"

"No," Beau muttered.

Charity smiled. "Don't be silly."

Beau loved his brother; of course he did, but he sure had a bad habit of turning up at the worst time.

Charity turned away. Her bed seemed to suddenly dominate the tiny room. She edged timidly toward the mattress while Beau banked the fire for the night.

Cass settled himself on the pallet.

Charity proceeded to pull the curtain across the room. Once she was assured of a modicum of privacy, she began to undress while listening to Beau bid his brother a good night. A few moments later, he parted the curtain and stepped into the small cubicle.

The intimate area suddenly looked stiflingly small.

"I'll get up with the baby for her night feeding," Beau offered. He sat down on a chair and began unbuttoning his shirt. "That way you won't have to . . . dress."

"Thank you." She mouthed the words, vividly aware of Cass sleeping in the same room. "It's so late; I'm surprised she hasn't awakened before now."

"I guess she's real tired."

Charity fumbled for her gown hanging on a small hook and glanced self-consciously at Beau. "Would you mind . . . ?"

Beau turned his head and she quickly readied herself for bed.

"All right . . . I'm through."

She busied herself turning back the blanket.

Beau remained in the chair.

She lay stiff with apprehension, awaiting the moment he too would be under the blankets. She had no idea where her earlier boldness had fled to, but it had completely deserted her now.

Beau leaned over and blew out the lamp, throwing the room into total darkness.

Charity lay perfectly still, thinking how much she'd always hated darkness. Fears tended to be amplified, doubts reborn, and small problems inflated to overwhelming obstacles when there was no light.

Many nights she'd slept with a lamp burning so she wouldn't have to face the emptiness. Now that she was married again, would that horrible loneliness finally be over? she wondered.

"Aren't you coming to bed?" she whispered.

"No. Best I sleep in the chair."

Frustration swept through her. She supposed he was right. She could still hear the wind howling outside, the tick of the clock, the baby making soft sucking sounds in her sleep, Cass's soft breathing as he dropped deeper and deeper into untroubled sleep. With Beau beside her, it was as if her life had been miraculously sorted out and put back into order.

For a moment he sat quietly, lost in his own thoughts.

She wondered if he was thinking of Betsy. It would be only natural, of course. She didn't expect him to forget his first wife, but she wanted him to think of her tonight. Ferrand's face floated through her mind and she sighed. Betsy and Ferrand were part of their past. Tonight was the beginning of their future. A future together, she prayed. It would be easier if she thought Beau loved her, but she knew he had only married her because he considered it the right thing to do.

He reached over and took her hand. His presence was comforting in the darkness. She remembered the sinewy muscles, the tuft of springy hair above the opening at the throat of his long johns. His familiar scent surrounded her and she clung tightly to his hand.

"I'm sorry about tonight," he whispered.

His voice sent a flood of sensations through her like warm honey, all breathtaking, all mysterious, all inexplicably exciting.

"I understand. I guess the only thing that's really important is that you're here . . . that we're together," she returned softly.

It occurred to her that neither she nor

Beau had mentioned to Cass that this was their wedding night.

Not that she supposed it would have made any difference. He was here, and they couldn't turn a man out in the teeth of a Kansas blizzard. He'd die out there. She could sense Beau's frustration, but Cass was here and they'd have to make the best of it.

He'd come in answer to the letter she'd mailed last month. She had a sudden fierce wish she'd thrown the envelope away, not mailed it, but of course she couldn't have done that. She had to do what was right, and keeping news of Beau from his family would have been terribly wrong.

She caught her breath when a horrible thought occurred to her. What if Cass had come to take Beau home with him? Could she give him up now? *Please, God, let me have this winter. If I have to give him up in the spring, I will, but let him be mine for a while.*

Cass was as strikingly handsome as Beau. If Cole, the older brother, was any more handsome, she didn't think her heart could stand it.

Not that she was expecting to ever meet

Cole or Wynne or any of the Claxton clan. Eventually Beau would leave, and she wasn't going to tell herself anything different. Today meant only that he loved Mary Kathleen enough to give her a mother.

Beau had been silent, but now he whispered, "I'm glad to see my brother, but his timing's a little off."

She laughed softly, feeling more at ease. "We couldn't turn him out."

"We can't? It sure is tempting."

She snuggled deeper into the sheets, savoring the moment. This wasn't the wedding night she had anticipated, but maybe it was best this way. Perhaps Beau had been right in the first place. They needed to take it slow, get used to thinking of themselves as husband and wife. Having him here was enough. For the first time in a long time she would fall asleep with someone holding her hand. For a while at least, she could feel loved again.

Beau sat quietly, wondering how he'd sleep in the straight-back chair. It would be a long night. This wasn't the way he had pictured their wedding night. Sitting here with Charity so close was pure torture. He thought of the way they used to talk into the night, Charity in the bed and him on the floor, sleeping on the pallet where Cass was now snoring. He'd never felt this passion then, this desire to hold her. Never wanted to kiss her.

What had made the difference? A few words spoken before a preacher? Evidently the marriage ceremony had resurrected feelings he'd wanted to forget. He breathed in lemon scent. Her scent. She always smelled good.

"What are you thinking?" he whispered.

"I was thanking God for sending you my way," she whispered back.

He felt humbled. She was thankful for him? He'd ruined her reputation and subjected her to a marriage with little hope of surviving. For all she knew, he'd be gone in a few months, and she was thankful? He sighed.

Lord, I don't deserve this woman. I don't deserve much of anything the way I've acted this past year, but it seemed like I couldn't help myself.

He had a feeling God knew what he'd gone through and understood. God always understood. Beau felt humbled. He'd always been so sure of what he wanted and knew how to go about getting it. Then he'd lost hope. Maybe he had to reach the place where God was all he had to realize God was all he needed. Beginning tonight, he intended to trust more and appreciate his blessings while he had them.

Like Job in the Old Testament, Beau had lost all he valued in one day. But God had given him new blessings, *"good measure, pressed down, and shaken together, and running over."*

"The Lord gave, and the Lord hath taken away; blessed be the name of the Lord."

He smiled into the darkness. *I don't deserve a second chance, Lord, but I'm glad You don't give me what I deserve. I'll try not to let You down again.*

Charity stirred and he pulled a blanket closer to her chin, feeling protective. He had a family now—Charity and Mary Kathleen. They couldn't take the place of Betsy and the unborn child he'd lost, but they could make their own place in his heart. He bent to kiss his wife good night.

"He'll only stay a few days," Beau promised when their mouths parted.

Charity nodded and returned the kiss.

"Just a few days," he whispered.

It was indeed a strange wedding night, but as the fire began to die down, Beau accepted the circumstances.

Wasn't like he hadn't encountered a change in plans before.

CHAPTER 12

Two weeks later, Cass was still there.

When Beau inadvertently mentioned the large amount of work he had to accomplish by spring, Cass decided to stay for a while and lend a hand. He insisted it was the only proper thing to do.

He couldn't stay much longer though, because the few storms they'd had would soon give way to howling blizzards, making travel impossible until spring.

When Cass had been there for three days helping Beau, Charity was amazed at the amount of work the two of them had completed despite the bad weather. They came in at the end of the day, laughing and talking. Charity had supper on the table; Cass stood in front of the stove basking in the brothers' friendship.

She was used to Cass's striking good looks now. He was handsome, but he didn't make her pulse race the way Beau did.

Beau washed his hands and reached for the towel. "I guess we're going to lose our favorite guest."

Charity glanced up from setting the table. "What do you mean?"

Beau grinned. "Cass has decided he'd better start home before we get snowed in."

Charity's heart hit the bottom of her stomach. Would Beau decide to go with him? If he wanted to go with Cass she wouldn't be able to hold him. She turned her back to the men, fumbling with the oven door. What would she do if he left? She could not face losing this man.

"That's right," Cass said. "I've helped Beau about all I can until spring. I need to be heading home."

Charity set a pan of steaming corn bread on the table. "We'll miss you." She was proud that her voice sounded so steady. "Supper's ready."

Grinning, Cass took a couple of steps before his left foot caught on the pallet where he slept at night. "Whoa!" he exclaimed, fighting to retain his balance.

Charity watched, horrified, as he fell, hitting the floor with the grace of a fallen oak tree.

Beau crossed the room in four steps. "You all right?"

Cass sat up, looking dazed and holding his foot. His face contorted in pain. "My ankle—I think it's broke."

Charity dropped beside the fallen man, her hands deft and sure as she probed the injured ankle. "Beau, help me. We've got to get his boot off before that foot swells so much we have to cut it off."

Beau took the boot in his large, capable hands, moving it gently back and forth while Cass sucked in his breath. "That *hurts.*"

"I know it hurts," Beau said. "But Charity's right. You want me to take it off this way or cut it off after it swells?"

"Take it off," Cass muttered between clenched teeth. He kept quiet until the boot was removed to reveal an ankle already swelling and turning blue. Charity moved the appendage experimentally back and forth. "It's not broken," she said. "Just badly sprained, but you'll have to stay off it a few days."

Beau glanced at Charity.

She looked back.

"Well, little brother, looks like we're going to have the pleasure of your company a little longer. You can't ride with that foot."

Cass shook his head. "I guess you're right. I just hope we don't get another blizzard before I'm able to leave."

Charity felt almost relieved that Cass had to stay. She'd be happy to keep him here until spring if it meant Beau would stay too. She'd seen the bond between the two brothers, and she knew if anyone could convince her new husband to leave, it would be Cass.

Beau had only married her to save the land and to provide a home for Mary Kathleen, and she appreciated it, but now that he was her husband for real, she wanted more.

Given time, she'd find a way to keep him here. God willing.

Nine more days passed. Beau and Cass were sitting at the table finishing breakfast, and Charity was getting the wash ready to hang out to freeze dry on the line.

She'd fixed a solid meal—cured ham and eggs with biscuits and gravy. Cass had eaten with enthusiasm, but Beau had been quiet. He hadn't talked much, and when she inadvertently touched him while serving, he had flinched away. She knew his brother's extended visit was getting on his nerves. It would have been different if they had any privacy, but in a room this size, there was no way to be alone. Beau's even disposition was beginning to suffer.

Even Cass was beginning to notice his brother's unusually sour behavior. Beau had snapped at him twice over something so trivial it had made both his and Charity's brows lift in astonishment.

"Would you mind watching the baby while I hang the wash?" Charity asked as soon as the last breakfast dish was washed and put away.

Beau was sitting in front of the fire, pulling his boots on.

"How long will that take?" he asked sharply.

Charity glanced up. "Not long. Why?"

"I can't get anything done if I have to stay in the house and baby-sit," he barked.

Charity sighed. Indeed he was in a very foul mood these days.

"I'll watch Mary Kathleen," Cass offered.

"You can't watch Mary Kathleen and drive nails at the same time!" Beau snapped.

Cass looked at Charity and shrugged good-naturedly. "I can't watch Mary Kathleen and drive nails at the same time. Sorry." He held his forefinger up as an afterthought occurred to him. "But I would, if I could." Charity detected a mischievous twinkle in his eye now as he tried to smooth over Beau's uncharacteristic bad humor.

"I'm capable of watching Mary Kathleen," Beau grumbled. "I merely asked how long it'd be before I could start on my work." The tone of his voice left no doubt that *his* work was far more important than hers, but she let the thinly veiled implication slide.

"Fifteen minutes at the most," Charity bargained.

"Make it ten."

"I'll pin as fast as I can." She shot him an impatient look, picked up the basket of wet clothes, and sailed out the door, letting it bang shut behind her.

Still seething, she marched to the clothesline, flung the basket on the ground, and began to haphazardly pin diapers and washcloths in a long, disorderly row. She knew what was causing Beau's ill temper, and she could sympathize, but she was getting tired of his sour disposition. The past two weeks hadn't exactly been a bed of roses for her either.

Her conscience bothered her; Cass still being here was her fault. His sprained ankle would have healed if it hadn't been for the poultices she carefully applied twice a day. She'd been careful not to choose anything that would hurt him—just a various mix of herbs plus a good handful of stinging nettle—with the results that, although Cass could walk better, his ankle was still red and swollen and he couldn't wear his boot.

The deception shamed her, and she knew only too well what Ferrand would have thought about her behavior.

For that matter, she didn't want Beau to know.

He wouldn't understand, and she wouldn't want to tell him the truth, but she had to keep Cass here. Beau would go with him when he left. Her new husband didn't love her the way she loved him. He was a one-woman man, and that woman was Betsy.

Submerged deep within her self-pity, she forgot to keep an eye out for danger.

A nut-brown hand suddenly snaked out and clasped her arm, and she nearly swallowed the clothespin she'd just wedged between her teeth. She jumped and squealed.

A tall, muscular brave was standing next to her. Where had he come from? She hadn't heard a thing.

"Mhhhhhhh?" Her wide eyes peered helplessly up at his imposing height. She prayed Beau was watching from the window, but she knew that was unlikely.

The brave eyed her impassively. "You White Sister?" His voice was deep and gruff. She was so terrified that if he'd asked her if she was Mrs. Wa-kun-dah, she'd have agreed.

Wordlessly she nodded.

The brave's eyes narrowed. "Why White Sister have stick in mouth?"

"Mhhh . . ." Charity hurriedly reached up

and removed the clothespin. "I—I'm hanging wash."

"Hanging wash?" His black eyes looked confused. "How White Sister hang wash? Red Eagle wash in water and water cannot be hung up with funny-looking sticks."

Charity hoped he didn't expect an answer. Her heart was pounding, and her knees had turned to pulp. He wasn't Kaw; she was sure of it. Cheyenne, maybe? Handsome, with high cheekbones, a proud, aristocratic nose, and long black hair that whipped freely about in the blustery wind. He wore buckskins, moccasins, and a massive buffalo robe draped over his broad shoulders to ward off the cold morning air.

"Did . . . can I do something for you?" she asked, wondering if he'd come here to harm her. Maybe he'd been hunting and when he noticed her hanging the wash he'd grown curious. She prayed that was the case.

"No can find Laughing Waters."

"Oh?" Why would a man who looked like this be hunting Laughing Waters? She could understand why Laughing Waters would be hunting *him.* The way the two sisters had latched on to Beau, she was sure they wouldn't let someone like this man get away.

"Laughing Waters tell Red Eagle, 'White Sister make good medicine.'"

"Oh . . . Laughing Waters said that, did she?" Charity felt a quiver of apprehension. She made terrible medicine. Beau would have died if Laughing Waters and Little Fawn hadn't stepped in.

The brave crossed his arms and stared. "Squaw heap big sick. White Sister make good medicine."

Charity decided he must be trying to tell her that his wife was sick and Laughing Waters was not available to tend her.

"I'm not very good. . . . Laughing Waters and Little Fawn are much better at this sort of thing," Charity hedged.

"No can find cuckoo sisters," he announced flatly.

"Well, I . . ." Charity searched for a reasonable excuse to deny his request but failed to think of one. "What's wrong with your . . . squaw?"

He rubbed his stomach. "Bad hurt."

"Oh. Well, come with me, then." She had no idea what the problem could be, but she figured a good dose of castor oil couldn't harm and might cure his under-the-weather squaw.

Charity traipsed into the cabin with the brave following close behind. Beau and Cass caught sight of the pair and their mouths dropped open.

Beau scrambled for his gun. Cass sprang to his feet, every muscle tensed and ready for combat. Charity ignored them.

Without a word of explanation, she hurried to the cabinet and extracted a large bottle, then poured a small portion of the contents into a fruit jar. Screwing the lid on tightly, she handed the jar to the Indian. "Make squaw drink."

The brave held the jar up to closely examine the thick, gummy substance. He scowled. "Make squaw drink?" He shook his head. "This not look like something to drink."

"I know. It looks awful, but it will help."

The brave, evidently taking her at her word, nodded. He cast a sour look in Beau and Cass's direction, his gaze flicking over them in a contemptuous manner, as if they weren't worth worrying about; then he turned back to Charity. "Red Eagle thanks White Sister."

If the castor oil didn't do the trick, Charity sincerely hoped that, at least in this particular instance, his gratitude would be short lived.

Red Eagle turned and marched with a royal dignity to the door and made a quick exit, the jar of castor oil held carefully in the crook of his arm.

"Just who was that?" Beau demanded as the door closed behind him.

Charity shrugged. "I have no idea. I was hanging the wash and he approached and said his squaw was sick and needed medicine."

Beau looked incredulous. "You mean, out of the clear blue sky, he walked up and asked you for medicine?"

"Yes, he did, but that isn't unusual," she pointed out. "The Indians around here are rather straightforward when it comes to something they need."

"You've never met him before today?" Beau challenged.

"If you mean is he a friend of mine, no, he isn't." She didn't appreciate the insulting insinuation in his voice. What right did he have to act like he doubted her word?

"But he was quite a striking man, don't

you think?" she added, with a flirtatious glance in his direction.

She was pushing her luck and she knew it.

Beau stared coolly back at her. "I hope you mentioned you were under a man's protection now—just so he doesn't get the idea of coming around when I'm not here," he countered tersely.

Charity saw Cass grinning at Beau's splendid performance of a jealous husband, which didn't make her feel any better. Undoubtedly that's all it was—an act.

Her chin lifted with unmistakable defiance. "I don't believe we got around to that subject."

Their eyes locked in a silent duel.

The silence stretched uncomfortably. Charity decided to wait Beau out. Let him speak first. But he was so stubborn he'd sit there until violets bloomed in the spring before he'd give in.

"Well, well." Cass awkwardly reached for his coat. "Guess we best be getting to those chores, Beau. We're burning daylight."

"I'm right behind you." Beau swiped his coat from the peg and opened the front door. He glared at Charity. "You're through hanging wash?"

"It certainly looks that way!"

The door snapped shut.

Charity watched from the window as the two men left. Cass favored his bad ankle, and she felt a sudden renewed stab of remorse for what she was doing.

God, I know it's wrong and I'm asking You to forgive me.

She knew He wouldn't though, because even at that moment she had a pan of herbs simmering on the stove, ready to apply a new poultice.

The next morning, bright and early, a sharp rap sounded at the door.

Both Charity and Beau went to answer it.

"I'll get it."

"I'll get it," Beau corrected.

"I'm perfectly capable of answering my own door."

Their gazes locked obstinately.

Beau gave in first and Charity opened the door.

The handsome brave who'd caused all the trouble the day before stood before them, his face wreathed with an ecstatic grin.

"White Sister makes strong medicine." He held up three fingers. "Many papooses!"

CHAPTER 13

The bell hanging over the door to Miller's Mercantile tinkled melodiously when Beau and Cass stepped inside. Cass wore a boot on one foot and a moccasin on the other. Seemed like those herb poultices of Charity's weren't helping much. The foot was still swollen. The store was empty, except for Edgar, who was busy putting turnips in a large barrel.

"Morning, Mr. Claxton." The storekeeper wiped his hands on his apron and stepped behind the counter. "What can I get for you today?"

"I need nails, wire, and a few more fence posts," Beau said.

"Sure thing. Just got a new load of posts

in yesterday. Who's that you got there with you?"

Beau introduced Cass to the friendly proprietor.

Edgar cordially reached out and shook Cass's hand. "Thought you two must be brothers. There's a strong family resemblance. Where you from, Mr. Claxton?"

"Missouri."

"Missouri, huh? Never been there. Always wanted to go; just never got the opportunity."

Beau told Edgar the amounts he needed, and Edgar wrote it all down on a large, thick pad.

"Got those raisins in," Edgar mentioned.

Beau glanced at the large glass jar of raisins sitting on the shelf. He could buy the raisins, and Charity could make a pie . . . or he could save the money and apply it toward a new plow this spring. He quickly tossed the temptation aside. Charity needed a plow more than he needed raisins. "Thanks, but I'll be passing up the raisins today, Edgar."

"Just thought I'd mention it."

"Appreciate it."

While Beau and Cass browsed, Edgar went about filling the order.

The door opened again, and a small, rather harried-looking man entered the store, accompanied by a girl who appeared to be his daughter.

She was a beauty with an exquisite figure and lovely amethyst-colored eyes. Her golden blonde hair, scooped up into a mass of ringlets, trickled down the back of her head beneath the brim of the latest Paris fashion.

She had a wide-eyed, innocent-looking appearance, but her full lips formed a petulant pout as if she'd just finished sucking a lemon.

Beau noticed Cass glancing up and taking note of the new arrivals before he promptly returned his attention to the shirts he was examining.

The bell tinkled again, and Reverend Olson entered the mercantile. Catching a glimpse of Beau, he immediately came over and struck up a conversation.

"How's Mary Kathleen?"

"Growing like a weed."

"And your new bride?"

"She's just fine."

The reverend chuckled. "I hope the baby is allowing the newlyweds some privacy by sleeping longer periods of time."

Beau flashed a tolerant grin. "She's not bothering us."

And Mary Kathleen wasn't. It was his own baby brother, who was right now eyeing the blonde beauty that'd just come in, trying to pretend all he had on his mind was buying a new shirt.

"Well, I haven't been able to locate any of Ansel's or Letty's kin. I've sent letters, but as yet, I haven't received an answer," Reverend Olson admitted. "Now, the Farrises have offered to look after the baby, if you and Charity want, but with nine in the family and another one on the way . . ."

"Mary Kathleen's doing fine with us," Beau dismissed abruptly. "Charity would be lost without her."

Reverend Olson gazed kindly back at Beau. "And what about you?"

Cass approached the two before Beau could answer. "I don't believe you've met my brother, Reverend. Cass, I'd like you to meet Reverend Olson."

The two men shook hands. The reverend's smile was as pleasant as always. "Will you be staying in Kansas long, Cass?"

Funny. That was the question uppermost in Beau's mind too.

"I will *not* have that *filthy, disgusting,* piece of slime on my back!"

The men pivoted at the sound of a woman's shrill voice raised in anger.

"Now, Susanne, dear . . ." A small, harried-looking man ducked hurriedly as a bolt of material came sailing over his head and landed with a thud at the feet of the three men, who stood watching the developing ruckus with growing curiosity.

"I am *sick* and *tired* of having to look like a—a common *peasant* all the time!" With one fell swoop, the young woman angrily cleared the table of calico, cotton, and muslin. The mercantile suddenly looked as if it had been hit by a cyclone.

Edgar made a sound between a gasp and a moan at the sight of his valuable bolts of fabric scattered on the floor.

Beau smothered a grin. Turn that little spitfire loose and she'd trash the mercantile in nothing flat! What she needed was a good spanking, but her daddy didn't look capable of administering it.

The girl turned tail and flounced over to rifle through the display of ribbons and fine laces. Beau noticed Cass staring after her. He'd better be careful. That one would be hard to handle.

Cass, Reverend Olson, and Beau haltingly resumed their conversation as the girl's father gathered up the bolts of material, mumbling something softly under his breath about having only suggested the material might look nice on her—nothing to get all that upset about.

"As soon as the swelling in my ankle goes down and the weather holds, I'm planning on heading back to Missouri," Cass said, answering the reverend's interrupted inquiry.

"Well, I'm sure Beau has appreciated having another set of hands to help with the work." Reverend Olson cautiously eyed Susanne, who, having moved to the rack of cooking utensils, was plainly trying to eavesdrop on the men's conversation.

"Susanne McCord is a high-spirited girl," he whispered. "Extremely spirited."

"Acts like a spoiled brat," Cass observed curtly, looking shocked by such an unladylike display of temper. "The woman has the manners of a goat."

Susanne heard his remark, and her perfectly arched brows lifted with disdain. When Cass shot her an impervious look that not only matched hers but topped it, she quickly moved on.

Beau grinned. His little brother wasn't used to getting high-toned looks from a woman. All the females back home had practically stood in line to talk to him. Could be the boy was a trifle spoiled.

"Oh, dear. Well, remember, *I* didn't say that," Reverend Olson insisted nervously. "The McCords are new in town. Leviticus is a retired circuit judge. He and his daughter came from back East, and it seems the girl hasn't quite made the adjustment her father had hoped she would."

The men drifted apart, trying to remain detached in the wake of a wildcat loose in their midst. Beau thought nostalgically of his own even-tempered wife waiting for him back at the cabin and thanked the good Lord he hadn't been rescued by an ill-tempered harridan like Susanne McCord.

His thoughts soured. Charity had been distracted lately. He had a feeling she was regretting jumping into this hasty marriage. A woman like Charity didn't give her heart lightly. He knew she still loved Ferrand. How did you compete with a dead man?

A few minutes later, Cass was forced to duck again when he heard Susanne scream and a bottle of perfume sailed over his head to smash noisily against the west wall.

His head shot up, and his hands moved defiantly to his hips. Beau watched with interest, figuring Cass was planning on teaching Miss McCord some manners. He hoped his brother was up to the task. The girl ignored the men, diverting her full attention to bullying poor Edgar Miller.

"Why don't you have something as simple as a spool of red thread? You have every other color," she accused. "Why don't you have *red*?"

"I did have red," Edgar said, eager to console her, "but Ethel Bluewaters came in yesterday and bought the last—"

"Incompetent fool! Sheer incompetence!" Her eyes narrowed threateningly. "It's a lucky thing you have the only mercantile in town, Mr. Miller, or I would certainly take my business elsewhere!"

Edgar had a scrunched-up expression, and Beau figured he prayed daily that such colossal good fortune would befall him.

"Miss McCord, I have a new shipment of thread coming in next week, and I'm sure there will be plenty of red—"

Edgar's apology was interrupted when she bombarded him with a barrage of spools. "I wouldn't buy your stupid thread even if you had it!"

He cringed and ducked, throwing his arms over his head protectively. The spools continued to bounce off the counter . . . and off his balding skull.

"Susanne, dear! You must stop this!" Leviticus sucked in his breath and drew up his slight five-foot-two frame to boldly confront his daughter. "Mr. Miller can't help it if Ethel Bluewaters bought his last spool of red thread!"

"The service here is *wretched*!"

Edgar looked like he was holding on to his temper by the grace of God.

Reverend Olson clucked. "Dear me. What an exhibition."

Cass shook his head. "Why would Edgar put up with that kind of treatment?"

Beau grinned. "I figure prudence is the only thing keeping him silent. The man values his life."

"Now, dear—" Leviticus balled his fists up

tight—"now, dear, we just can't have this! You'll just have to go back home until you can get yourself under control."

Cass leaned against the doorway, arms folded. "Would you look at that? She's managed to tree two grown men without firing a single shot."

"Amazing," Beau agreed. "But you have to consider the men. Neither Leviticus nor Edgar are a match for her."

"That's perfectly all right with me." Turning her nose up haughtily, Susanne lifted the hem of her skirt and swept past her father with the regal air of a queen holding court.

She paused momentarily when she came face-to-face with Cass, who by now had stepped over to deliberately challenge her path through the door.

"Get out of my way, cowboy." She spat the words out contemptuously, her eyes flashing with renewed anger.

Cass grinned insolently and his dark eyes glittered. He reached up and pushed his hat back on his head. "And if I don't?"

Beau, watching, figured this would be a battle of the wills. No way would Cass allow any woman to push him around.

After a tense pause Susanne hauled off

and hit Cass squarely between the eyes with her purse. The blow was unexpected and explosive. Cass staggered, groping blindly for support. Beau tried to grab him before he fell, but missed. Susanne slammed out of the mercantile, rattling windowpanes and sending jars dancing merrily across the shelves.

Cass slid to the floor. Beau looked down at his brother. "I don't suppose you've ever heard 'Hell hath no fury like a woman scorned'?"

Cass shook his head.

"Well," Beau sighed, offering him a hand, "you have now."

Charity opened the front door and scanned the flawless expanse of blue sky. It was an extraordinarily beautiful day.

She wished now she'd ridden into town with the two brothers when they'd asked her this morning. Instead, she'd stayed behind to do her weekly baking. By late morning she'd finished six loaves of bread, and three sweet-potato pies were cooling on the windowsill.

The pies reminded her of Beau's penchant for raisins, and the idea suddenly came to her. By now Mr. Miller should have received the shipment from Hays.

First thing tomorrow morning she'd bundle up Mary Kathleen and make the hour's ride into Cherry Grove. Beau would be overjoyed when he came home to find his favorite pies bubbling in the oven.

"You feeling any better?" Beau noticed Cass wasn't quite as pale as he'd been earlier, though he still complained of a throbbing headache.

"That woman's meaner than a two-headed snake," Cass grumbled.

"You shouldn't have provoked her," Beau reminded him. "You need to leave a woman like Susanne McCord alone."

"You don't have to worry about that. I hope I never meet up with that spitfire again."

They rode on for a few moments in silence, enjoying the unseasonably warm afternoon. "You know, you've been as testy as an old cow missing her calf," Cass accused, reminding Beau of his own display of bad temper of late.

"I know," Beau said simply.

"Well?"

"Well what?"

"Well, what's gotten into you? You never used to be so short fused. I don't know how Charity puts up with you."

Beau shrugged.

"Exactly how long have you two been married, anyway?"

"How long have you been here?"

Cass looked confused. "What's that got to do with anything?"

"Because we'd just gotten married the afternoon you arrived," Beau said curtly.

Cass's jaw dropped. "Are you—you've got to be pulling my leg."

Beau shook his head.

"You mean to tell me . . . you and she . . . ?" Cass sputtered.

Beau nodded. He watched Cass put two and two together.

"Well, well." Cass mulled over this surprising bit of news. "It's beginning to dawn on me what your problem might be. No wonder you've been on edge. Why didn't you say something?"

"I don't know. Maybe I wasn't exactly sure if I would be doing the right thing if we consummated our vows," Beau confessed.

"Now what's that supposed to mean? She's your wife, isn't she?"

"Yes, but the marriage isn't what you think."

As the two men rode along through the bright sunshine, Beau filled Cass in on the past year of his life. At times his voice filled with emotion as he relayed how miserable he'd been until that fateful day the wolf attacked him in the stream.

He spoke of how Charity, along with two Indian squaws, had worked to save his life. "I'm real grateful to all three of them. I guess it was touch and go for a while. I don't remember much about it. Most of the time I was out of my mind."

"We never knew you were hurt so bad," Cass said.

"I wasn't in any shape to write letters," Beau admitted. "Charity insisted I send word home and even wrote the letter for me."

Cass looked at him. "Seems like Charity has done a lot for you."

"She saved my life, with a little help from Laughing Waters and Little Fawn." Beau thought about the two Indian women's determination to marry him, but decided not to mention that. If he knew his brother, Cass would rib him about it, and you could count on him to spread the news to Cole as soon as he got home. They'd never let him hear the last of it.

"What happened to her husband?" Cass asked.

"He was killed in the war." Not every family had been as fortunate as the Claxtons. All three brothers had gone off to fight, and they'd all come back home in reasonably good spirits.

He told Cass about Mary Kathleen and about Ansel's untimely death. "You know, Cass, I felt just about that hopeless myself for a long time. I figure it's pure luck that I'm still alive."

Cass frowned. "I think Ma's prayers had more to do with it than luck. You know she wouldn't want to hear you talking like that. Neither would Betsy, for that matter."

Beau sighed. "You're right. God's been

good to me, and I haven't thanked Him enough. I'm realizing it more every day."

"Are you going to stay here in Kansas, or are you bringing Charity back home to Missouri?"

"I figure I'll stay here. Charity needs a lot of work done before she can claim her land. I should have it in good shape by spring."

"Charity seems like a good woman," Cass ventured.

"She is; one of the best," Beau agreed.

"There's something that bothers me," Cass said. "You've said you were sorry for her. You're grateful she saved your neck. You told me all the reasons you married her, but you've never once said you love her, and you've never said you intend to make this marriage permanent. Are you saying you plan to leave once Charity has the title to her land?"

Beau fixed his gaze on the winding road. A muscle twitched in his jaw. "I'm saying I'm not sure what I'm going to do."

"Well, look here, Beau. If you're not going to stay with her, do you think it's fair to . . . to . . . well . . . act married?"

"I don't know."

"Do you love her?"

Did he love her? It had been such a long time since Beau had felt love, he wasn't sure he would even recognize the feeling again. But yes, he thought he did.

"I don't know. . . . I still think of Bets. . . ."

"She's gone, Beau," Cass reminded him gently. "We all loved Betsy, but you have to go on. She'd want it that way."

"I know. It's been real hard for me, Cass."

"I think Betsy would approve of Charity," Cass said. "I don't think your conscience ought to bother you there. She seems like a fine woman. And she's beautiful. You have noticed that, haven't you?"

"Of course I have," Beau admitted. "Living together all winter . . . well, it would be impossible not to."

Yes, Charity was beautiful. He knew other men found her desirable. Even his baby brother had sent a few glances her way.

That was another thing that bothered him, the way Charity didn't seem in a hurry for Cass to move on. The way she fussed over him sometimes, putting poultices on his ankle, set Beau's teeth on edge. He wasn't a jealous man; still, Cass was the best-looking one of the Claxton men. He couldn't help wondering if Charity hadn't noticed.

Cass interrupted his thoughts. "But you're not sure you love her enough to make a lifetime commitment?"

Beau laughed mirthlessly. "Who knows how long a lifetime is going to be?"

"Well—" Cass sighed—"you'll have to decide what to do about Charity, but I'll make it a little harder on you." He flashed his brother a grin. "The weather's real nice, and it looks like there's going to be a full moon tonight. I'll saddle up and ride out to do a little . . . uh, fishing." He winked knowingly. "Been meaning to do that, anyway."

Beau shook his head, but he couldn't deny the thrill of expectation that shot through him at the thought of being alone with his wife. "Leaving me and Charity all alone," he concluded dryly.

"You'll still have the baby—unless Mary Kathleen wants to go hunting with me."

"I doubt she will. She's out of bullets."

Cass grinned and spurred his horse into a faster gait. "Well, what are you waiting for, big brother?" His grin widened. "We're burning daylight."

CHAPTER 14

Charity turned from feeding the chickens when the horses galloped into the yard. Beau threw the reins to Cass and announced that he was in need of a hot bath. She looked surprised by his strange request, especially since he seldom took a bath in the middle of the week, but she quickly set about filling kettles and putting them on the stove to heat.

After supper Beau dragged in the old washtub, laid out a bar of soap and a fresh towel, and drew the privacy blanket.

He then proceeded to bathe, shave, comb, and brush. By six o'clock he was clean as a whistle, though he wasn't sure what he was hoping to accomplish with the

improvement. Throughout his preparations
he'd weighed the dangers of embarking
upon the course lurking in the back of his
mind. Was it wise to wholly enter this marriage?

They were married in God's sight. But
Beau needed to be committed in his heart.
Irreversibly faithful.

Neither he nor Charity had false expecta-
tions concerning their arrangement. He'd
been honest with her; he knew she needed
his help to gain the title to her land. He was
willing to do that. It would be impossible for
him to remain under her roof as long as they
were both single. Marriage was the only answer to their immediate problems. Yes, they
desired each other. The past month had
proven that, but would desire be enough to
get them through a lifetime, if he chose to
remain here come spring?

Bets had died over a year ago. Sixteen
months. It seemed like a lifetime. Would it
make a mockery of his vows to Betsy to
bring another woman into his heart this
soon?

He wrestled back and forth with the
weighty questions until he grew short-
tempered again.

"I thought you were going hunting!" he snapped. Cass was sitting in the rocker playing with Mary Kathleen when Beau's accusation ricocheted across the room.

Charity glanced up from the sampler she was working on and frowned. "My goodness, Beau, why would he be going hunting tonight?"

"How should I know? He said he was going." Beau sent a pointed look in Cass's direction. With typical Kansas unpredictability the weather had warmed, melting the snow. The temperate weather wouldn't last, but hunting was possible.

Charity frowned. "How can he hunt in the dark?"

"He's coon hunting," Beau said. "Best time to hunt coons is after dark."

Cass sprang to his feet and carried Mary Kathleen back to her crib. After nuzzling her fat cheeks affectionately, he kissed the baby good night, then reached for his coat.

"Don't look for me to be back till late," he warned. "I may even do a little fishing while I'm out."

"Don't rush on our account," Beau grumbled.

Charity's expression suggested that she

found Cass's odd behavior as puzzling as Beau's. "Fishing? Tonight?"

"Thought I'd take advantage of the mild weather. Won't be many more days like this one," Cass predicted. He eased the brim of his hat back on his forehead. "You two have a nice evening."

"Beau?" Charity laid her needle aside, clearly concerned.

Her husband shrugged. "A man's got a right to go fishing if he wants."

When Cass opened the door, he came face-to-face with Susanne McCord.

He drew back in defense. "What are *you* doing here?"

"Mr. Claxton?"

"Yes."

"Mr. *Cass* Claxton?"

He frowned. "That's right."

Susanne glanced from Beau to Cass, clearly confused. "Oh . . . I didn't realize *you* were Cass," she murmured.

Cass's expression was about as friendly as a head cold.

Susanne took a deep breath and primly drew up her shoulders. "It really doesn't matter. I'm here on a purely business matter.

I wonder if I might have a word with you, Mr. Claxton."

"What do you want with me?"

"Our conversation will be brief," she assured him.

Charity approached the doorway, pulling a wrap closer. "Won't you come in, Miss . . ." She smiled and looked to Cass to provide the guest's name.

The set of his steel jaw indicated he wasn't going to hand out any information.

"Why, yes, thank you. I will come in." Susanne quickly stepped into the cabin before Cass could argue. She nodded pleasantly at Beau when her skirts brushed past him.

Beau closed the door and wondered why the spitfire wanted to talk to Cass. Had she come to apologize for her outrageous behavior this morning? The idea seemed unlikely; the woman didn't look to be the type that would admit she was sorry for anything.

"May I get you something warm to drink, Miss . . . ?" Charity glanced helplessly to Cass again. "A cup of tea or coffee to help ward off the chill?"

"Miss McCord won't be staying long enough to socialize," Cass said.

Charity looked shocked by Cass's rude behavior. Her eyes switched to Beau, and he grinned and shook his head. Cass and Susanne reminded him of a couple of hound pups, snapping and snarling for no reason.

Charity wasn't aware of Miss McCord's earlier behavior; he'd have to inform her. Cass hadn't been in any mood to talk when they got home, especially about how he had been bested by a woman who didn't reach to his shoulder.

Susanne returned Cass's fixed gaze, her nose lifting a notch higher. "Why thank you, Miss . . . ?"

"Mrs.," Charity supplied. "Mrs. Claxton."

Susanne's eyes reverted coolly back to Cass. "I was about to say, I don't care for anything to drink, Mrs. Claxton. I'm here to speak with Cass."

"Then Beau and I will take a short walk and let you two talk in private."

Cass objected. "No need to do that. Whatever Miss McCord has on her mind won't require privacy."

"I would like to speak to Mr. Claxton alone," Susanne reiterated stiffly.

Charity checked on the baby, then smiled

encouragingly at Susanne and reached for her shawl. "Take all the time you need. My husband and I will enjoy the outing."

"Thank you ever so much." Susanne moved closer to the stove. Shortly afterward, Beau and Charity closed the door behind them.

"Who is she?" Charity asked when she and Beau stepped off the porch and began their walk.

"Susanne McCord. She and her father were in Miller's Mercantile this morning where she made quite an entrance."

The recollection of Cass's unfortunate encounter with the highly temperamental Miss McCord brought a grin to Beau's face.

"She seems like a lovely young thing."

Beau wrapped his arm around his wife's waist and drew her close to his side. "You think so? Well, let me tell you what that 'lovely young thing' did to my little brother."

When the door closed, Cass squared off to meet his adversary. "What do you want, Miss McCord?" There was no time for mundane pleasantries; he did not like this woman. His gaze impersonally skimmed her petite frame elegantly sheathed in an outfit he figured had set poor Leviticus McCord back a pretty penny.

Susanne cleared her throat. "I understand you're from Missouri?"

"That's right."

"And you plan to return there soon?"

"I might."

"You're not being the least bit cooperative. But it really doesn't matter." She smiled, flashing dimples. Cass figured that was the way she dazzled the young men in Cherry Grove. Unfortunately, he'd been around a while; he was tough to dazzle.

She fluttered her eyelashes. "When you leave, I want you to take me with you."

He shifted his weight to one foot, staring at her as if he hadn't heard her correctly. "You want what?"

"I want you to take me to Missouri," she repeated.

Cass laughed. He pulled off his coat and draped it over a chair back.

Susanne tapped her foot. "I'm prepared to offer you five hundred dollars provided that you'll safely escort me to my aunt's home in Saint Louis."

Cass knelt in front of the stove, poker in hand. "Where would you get that kind of money?"

"That's none of your business," Susanne informed him. "But I assure you I have it. It's imperative that I leave this gopher hole they call a town and leave it immediately!"

"Imperative to whom?"

"Imperative to my sanity," she snapped. "I cannot stand the thought of living in Cherry Grove, Kansas, another moment."

She eased forward, her eyes mirroring desperation. She reached out to clutch the sleeve of his coat. "You *must* help me. You are the only sane person in this backwater town who is smart enough to leave." She spat out the observation as if the words left a bad taste in her mouth. "When I overheard Reverend Olson telling Edgar Miller that you were planning to return to Missouri, I knew this was my chance to escape."

Cass coolly eyed the hand clutching his sleeve. Susanne released the fabric. Her expression went from arrogant to pleading.

"Mr. Claxton. If you would be so kind to see me safely back to Saint Louis, I will pay you handsomely. Once I'm there, Daddy will understand how unhappy I've been in this— this rat's nest, and he'll let me stay. Oh! There will be parties and balls and lovely gowns when I'm under Aunt Merriweather's supervision." She gaily whirled around the hearth, caught up in her flight of fantasy. "Daddy will be overjoyed to let me stay in Saint Louis once he knows that I will never come back to Kansas. Never." She paused, her face flushed prettily from the heat. "Well?" She tipped her head flirtatiously. "Will you do it?"

Cass's expression was calm and aloof. "I'd rather be horsewhipped."

Susanne's brows shot up. "You mean you won't?"

"Not on your life, sweetheart."

"And if I increase my offer to six hundred dollars?"

Cass shook his head. "You don't have six hundred dollars."

Her eyes darted away momentarily, but seconds later they switched back to meet his with defiance. "I do have the money and more, and I'll pay whatever you ask if you'll take me with you."

Cass sighed. "Miss McCord, not only will

I not take you to Missouri for six hundred dollars, but you could sweeten the deal with a herd of longhorns, a ranch in Texas, and a chest of gold, and I still wouldn't take you to a dog fight."

Her eyes dripped ice. "You're despicable."

He shrugged. "So are you."

"Why won't you take me?" she demanded.

He smiled. "Because I don't *like* you, Miss McCord."

She cocked her chin rebelliously. "I didn't ask you to like me. I don't *like* you, either, but I see no reason why personal feelings should interfere with a business arrangement. If it would help, I'll promise not to even *speak* to you during the journey."

Cass walked over to stare thoughtfully out the window. "Does your daddy know you're running around asking strangers to take you to Missouri?"

"What do you think?"

"What would he do if he found out?"

"He'd be upset, naturally. But he isn't going to find out—unless you tell him, and I doubt if you will. Apparently, you're not the sort to involve yourself in other people's business."

"I'm not going to tell him." Cass turned and walked back to the fire. "Nor am I going to take you to Saint Louis."

She shot him a scathing look. "Exactly why don't you like me? Until this morning, we didn't know the other existed, so how can you not like me?"

"I know you about as well as I plan to know you." The scene in the mercantile said about all he needed to form an opinion of Susanne McCord.

"Why?" she persisted.

"I don't like little girls with nasty tempers."

She sighed. "You're upset about what happened this morning. Well, it was your own fault. You should never have blocked my way."

"You're lucky you're still standing," he reminded her. "What kind of woman goes around hitting a man for no reason?"

Her face colored, which surprised Cass. He hadn't figured she had a repentant bone in her body. "Then you refuse to take me?"

"That's about the size of it."

"For any price?"

"For any price."

"You won't change your mind?"

"No, ma'am."

"Then I suppose I've said all I came to say."

Cass tipped his head politely. "It's been a real pleasure, ma'am."

Susanne walked to the front door, pausing with her hand on the latch. "If you should change your mind—"

"Do you have a hearing problem?"

She yanked the door open. "I'd appreciate it if you'd take a look at my mare before I return to town."

"What's the matter with her?"

"She developed a slight limp just before we got here."

Cass grumbled something uncomplimentary under his breath, but he followed her out to the sled.

"She's thrown a shoe," he said a few minutes later.

"What does that mean?"

"It means the horse will need a new shoe before you can leave."

She sighed, drawing her collar tighter. "Can you fix it?"

He straightened. "Lady—"

"I'll pay you for your services, sir!"

There wasn't enough money in the world— Cass took a deep breath. "I'll see what I can find."

Smiling, Susanne slumped lower onto the seat.

Thirty minutes later Cass had the horse reshod and ready to travel.

"Which direction is Cherry Grove?"

Cass glanced up from a final check of the hoof. "What?"

"Do *you* have a hearing problem? *What direction* is Cherry Grove?

The muscle in his jaw tightened. "You don't know?"

She shook her head. "It was still daylight when I came. My father only moved me to this horrible area three months ago. This is the first time I've ventured out on my own."

"And you chose to come two hours before dark? To the west," he said curtly and turned back to the horse. "Okay," he said a minute later. "You shouldn't have any trouble."

He glanced up to confront two large, violet pools swimming in tears.

"Now what's wrong?"

"I'm afraid. I don't think I can find my way back to town." She sniffed.

"Just follow the road, lady."

"I—I have a terrible sense of direction," she confessed. "And this is the first time I've ever traveled . . . alone."

"You'll make it fine," Cass said. His chin set in a stubborn line. "Light your lantern, and give the horse her head. She'll find the way."

Susanne's hands trembled when she reluctantly accepted the reins he offered.

"What if she doesn't? What if I become lost—and it snows again. I could perish—then my father would hold you responsible for my death." Her small teeth worried her lower lip. "Knowing Father, he would sue for lack of responsibility—"

Cass glanced down the darkened road, then back to her. "Stop the 'poor me' act, Miss McCord. I'm not buying it. You'll be all right. You have a gun, don't you?"

She shook her head. "I never thought of bringing a gun. Besides, I wouldn't know how to use one."

Her sniffling grew more pronounced. "Suddenly I have this most wretched headache, and I'm beginning to feel faint." She sounded ready to collapse on the spot.

Cass shook his head. She actually thought he was buying this performance?

She sniffed and blew her nose daintily into a lace handkerchief. "I do hope I don't just faint dead away and have to remain here—with you—in that small cabin for . . . well, who knows when I might be able to travel?"

Resigned, Cass helped her out of the sled and they walked toward the house. He was whipped. She'd have to stay the night. But not a moment longer. Her little tricks wouldn't work on him.

"Will Mr. and Mrs. Claxton mind having an unexpected houseguest?" she asked.

"They won't mind," Cass lied.

Charity looked up in surprise when they entered the room. She and Beau had gotten back from the walk. "You haven't left yet?"

Cass strode to the fire. "Miss McCord's horse threw a shoe."

"Oh . . . I'm sorry."

"But you fixed it," Beau prompted.

Cass met his brother's eyes. "I fixed it, but now it's dark, and she's afraid she can't find her way back to Cherry Grove."

"Can't you drive her back?"

"She's developed a wretched headache and she feels faint."

The brothers exchanged a series of trapped looks.

"You do?" Charity immediately moved to welcome her guest. "May I do something for you?"

"Maybe . . . if I could just rest a spell," Susanne said softly. She glanced at Cass and smiled.

Beau looked on helplessly when Charity moved Susanne to the bed. "You just lie down in here. I'll bring you a cup of tea— nothing like a cup of hot tea to chase away a headache."

"You're ever so kind."

"Can't you do *something*?" Beau hissed when the two women disappeared behind the privacy curtain.

"What do you expect me to do? Let her wander around on the road in the dark? That woman doesn't know up from down."

Beau's lips thinned. "I suppose the hunting trip is off."

"Would it accomplish anything now? I'll stay by the fire, thank you."

"Well, it's going to be another long, miserable night," Beau predicted.

Cass glanced at the drawn curtain where female voices could be heard. "Tell me about it."

CHAPTER 15

The women carried on the brunt of the conversation over breakfast. Beau and Cass ate steadily, commenting only out of necessity. The moment the last egg was eaten and plates were removed and washed, Susanne announced that she was leaving.

Cass refused to look up from his plate. "Tell Leviticus that he has my prayers."

"I will indeed, sir." She flounced away from the table, addressing her remarks to Charity. "I so appreciate you letting me spend the night. If I ever do get to Saint Louis—" she paused to give Cass an aggrieved look—"you must come for a long visit."

"Oh—I don't think I'll ever get to Saint

Louis," Charity admitted, "but thank you for the invitation. Perhaps we can correspond occasionally?"

Beau thought his wife's smile seemed a trifle strained. A little of Susanne McCord went a long way.

Cass hitched the McCord sleigh, and without further ado Miss McCord set off for Cherry Grove—concocting, Beau suspected, a lofty explanation for a father who was sick with worry. Leviticus would have no way of knowing that his daughter had spent the night at the Burk homestead. For all he knew, the willful Miss McCord was off in a ditch somewhere.

Beau and Cass left shortly after to spend the morning repairing fences on the north section. The morning had dawned sunny and bright and promised a mild day for late January, though snow lay deep on the ground.

Before he rode out, Beau managed a rare moment alone with his wife. Drawing her into his arms, he kissed her soundly.

"My, my," Charity murmured, breathless when he finally relinquished his embrace. "What's this all about?"

Beau rested his cheek on the top of her

head, nuzzling her hair. "I'm thinking how lucky I was that day at the stream."

"Lucky!"

"Sure. You found me. What if someone like Susanne had come along first?"

"Are you suggesting Susanne McCord isn't your ideal companion?" She grinned, closing her eyes when his lips lightly traveled the base of her throat.

"The good Lord must have been put out with Leviticus the day that woman was born." He stole another kiss, interrupted by Cass, who'd returned to the house to search for his forgotten gloves.

With a regretful sigh, Beau released her. "I wish Ferrand had built you a bigger house."

"He would have if he'd known I'd need one so badly," she bantered back.

Beau winked and kissed her forehead, then reached around her for his coat. "See you at dinner time." Looked like the weather would hold a while longer. It had been days since the last snow; maybe spring would come early this year. "I won't be back until dark."

"Mary Kathleen and I will be waiting for you."

When the horses rode out, Charity quickly finished her chores and dressed Mary Kathleen warmly. If she hurried, she could make the trip into Cherry Grove to purchase raisins and be back before Beau discovered she'd gone.

Sun was streaming brightly among a scattering of fleecy clouds. It would be a perfect day for a short winter outing.

She put on a lightweight jacket, which she wouldn't need but wanted to take along just in case. Kansas weather could be fickle—just like a man's affection.

She led the harnessed horse from the lean-to, then went back to the cabin and carried Mary Kathleen to the waiting sled.

"Easy now, Jack." She spoke to the horse while she settled the infant on the board seat, then climbed up and took hold of the reins. Suddenly she thought to take the shovel along in case she might need it. She retrieved the shovel, tossed it in the back of the wagon, and climbed onto the seat again. After checking to make sure Mary Kathleen was warm enough, she gathered up the reins and set off for the hour's ride to Cherry Grove.

Charity lifted her face to the sun, drinking in the marvelous treat. She couldn't remember when she had felt this good. She hummed the hauntingly sweet melody "Aura Lee" to the baby as the horse trotted briskly down the snow-packed road.

The sled runners skimmed effortlessly through Fire Creek and picked up speed when Charity urged the horse into a fast trot. If she didn't dawdle at the mercantile, she'd have plenty of time to share a cup of tea with the Olsons before starting back. Beau wouldn't be home until dark. By then she'd have the raisins tucked away and dinner on the table. He would never suspect she'd made a trip to town.

A small, puffy cloud passed over the sun, but Charity didn't worry about it. What was a cloud on a lovely warm day like this? Besides, she was having too much fun thinking about her husband's sheer joy when she brought those two hot pies out of the oven. Though a small, insignificant token, the celebrating of their marriage would not go unnoticed.

Charity glanced up when an unexpected

chill crept into the air. A second cloud now skimmed the sun. Even as she watched, the cloud was joined by two more, then three. The sky had been perfectly clear a few minutes ago. Now it was clouding up and the wind had a sharp bite.

She decided she'd better stop long enough to readjust Mary Kathleen's blankets and put on her light jacket. It only took a minute to perform the simple tasks, and she was ready to move on.

A Kansas blizzard could move in faster than a jackrabbit outrunning a prairie fire. After careful study of the darkening clouds, she concluded they were nothing to be overly concerned about. But just in case . . . instead of sharing a cup of tea with Rebecca and Reverend Olson, she would buy the raisins and start home immediately. She clucked her tongue, and Jack's big hooves clopped noisily back onto the road.

Thirty minutes later, the first minuscule flakes started to drift lazily down, melting as soon as they touched the ground.

Charity still wasn't concerned about the abrupt change in weather. It would be about as far to turn back as it was to go on, and the snow appeared to be nothing more than flurries. But it was getting noticeably colder, so she set the horse to a brisker gait. Mary Kathleen, cuddled in her warm cocoon, stared with big eyes at the snow drifting down like tiny feathers to dot the wagon seat. Charity reached over to brush the accumulation off the infant's blanket.

"It's getting cold, isn't it, darling? We'll sit in front of Edgar's fire and toast our toes when we get there."

Snow continued to fall in the same gentle manner. The pristine beauty had always fascinated Charity. She watched the pea-sized flakes float peacefully from the heavy, leaden sky, marveling at yet another one of God's wondrous creations. She hoped this was the last snow of the season, but she knew that was wishful thinking. They still had February and March to contend with— months when they got their biggest snowfalls. The wind suddenly shifted directions, and the snow fell in earnest now. Periodic wind gusts whipped the wagon about on the road. Charity gripped the reins tighter and urged Jack to greater speed.

The wind steadily picked up strength, swirling snow back into her face, taking her breath away with its growing ferocity. It was increasingly evident that once she reached Cherry Grove, she'd be forced to wait out the blizzard. Beau would be worried—she hadn't left a note saying where she was going.

She was a mile from the town when panic set in. By now, Mary Kathleen was cold and crying, and Jack was becoming increasingly spooked by the storm's freakish nature.

Drifts built beside the road so quickly that Charity found herself losing her sense of direction. If it weren't for the aid of familiar landmarks, she knew she'd soon be hopelessly lost.

She reached a hand over to soothe Mary Kathleen's frightened screams, finally admitting to herself that the trip had been a mistake. At the first sign of trouble she should have turned around and gone back home.

From all indications this was going to be a full-blown blizzard, and she and the baby would never survive the storm if she didn't find shelter—and soon.

Above all she must keep her head. She'd reach appropriate shelter and wait for Beau to find her.

But Beau has no idea where you are, her

mind shouted. Stinging sleet lashed her face. She had been so intent on keeping the trip to town a surprise she hadn't thought of possible danger and the need to leave a note.

She stopped Jack in the middle of the road and gazed helplessly at the chilly alabaster prison in which she found herself. She realized with sinking despair that Beau wouldn't know where to begin looking for her.

Not the vaguest idea.

The blizzard hit full force as Beau and Cass finished setting the fourth fence post.

"Looks like it's going to be a bad one!" Cass shouted above the rising wind.

"Let's head in!"

The two men quickly gathered their supplies, loaded up, and kicked their horses into a full gallop.

Snow swirled around the riders. Once the two men stopped and tied bandannas around their noses to ward off the stinging air. By the time they reached the cabin, the horses were having difficulty navigating the deepening drifts.

"I've never seen a storm move in so quickly," Cass remarked. They rubbed down the horses and secured the lean-to. "I wonder if that snippy little twit made it home before the storm hit."

"Susanne?"

"Do you know another snippy little twit?"

"She started early enough to outrun the storm. I've heard of freakish blizzards, but this is the first one I've ever dealt with." Beau glanced over and noticed Jack's stall was empty. "Where's Jack?"

"I don't know. Maybe Charity turned him out to pasture before the storm."

The men bent into the wind and slowly made their way to the house. Beau shoved the door open and was surprised when Charity wasn't there to greet him.

The brothers stepped inside. Beau paused when he saw the room was empty. The fire burned low in the chilly room. There was no sign of Charity or the baby.

"Charity's not here. Where is she?"

"I don't know. Maybe she's out trying to help the stock?"

"She wouldn't have taken the baby with

her." Beau jerked the door open and scanned the swirling mass of white. Encountering nothing but endless drifts of mounting snow, he felt the knot in his stomach tighten. Where was she?

He stepped out of the house and made his way back to the lean-to, oblivious now to the howling storm. There wasn't a sign of the stock, except for the two oxen, Myrtle and Nell, contentedly munching hay in their stalls.

He strode behind the lean-to, and his heart sank when he discovered the sled missing.

He quickly threw a saddle across the mare. Cass entered the lean-to and automatically started saddling his animal.

"She's probably fine, Beau. She may be caught at one of the neighbors'—"

"Charity wouldn't be out on a day like this," Beau said shortly. "If she'd planned to visit anyone she would have said something about it this morning. Or left a note."

The men remounted. Cass handed Beau one of the two wool scarves he'd brought along. He tied one around his neck and pulled it up to cover his mouth. "Where do we start?"

Beau shook his head. The full implication of Charity's unexplained absence closed in on him. "I don't know."

"I say we try the neighbors first and then head toward Cherry Grove," Cass suggested.

"Cherry Grove? She wouldn't be going to town."

"You don't know that."

"And you do?"

"No," Cass admitted, "but I figure that's where I'd be going if I had a husband and a small baby and I'd been cooped up in the house for a spell."

"In the middle of a blizzard?" The horses shied nervously when a violent gust of wind threatened to collapse the drafty lean-to.

"The weather was like a spring day three hours ago."

Beau wasn't going to waste time arguing. Cass's reasoning might seem insane, but it was bound to be better than his own right now. He pulled up into the saddle. Charity and Mary Kathleen were out there somewhere. "Let's get moving."

"We'd better stay together," Cass warned.

Beau was well aware how crazy it was to

ride off in a storm. They could be risking their lives, but Charity's and Mary Kathleen's lives were at risk. He felt sick to his stomach when he thought about losing them.

"Let's go." Beau viewed the worsening storm. A fresh feeling of despair threatened to engulf him. "Where are you, Charity?" he whispered. "Where are you . . . sweetheart?"

Charity's feet and hands were numb. She'd searched for over thirty minutes, but she had found nothing in the form of shelter. During the process, she'd managed to run the sled off the road and into a steep ditch. One runner had sunk into a deep drift, and the rear end was tilting grotesquely to one side. She crawled to the back of the sled and laid Mary Kathleen on the floor, then lay down beside her. Huddled in the warmth of the baby's blankets, she began to pray.

Dear God, help us. That's all her mind could repeat. *God, help us.*

The day wore on. Snow continued to fall

in wet, heavy sheets. Charity managed to stop the baby's periodic crying by letting her nurse from the cloth she'd brought along. Ice had formed in the milk, and Mary Kathleen angrily spit the liquid out of her mouth, but Charity forced her to drink enough to momentarily pacify her. She wondered what would happen when the milk was gone. She'd only brought one jar.

Mary Kathleen eventually cried herself out. She now seemed fascinated by the snow. Charity knew the child was getting colder, and she had no idea how much longer an infant could survive in the falling temperatures.

By afternoon both she and the baby had started to doze.

Charity lay next to Mary Kathleen, vacantly watching the snow slowly begin to bury the sled. She tried to make herself stir, recalling how Ferrand had once told her about a man who'd frozen to death. The man succumbed to the temptation to sleep; a deadly mistake, he had warned her.

Charity forced her eyes open, but her lashes were becoming frozen. Soon they drifted shut on her snow-covered cheek.

Beau . . . don't let me die. . . . Don't let me die.

Beau and Cass searched the back roads, methodically wading their animals through deepening drifts, checking nearby home-steads. Beau's worry amplified with each negative shake of head. Not one person knew of Charity's whereabouts.

They stopped at Bill Cleveland's only to find he hadn't seen her either. No one had, Beau thought in despair. *Charity, where are you?*

Bill followed them out to the horses. "I've been abed for a couple of days. Just got up the first time about an hour ago." He coughed a deep, rasping noise that threat-ened to tear through his chest wall. "Let me get old Duke saddled and I'll go with you."

Beau shook his head. "You wouldn't last an hour out here, Bill. Go back to the fire."

"But I want to help," Bill argued. "The widow Burk's been such a good neighbor to me. Bought food when I was flat on my back last fall."

"You can pray." Cass held out his hand and Bill reached to take it. "We'll find her."

Bill nodded. "I'll be praying. Never doubt it."

Beau had been brought up to believe in the power of prayer, though he'd gotten out of the practice. That was about the only thing they had going for them right now.

Next stop was Jacob Peterson's dugout. Beau banged on the door. Jacob stuck his head out and blinked snow out of his eyes. "What's all the commotion?"

Beau quickly dispensed with the introductions. "I've been helping Mrs. Burk around her place."

"I know who you are." Peterson motioned for the two men to come inside.

Beau entered the dugout with Cass following behind. Both men stomped their boots, knocking off the wet snow.

"Charity's missing. She didn't happen to stop by here today, did she?" Beau asked.

Jacob turned thoughtful. "Missing, you say? In this weather? That's bad."

"Yes, sir." Beau knew how bad. If they didn't find her soon, Charity would die out here. The baby too.

Jacob stooped to add another piece of

wood to the fire. "Haven't seen her. You checked with the Joneses? They live 'bout a mile on down the road."

Beau shook his head. "Not yet. She didn't leave a note; that's unusual. It started out to be a nice day, so I suspect she decided to go for a visit."

Dear God, let that be true. Right now, let her be holing up somewhere drinking hot tea and eating cookies in a safe haven— though where that would be Beau didn't know.

Folks were talking; they wouldn't take kindly to Charity and the baby showing up on their doorstep.

"Kansas weather's as fickle as love," Jacob said. He took a couple of cups from the board shelf fastened to the wall and filled them with hot coffee. "Get this inside you. Maybe it will warm you up a little, anyway. I'll saddle my mule and help you look."

"You can't do that," Beau protested. The man was eighty if he was a day. He wouldn't last thirty minutes in this weather.

Jacob paused in the act of reaching for his coat. "Son, I ain't got many more years left. If I die trying to save a woman and a baby, then so be it."

"You wouldn't get past the lane and I'd have to bring you back. Sorry, but you'd just slow us down."

Jacob's expression turned old and defeated. "I know you're right, but I can't hardly stand by and do nothing."

Cass spoke up. "You'd be more help if you'll join Bill Cleveland."

"How's that?"

"He's praying right now."

"I can do that," Jacob said. "I'll sure be bending the good Lord's ears tonight." He paused. "Lot of talk going around—some real unkind towards your lady. But I never believed a word of it. If I'd been in Mrs. Burk's shoes I'd likely have done the same thing. You boys take care. I'll be on my knees before you're out the door."

Seconds later, Beau and Cass rode off, wool scarves thrashing in the wind.

"We have to split up!" Beau had to shout to make himself heard above the shrieking storm. "Charity and the baby are out there somewhere. I know it, Cass. We'll have a better chance of finding them if we ride in different directions. It's risky to separate, but we're running out of time."

"Agreed!" Cass shouted. "I'll veer east; you take the road to town!"

Beau reached across his saddle horn and clasped his brother's hand. "Be careful."

"You do the same." Their eyes silently conveyed both men's fear.

"If we don't find them before nightfall, go back to the house. I'll meet you there."

Cass nodded.

It made Beau ill to consider the possibility, but he knew if they didn't find Charity and the baby by dark, they would have to wait until morning. By then it would be too late.

"Don't worry. We'll find them," Cass said.

With a brief nod Beau acknowledged the hope, then reined his horse away and disappeared into swirling snow.

Cass reined in the opposite direction.

Charity woke with a sudden start. She was in some sort of cave. A white one. And she was warmer.

Outside she could hear the wind screeching, but the sound was muted, softer somehow. Less terrifying.

She cautiously flexed her fingers, trying to determine if they were frozen. To her relief, they moved. Though bright red and stiff, she could wiggle the appendages, but the effort was painful.

Her gaze circled the cubicle; she and the baby were completely buried beneath snow.

Buried alive.

She bit back a scream when panic seized her. She had to get out. Their body heat had melted enough space to shift positions. The sled bed provided some protection. A dim light filtered in from overhead.

She clawed at the drifts, trying to dig her way out, but gave up after a few futile attempts. She sank back down beside the baby. It was hopeless. She didn't have the strength to break through the packed layers of snow. Her gaze searched Mary Kathleen's face. The baby's eyes were closed. She lay deathly still. Charity's heart caught in her throat. Was she still breathing? She touched the round baby cheek and found it warm to the touch. Mary Kathleen's breath was feather soft against her hand. Charity sighed in relief. She was sleeping.

Thank You, God. Don't let her die, please.

Somehow she had to keep the baby warm until help came.

Tears pooled in her eyes. She felt a tremendous sadness overtake her, and she laid her head beside the baby and lovingly patted the helpless infant. Help? Who could find them now with the snow piled high above them? No one could see them.

No one would find them until spring thaw.

Charity knew she couldn't survive the elements for long, and she would die. She lay across the foot of the blanket, warming Mary Kathleen with her body heat, peacefully awaiting the moment her life would slip away. She'd heard of small children's lives being saved by parents sacrificing themselves to keep their little ones safe. She was prepared to do that for the precious baby Letty had left in her care.

Oh, Letty, I'm sorry. I should have taken better care of your daughter.

She thought of Beau and how much she loved him. *Loved him.* She loved him! As much as or more than she'd loved Ferrand. How she wished now that she'd told him how much she cared. She'd started to, many times, but she'd always stopped herself because she was afraid he'd think she wanted him to make a similar declaration. She'd convinced herself he didn't want to hear her foolish prattle, and if he ever said those words she wanted it to be because he meant them, not because he felt obligated to speak. Betsy still lived so deeply in his heart that no other woman would ever be able to exorcise her ghost.

Oh, Beau . . . Beau . . . I love you. . . .

Would Ferrand be there to meet her when she passed from this life into the next? And Letty? Would she be waiting to hold her precious daughter? She heard herself chuckling, her voice sounding hollow against the walls of snow. Would she even remember what her first husband looked like? The Bible seemed to indicate that she would, and yet there would be no marriages in heaven.

Would Beau be saddened by her death? Had he made it back before the storm hit? If she survived, would she ever be able to win his love? Her mind turned from tormenting her to playing tricks on her. Strange tricks.

She saw Beau coming to her. She could see the way the corners of his eyes crinkled endearingly, and a sigh escaped her. She eagerly reached out to touch him.

He caught her hand and brought it to his mouth. His eyes, his beautiful blue eyes, probed deeply into hers. They were in a room . . . alone . . . a lovely, quiet room with candles burning low in crystal holders and flowers, lots of beautiful flowers filling the room with their perfumed fragrance.

Her breathing turned shallow. His mouth caressed hers.

Charity could feel her sleep deepening. Her strength slowly ebbed as the illusion wove its way in and out of her mind. In the rare moments when she was lucid, she realized she was hallucinating . . . but oh, such lovely agony.

If she had a pencil and paper she would leave Beau a note. A simple message: *I love you. Forgive me for never telling you so.*

She should have told him.

Sometime during the fantasy it occurred to Charity that even if Beau was looking for her, he wouldn't be able to find the sled. Snow completely covered it now.

Feeling as if she were suspended from

somewhere far above the sled and looking down, she saw herself struggle out of her petticoat. She watched, spellbound. She saw herself sit up and begin to feel around in the sled for something to slide the dark muslin onto. She'd made the garment from some of Ferrand's old shirts.

Her hand found the shovel she'd brought along, and with stiff fingers she tied the piece of fabric around the handle and hoisted the shovel into an upright position.

In the smooth, unbroken surface of snow, a long makeshift flag began to flap at half-mast.

She lay back, watching the fabric whip in the icy wind. Curling around Mary Kathleen, she closed her eyes. Pictures in her mind faded. She gave herself over to the question that haunted her.

Would she recognize Ferrand? . . . He had blue eyes . . . no, green. . . .

Darkness was closing in.

Beau's horse plowed laboriously through deepening drifts, moving noticeably slower.

He knew the animal was close to dropping from exhaustion, and yet he couldn't make himself turn back. He'd die with Charity— but he wasn't turning back until he found her.

He was running out of time, and he blamed himself for listening to Cass. He should be searching south or west, not north. Charity had no reason to go to town. She had supplies to last the winter. Why had he let Cass talk him into riding to Cherry Grove when he knew better?

He pushed on, pausing frequently to cup his hands around his mouth and shout, "Char-i-ty!"

"Char-i-ty!"

Time after time, the wind blocked his effort and flung the words mercilessly back in his face. He nudged his horse forward, his shoulders hunched against the howling gale.

The horse squealed. She stumbled and suddenly went down, her heavy weight dropping into the folds of the wet snow. Beau exclaimed under his breath and waited until the horse struggled to regain her footing.

This was insane. He was going to kill both

the horse and himself if he didn't turn around soon; yet he couldn't turn back. *Charity. Mary Kathleen.*

He suddenly realized he was in love with Charity and that child.

He set his jaw. He wasn't going back until he found them. If the storm took his life, so be it. God had already taken a wife and child; this time he was going to fight with everything he had to keep this one.

He steeled himself against the bitter wind and rode on. His gloves had frozen to the reins, but he was past feeling the cold. He was aware of nothing except the pitch and sway of his horse as she labored through building drifts. He ignored the growing ache in his heart.

Hope was starting to dim when he spotted the flag.

The horse slowed. He squinted through the blowing snow at the piece of dark fabric flapping crazily in the wind. Inching forward in the saddle, he peered through the swirling flakes and then clucked to his horse and the mare eased forward. Holding the lantern high above his head, he followed the mellow beams across the snow-crusted

earth. He inched closer. The flag—the signal—was a woman's petticoat.

Sliding off the horse, he began to run.
Deep drifts impeded his progress, but he
ran on. When he reached the flag, he
dropped down on his knees and began furrowing through the packed snow.

"Charity! Charity? Are you in there?" He
ripped off his gloves with his teeth and dug
faster.

His fists frantically busted drifts, tears
blinding him. Gut-wrenching fear turned to
searing, white-hot anger and frustration.
She had to be in there. She had to be!

"Charity! Are you in there? Answer me!"
Snow flew in a furious white cloud.

Howling wind hammered him. He bowed
his head, turning his back on the gale, and
continued to dig, his hands frantically claw-
ing at the packed snow. She was there, beneath the heavy drift. He could sense her
presence.

God, help me. Let me be in time.

Snow had not only drifted in dense
ridges, the wind had twisted it until it was
almost impossible to tunnel through.

When his hand hit the side of the sled, his
motion ceased. For a moment he sat back

on his heels, breathing heavily. Large red stains dotted the snow. His hands were raw and bleeding.

Then he heard her.

A weak voice snatched away by the wind, but recognizable, and the sweetest sound this side of heaven. "Here—I'm here, Beau."

His sobs turned to hysterical laughter and he dug faster, unaware of the cuts on his hands, scooping the snow up in large armfuls and flinging it wildly into the wind. He shouted her name. "Charity!

"Chariiittty!"

He saw her hand first and then caught a glimpse of her sleeve. Alternately laughing and crying, he uncovered her and the baby and caught them both up tightly to his chest.

"Oh, God . . . oh, God . . . thank You. . . . Thank You. . . ."

He held the baby in one arm and covered Charity's face with kisses, clasping her close against his chest, then releasing her long enough to claim her mouth again and again.

"I didn't think I was going to find you." He cupped her face with one hand, meeting her eyes in the weak lantern rays. "Are you hurt? Are you all right?"

"I'm . . . co-co-ld, B-B-B-ea-u."

"Oh, sweetheart, I'll take you home where it's warm," he promised.

"Th-th-the ba-b-by?"

Beau gently uncovered the thick layers of blankets to encounter a tiny pug nose, which suddenly wrinkled in disgust at being awakened so abruptly. Mary Kathleen let out a wail that threatened to permanently impair his hearing.

The familiar bellow was music to Beau's ears. His face broke into a radiant smile. "She's fine!"

He pulled Charity and Mary Kathleen back to his chest and squeezed his eyes shut in pure joy as he held his family tightly in the shelter of his arms.

"Both my girls are fine, Lord." His voice broke before he finished in a ragged whisper. "This time I'm not going to be forgetting Your mercy."

CHAPTER 16

Beau shifted Charity, who still held tightly to Mary Kathleen, to one arm and knocked on the Olsons' front door. They'd made it this far. God had been good. Snowdrifts nearly blocked the road now, but once he got Jack unhooked from the sled he'd put Charity and Mary Kathleen on his horse, and they'd managed to come through the storm with their lives intact.

Reverend Olson opened the door, shock registering on his features. "Beau? Come in!" He quickly summoned Rebecca, and they welcomed the half-frozen family in from the storm's fury.

Beau explained what had happened, but before he had finished, Rebecca was helping Charity and the baby into the bedroom. Reverend Olson was already pulling on his coat to go for the doctor.

He returned within the hour after rooting Dr. Paulson from a deep sleep. The good doctor had then made the cold trek to the parsonage to examine the weary travelers.

An hour later the doctor entered the parlor and set his worn leather bag down on the piecrust table. A fire blazed high in the hearth, and the smell of fresh coffee permeated the air. "I think they're both mighty lucky," he told a haggard-looking Beau. "Another hour out there in this storm and it could have been too late."

Exhausted, Beau could barely keep his eyes open. The fresh cuts on his hands were pure agony, but he hung on the doctor's words. "They'll be all right?"

The doctor smiled. "Mother and child are doing fine. With proper care, they should regain full strength."

Beau slumped with relief, realizing he had been holding his breath. "Thank you. . . . Thank you, Doctor."

"Don't thank me, young man; only God could have pulled this one off. I'm glad I could help. That's a right nice family you have there, but I'm guessing you already know that."

Beau knew his eyes were brimming with tears and he didn't care.

Rebecca came in from settling the infant. "Happen to have an extra piece of chocolate cake, Harlow. Couldn't interest you in it, could I?"

"You know I'd risk any kind of weather for a piece of your chocolate cake, Rebecca. Thank you; I'd love some."

"How about you, Beau—won't you join us?"

"No thank you, Mrs. Olson. I'd like to talk to my wife, if I could."

Dr. Paulson followed Rebecca to the kitchen. Beau walked to the window and lifted the thin curtain. The storm still raged, but he felt an inner peace that he hadn't known in a very long time.

Thank You, God, for giving them back to me. I'm going to take good care of them from now on. I've learned my lesson; I should have studied Your Word more when I lost Bets, not less. I should have held on to hope instead of bitterness.

"You comforteth us in all our tribulation, that we may be able to comfort them which

are in any trouble, by the comfort wherewith we ourselves are comforted. For as the sufferings of Christ abound in us, so our consolation also aboundeth by Christ."

How many times had Beau heard Ma recite 2 Corinthians 1? Enough for the verse to have stuck with him. The wisdom had gotten lost in his grief. It was going to be up to him to regain his trust, but he could do it. God had given him another chance for love.

He swallowed hard against the lump in his throat. He felt like the prodigal had come home.

"You say your brother's still out there?" Reverend Olson inquired.

"I hope that he's found shelter by now. I've been praying that when it got dark, he returned to the cabin." Cass was a reasonable man; he'd have given up the search at dark, as agreed.

Reverend Olson cleared his throat. "By the way, Beau, I've heard from Ansel's and Letty's families."

Beau turned slowly from the window. "And?"

"It turns out that Ansel's father passed away a few months back. Phedra Latimer is finding it hard to cope with her husband's death. I'm afraid she'll be unable to take care of Mary Kathleen at this time."

"And Letty's kinfolks?"

Reverend Olson sighed. "Letty's parents would love to take the child, but poor health makes it impossible. They regretted to inform me that they are not able to care for a youngster." He shrugged apologetically. "Children are for the young and healthy, Beau."

Beau turned back to the window, deeply troubled. "Put Mary Kathleen with strangers?"

"They wouldn't be strangers. They'd be Letty's kin. Of course, Mary Kathleen would have to grow to love them. And then there'd be the problem of sending the child back East, but these decisions don't have to be decided tonight. You're sure I can't have Rebecca fix you a bite to eat?"

"No, thank you. I'd like to see my wife."

"Then you run along. Rebecca and I will look after the baby. Mary Kathleen's sleeping soundly. The doctor says she shouldn't have any lasting effects from her adventure." A tender light entered the reverend's faded gray eyes. "You know, Beau, it was the Lord's hand that allowed that sled to be buried in the snow. It surrounded your wife and the child and conserved their body heat. It saved their lives."

Beau's eyes met the reverend's. "I know where the credit belongs, sir."

"Just wanted to make sure you did." Reverend Olson smiled. "See you in church when weather permits?"

"Yes, sir, you will."

"Now, I believe you have a wife you want to see."

Beau smiled. "Yes, sir."

"Then why are you hanging around here talking to an old codger like me? Go to her, young man!"

Charity's room was dark when he stepped inside. She stirred and opened her eyes as he cautiously approached the bed.

"Hi."

"Hi. I thought you might be asleep."

She sighed. "Just getting warm."

The bed creaked when he sat down on the side of the mattress.

"Baby all right?" she asked.

"She's sleeping. Reverend Olson said he and Rebecca would look after her tonight. You need your rest. Are you warm enough?"

She nodded. "Finally."

"Good."

Charity reached out and gently took hold of his hand. "Lie down beside me."

Beau shook his head. "I—I don't want to disturb you. The doctor says you need your rest." He couldn't see her face in the dark, but the plea in her voice drew him like a moth to a flame.

"Please. I need you beside me."

He carefully eased to his side and lay down beside her. Then he wrapped his arms around her small body and drew her close.

She sighed, burying her face in the warmth of his chest. "I love you, Beau."

"I love you too, Charity."

His mouth searched and found hers, and he kissed her with a passion that words could not convey. The will to fight was gone. The war that had been raging inside for over a year was over.

"Tomorrow we go home." Beau sat on the side of Charity's bed, an air of excitement in his voice.

"I know and I can hardly wait."

She had weathered the close call amazingly well, and this afternoon the doctor had pronounced her fit enough to travel. Beau leaned over to steal a kiss, his eyes sparkling like a small boy's. "Cass was afraid you wouldn't make it home before he left, so he brought you and Mary Kathleen a present by this afternoon."

"He did? A present for me! Where is it?"

"Not so fast." Beau held up his hand. "I'd like to give you *my* present before you open his."

Her eyes widened with excitement. "Why?"

"Because mine's better than his."

"Beau!" She laughed. "How do you know?"

He shrugged. "I asked him what he got you, he told me, and so I know mine's the best."

"You're terrible."

"Yeah, I know that too." He grinned and stretched out beside her, waving a small, wrapped box before her eyes.

She started to reach for the box, and he playfully drew it back. "Not so fast."

"I thought you wanted me to open it."

"I do, but I want you to beg for it first."

"Beg for it?" Charity laughed. "It's that nice?"

"I think so."

She rolled over to face him and traced a lazy finger across his cheek and over the outline of his lips. "Please, please, please, please, please. How's that?"

"So-so."

Her eyes softened to liquid pools. "Oh, Beau. I love you. I don't need presents; God has given me everything I ever wanted."

Catching her hand, he held it tightly. "When I thought I'd lost you and Mary Kathleen I knew—well, again I thought I didn't have anything left to live for." His voice cracked with raw emotion, and he remembered what it had been like looking for her, the gripping fear that had ridden through the night with him. He saw the tears in her eyes.

Her lips quivered. "I love you so very

much. That's all I could think of while I waited for you to find me and the baby— and how I so desperately wished that I had told you of my love, long before now."

Beau toyed absently with a strand of her hair, intrigued by its softness. "You know, I'm kind of glad it happened this way."

"What way?"

"This way. God showed me how easily I could lose love again. I'd been a blind, stubborn, bitter fool until two days ago." He squeezed her hand tightly. "I'm sorry. I should have told you how I felt sooner, but I still had Bets in my heart."

It was a hard thing for a bride to hear, but she had to know.

"And now?"

"Now I've let her go. Though I suppose she'll be with me from time to time, I realized that God had given me a second chance at love." He paused, still trying to sort through his new feelings.

Charity smiled. "I don't resent your feelings for Betsy. Betsy and Ferrand were our first loves, and they'll always hold a special place in our hearts. But we're older now. We share a different kind of love. I'm content with that."

"I love you, Charity. Deeply and forever. Maybe not in the same boyish way that I loved Bets, but what I feel for you in some ways is bigger and more—well, downright scary, to be honest."

She grinned. "And that frightens you?"

He pulled her ear closer, whispering, "It *should* scare the dickens out of you. Now, what about Ferrand?"

"I will forever hold him in my heart." Her hand reached out to gently caress her husband's face. "He was my first love; you are my last."

He reached for the small box. "This is your wedding gift."

She took the box and slowly slipped off the ribbon. "I'm afraid I have nothing to give you. I was going into town to buy raisins to make you a pie when the storm came up."

"You almost got yourself killed over raisins?" She was doing that for him? The realization only made him love her more.

"I wanted to do something special for a wedding gift. You saved my life . . . and I had nothing to offer you."

He shook his head. "You've given me back my life. That's enough."

Smiling, she removed the paper and

opened the box. Her eyes widened and she gently fingered the emerald brooch. "Oh, Beau."

"I hope you like it. I got it at the mercantile the day we got married, and I've been waiting for the right time to give it to you. A couple of squaws traded it for food and blankets." He reached out and gently stemmed the moisture suddenly streaming down her cheeks. "The color of the stones reminded me of your eyes."

Charity cradled the brooch in her hands, Ferrand's grandmother's brooch, and then pressed it to her heart. Laughing Waters and Little Fawn must have tired of the trinket and traded it off. She wouldn't dream of telling Beau that long ago another man had given her the same gift; Beau's gift meant just as much. She would cherish the token as deeply as she'd treasured Ferrand's gift.

"My beloved husband, have I told you how very much I love you?"

"Yes, Mrs. Claxton, but I'd have no objections to hearing it again." He smiled. "For the rest of my life."

"I still say you should wait till all the snow's melted." Charity frowned when she passed the sack of ham sandwiches up to Cass. "It's February. There could be another storm any day!"

Cass glanced at Beau and shook his head. "Your woman frets too much."

Beau grinned. "I love her anyway."

"I've hung around over a week waiting for you to get home, and now you don't want me to leave." Cass grinned and then softened his banter. "My ankle's fine now—strangest thing—the swelling's gone down, and I need to be getting home before another blizzard hits. You two don't want me underfoot all winter now, do you?"

"No," Beau said.

Charity shrugged. She couldn't put those poultices on him forever.

"That's what I thought." Cass climbed into the buckboard and tapped his hat back on his head. "I'll be seeing you again one of these days. Ma'll have me dragging another sledload of pickles and preserves out to you, thinking you all will be starving to death."

Charity pulled the blanket up closer around Mary Kathleen to shield her from the sharp wind. "You're welcome any time. And thank you again for the lovely handkerchief. I'll wear it close to my heart."

Beau leaned over and kissed his wife. "I'm going to ride out a ways with Cass. I'll be back."

She smiled. "Take your time. We'll be waiting."

He swung into the saddle. "Let's go, little brother. We're burning daylight."

The sled and rider moved out of the yard down the snowy pathway. For several miles the two brothers rode in compatible silence. Then as they crested a small rise, they reined their horses to a stop. Beau swung out of his saddle and stood beside the sleigh.

"Well, looks like I'll be going it alone from here on."

"Yeah. I'd best be getting back to Charity and the baby. Tell Ma I won't be coming home this spring."

Cass grinned and reached for the reins. "Didn't figure you would be."

"Yeah." Beau stared contentedly at the snow-covered plains. "Sorta feels like I am home."

"You got yourself a fine woman," Cass admitted. "You going to adopt Mary Kathleen?"

"Figuring on it. Then planning on having a couple more sisters, and maybe two or three brothers to look after the girls."

Cass chuckled. "That's good. Ma likes being a grandmother."

"Yeah, can't wait till she sees my baby." Beau met his brother's gaze evenly. "Mary Kathleen's about the cutest little thing you've ever seen, isn't she?"

"She's cute, all right."

Beau's grin widened. "I think so too. One of these days you'll settle down and have one almost as cute," he predicted.

Cass hooted merrily. "Don't count on it. No woman's going to rope and hog-tie me until I'm good and ready."

Beau shook his head skeptically. "Don't be too sure. A thing like that can slip up on a man before he knows it."

"Not on me, it won't." Cass released the

brake. "Best be moving on. I'm burning daylight."

"You take care. Tell Cole and Wynne we'll write. Maybe they can make the trip out to see us someday."

"Sure thing. You behave yourself, big brother."

"You do the same, little brother."

Cass shot him an arrogant grin. "Not a chance."

Beau threw his head back and laughed, his merriment rumbling deep in his chest.

Cocky kid, he thought affectionately. *Someday some woman will come along and tie his tail in a bowknot.*

He took a deep breath and held it, tipping his face up to drink in the cold sunshine. It felt good to be alive.

Real good.

NOTE FROM THE AUTHOR

Dear reader,

I hope you have enjoyed Beau's story. It's an adventure telling the stories of the lives and loves of these Men of the Saddle for you. I pray the struggles they endure and the lessons they learn will cheer you. The men have their troubles—and their fears—but I hope I've shown them taking comfort in the knowledge that they're never without help in their faith walk. And neither are we.

If you identify with Beau and his loss of hope, don't feel alone. There are seasons in all of our lives when we struggle to keep the faith—even this author. When you need a good dose of God's Word during difficult times, here are some of my favorite Scripture passages: John 14:27; John 14:1; Hebrews 10:35-36; and Galatians 6:9.

God bless you! And keep the hope—joy comes in the morning.

Lori Copeland

ABOUT THE AUTHOR

Lori Copeland, Christian novelist, lives in the beautiful Ozarks with her husband and family. After writing in the secular romance market for fifteen years, Lori now spends her time penning books that edify readers and glorify God. She publishes titles with Tyndale House, WestBow, and Steeple Hill. In 2000, Lori was inducted into the Springfield, Missouri, Writers Hall of Fame.

Lori's readers know her for Lifting Spirits with Laughter! She is the author of the popular, best-selling Brides of the West series, and she coauthors the Heavenly Daze series with Christy-award–winning author Angela Elwell Hunt. *Stranded in Paradise* marked her debut as a Women of Faith author.

Lori welcomes letters written to her in care of Tyndale House Author Relations, P.O. Box 80, Wheaton, IL 60189-0080.

Turn the page for
an exciting preview from
Lori Copeland's next book,

MEN *of the* SADDLE

the Maverick

the Maverick

Cass fought the unseemly urge to strangle Susanne. He knew it was useless to try to outwit her in a war of insults—he'd tried that six years earlier and had lost, hands down. All he could do was stand his ground.

She watched warily as he ran a hand through his hair. "What are you still doing in Saint Louis, Susanne?"

"I live here, remember?"

"I remember." But he'd tried to forget. He assumed she had married and was by now in the process of tormenting her husband to death. "I thought you might have moved on."

"Ah, then you've thought of me over the years," she said.

A wicked smile curved the corners of his mouth. "Not even once." That wasn't true; he'd thought she would be civil enough to send him a copy of the annulment, but she hadn't. Other than that, he hadn't thought of her.

She sighed. "A pity. And here I thought you were pining away for me all this time."

Cass chuckled mirthlessly. "What a dreamer."

"I would think the more proper question is what are *you* doing here in Saint Louis? I thought you'd be in River Run."

Cass casually set a booted foot onto the rail next to her. He stared into the darkness for so long Susanne thought he intended to ignore her again.

"It's none of your business," he finally said, "but if you must know, I returned to River Run for a few months before an old friend wrote and asked me to join him in a business partnership here in Saint Louis. So I came back."

"Josiah Thorton," she murmured absently.

His eyes snapped back to meet hers. "How did you know Josiah Thorton?"

"I didn't. I just know that he was your business partner . . . and that he died, leaving you heir to his estate."

Cass didn't fancy her knowing anything

about his business. "Where did you hear that?"

"Never mind how, I just did. Actually, it's Josiah's house that I came to see you about earlier."

"Josiah's house?" Cass studied her guardedly. "What about it?"

"I want you to rent the house to me."

"Rent the house to you?" Cass found the request odd, even for Susanne McCord. "I wouldn't rent my horse's leavings to you."

"Nor would I accept them," she snapped.

"Then what makes you think I would rent Josiah Thorton's house to you?"

"I know you won't rent me the house, but I'm hoping—and praying—that when you hear that I have nine children who desperately need that house, you'll be willing to at least listen to what I have to say."

For a moment silence filled the air as Cass slowly digested her words. Nine kids? Suddenly he threw his head back and laughed uproariously, his white teeth flashing in the moonlight. His jolity continued to grow, and by the puzzled look on Susanne's face he could see that she was frantically reviewing her remark to see what was so amusing that it could send him into fits of mirth.

"What's so funny?" she challenged.

Cass pointed at her, his eyes filling with tears. "You . . . and nine children!" He slapped his hand on his thigh and broke into another boisterous round of laughter. She watched with a jaundiced eye.

"What's so funny about the children and me?"

As quickly as his gaiety had erupted, it came to a sudden halt. He studied her dispassionately. "I can't imagine any man living with you long enough to father nine children. Did you marry a simpleton?"

She smiled. "Yes. But that's beside the point. The children don't have fathers."

His jaw dropped.

"Not *that*," she accused. "They aren't *my* children. Technically."

"I didn't think so!" He burst into laughter.

"If you can pull yourself together, I'll tell you why I have them," she said curtly.

"Oh yes." He wiped tears from his eyes. "I'm all ears."

"The children are orphans. My Aunt Merriweather took them into her home to raise, and after she died I assumed responsibility for their care."

He'd believe that when it was announced that, through an unforeseen technicality, the South had won the war! "Of course you did! Grasping, conniving, spoiled Susanne McCord giving unselfishly of herself to nine homeless children. Sounds exactly like you, my lovely."

"You don't believe me."

"I couldn't hope to live long enough to believe you, Susanne."

"Then I suppose it would do no good to plead with you to lease Josiah Thorton's house to me?"

"None whatsoever." Cass was not a heartless man, and he regretted that innocent children would suffer from his refusal—if she was telling the truth—but the truth was foreign to this woman. He wouldn't help Susanne McCord cross the street, let alone rent Josiah Thorton's house to her. She was out of his life and he intended to keep it that way.

"Mr. Claxton—" Susanne's eyes locked stubbornly with his—"I know you and I haven't exactly been friends." She stoically ignored the choking sound he made in his throat and continued, "But I fail to see how you could let our personal differences stand in the way of providing a home for nine helpless children. I *beg* you to reconsider. I understand you have accumulated wealth beyond what most people can imagine, and you surely have no need for such a large house. Please reconsider; I'm desperate."

"Come now, Miss McCord, if what you claim is true, and you've turned into an unselfish saint, which I don't believe for a minute, then why are you making it sound as if I'm the one responsible for the children's misfortune?"

"You have the house," she said simply.

He lifted his brows wryly. "There are no other houses in St. Louis with twenty-four rooms?"

"I'm sure there are, but none so ideal and none that I can afford. I'm afraid I can only offer a pittance to repay you for your kindness and generosity." She nearly choked on the praise. "But the children and I will paint and clean and weed the gardens for a portion of our keep."

"What makes you think you could afford what I would ask?"

"I'm not sure that I can, for we have very little money. But when I saw the house, I knew it was exactly what the children needed, even though it's old and run-down and needs a mountain of repair. Why, no one would think about purchasing it in the condition it's in now. Of course, I had no idea you owned it—"

"I don't. It belongs to Josiah Thorton."

"But he's dead, and you're the heir to his estate and the one most likely to inherit it, along with the rest of Mr. Thorton's vast holdings."

Cass's eyes narrowed. "And who told you that?"

"I can't say who told me, but wouldn't it be to your advantage to have people living in Josiah's house, people who would maintain the dwelling until the estate is settled?"

"And what happens once the estate is settled? Suppose I have a potential buyer interested in purchasing Josiah's house. Would the kindhearted, generous 'weasel' then throw you and your nine little orphans out of the maintained dwelling?"

"Well . . . I'm not sure what would happen in that case." Susanne had learned long ago to take life one day at a time. "It's possible . . . if I can't find another house at that time, I might be forced to take the children to my father in Cherry Grove, but I don't want to do that right now. With winter approaching, the long journey would be extremely difficult for the elderly couple who helps me run the home," she confessed.

"I hate to hear that, Miss McCord, because I'm not going to help you." Cass straightened to face her. "It looks like you're going to have to trick someone else into helping you out of your mess this time."

She felt her temper rising. "You can't help me—or you won't help me?"

He grinned. "Both. I can't because Josiah's house is not mine to do with as I please—his estate won't be settled for months yet. And I won't because . . ." His eyes skimmed her insolently. "Well, I think we both know why I won't, don't we? Oh, by the way, I never received those annulment papers. Where are they?"

"You are heartless," she spat out. "Cold, uncaring. Selfish!"

"Weasel," he mocked. He touched his index finger to her chin in silent warning. "Watch it, sweetheart—your halo is wobbling."

She was going to explode. He'd really done it this time. Years of prayer and steel resolve to forgive him melted. Squaring her shoulders, she called out to his retreating form. "We don't *have* to have twenty-four rooms, you know. We can make do with far less!"

"Forget it."

"Don't you have *any* house you could rent to me and the children?"

"Not even one. Good evening, Miss Mc-Cord." He threw his head back and laughed merrily.

Susanne stamped her foot. Good evening, indeed!

The man was an intolerable muttonhead who was going to pay for his high-handedness.

And pay dearly.